LEARNING TO FALL

PEACH MORRIS

This book is a work of fiction. Names, characters, places, and incidents are the product of the author's imagination or are used fictitiously. Any resemblance to actual events, locales, or persons, living or dead, is coincidental.

Published by 8th Note Press

ISBN: 978-1-961795-37-2

Manufactured in the USA

Cover art by Bex Glendining
Typeset by Typo•glyphix

10 9 8 7 6 5 4 3 2 1

For Finn

Chapter 1

The girl is scrambling for her clothes while my boyfriend just stares at me. He doesn't have apologies tripping off the end of his tongue like she does, and he isn't rushing to explain that this "isn't what it looks like," because this is definitely Ryan in bed with someone who isn't me.

"Um," I say.

"Um," he replies.

I turn around and walk out.

This is a love story.

I've nearly reached the main road when I hear pounding footsteps behind me. I turn around, expecting to see Ryan making his way toward me, but instead find the girl who was with him. She stumbles the last couple of steps in checkered slip-on Vans straight out of a nineties pop punk band, the backs of the shoes flattened as she's shoved them on in a hurry.

"You're fast!" she exclaims. "Long legs."

I blink and take a step backwards, which is apparently all the invitation necessary to allow her to barge right into my personal space and squeeze the side of my arm. She's only a couple of inches shorter than me. The neon orange tank top she's wearing sparks a warning in my brain and I am reminded of the image of that tank top draped over Ryan's desk chair. My brain also pulls up my biology GCSE coursework on aposematic warnings: when a dangerous animal is brightly colored to warn others not to mess with it. A delicate gold chain hangs around her neck, a locket resting in the hollow between her collarbones. Her skin is a deep warm brown. I'm sure I know her from somewhere.

"Look, I want to explain, I didn't know he had a girlfriend. I'm so sorry. I never thought I'd be this kind of person. I'm in a really shitty place at the moment and it all just kind of happened. He got some food at the cafe where I work and I felt really bad about myself and he was really nice to me and—" She breaks off and takes a deep, shaking breath.

She makes a passing effort to smooth out her mass of black hair, but the tight curls stay spilling out of her headband. The action fires a memory, a mannerism I've seen before.

"I just … He didn't say anything. About you. Until we heard you coming up the stairs."

I blink and give my head a small shake, pushing deep into the pockets of my jeans to stop myself from fidgeting. The way she's anxiously wringing her hands together makes it difficult to resist doing the same, but I settle for pulling my sleeves over my fingers and worrying at a loose thread on the right cuff.

"No, I get it, it's okay," I say, cursing myself for accepting her apology so readily.

"I'm not this person, I swear. It's just been … a bad week. Very bad."

I remember where I know her from. We were in the same

psychology class at sixth-form college for the last two years. She didn't say much in class, but when she did, it was thoughtful. Her comments often made it into my immaculately color-coded revision notes—succinct ways of phrasing tough concepts.

"Imogen," I blurt out without meaning to.

"Do we know each other?" She cocks her head, takes a step back (phew) and pops one hand on her hip. I still don't know what to do with my hands. I swear sometimes it's like I'm an alien wearing human skin.

"We went to college together. We were in the same year," I explain, hopefully without flapping my arms around too much. "We were in that psychology class with Claire."

"Yeah, I remember the class. I don't remember you." She narrows her eyes a little, looking at me in a way that makes me feel like I'm being x-rayed.

"I wasn't there very much; I did a lot of the work from home. My mum … I have to look after her." She didn't need to know that. I screw my eyes shut briefly, hating myself for revealing something so personal to the girl who, a few minutes ago, was in bed with my boyfriend. Or, I guess, my ex-boyfriend now.

"Oh, I'm sorry," she says.

"It's okay."

"I remember Ryan. Why don't I remember you?"

I shrug.

"When did you start dating? Was it recently?" she asks.

"At the start of the year." I was relieved when Ryan asked me out because he provided me with a ready-made friendship group so I could stop eating lunch by myself with my earphones in and Mum would stop worrying about how much of a loner I naturally am. "We've been together about eight months. Well, until he … cheated on me?" I want it to be a firm statement but it comes out like a question, even though I was there as it happened.

"It's my fault," she says. "I'm the one who suggested going back to his place after I finished my shift. I'm the one who made the first move. I'm the bad guy here."

"Maybe. I don't know."

"I'm surprised he didn't run out after you to be honest. He was just sitting there telling me he forgot he invited you over tonight. I couldn't get out of there fast enough."

"He didn't even wait until uni," I say, mostly to myself. "We haven't even got our A-level results yet."

"He's a knobhead."

I look up at her and she looks genuinely concerned for me. "Fuck him," Imogen says.

I grimace.

"Or not!"

We both laugh.

She reaches over and squeezes my arm again, but it doesn't feel like as much of a push into my space as before.

"Thanks for coming after me," I say.

"It's the least I could do, after such a monumental fuck-up on my part."

"It's not your fault. I'm gonna …" I gesture at the road behind me.

"Oh, yeah, me too. I'm this way." She sticks a thumb out toward the opposite direction.

"Okay, well, see you around, I guess," I say, turning to go.

"Wait!"

I turn back.

"I don't even know your name," she admits.

I smile. "Casey."

"Well, Casey, what a horrible way to meet you. Hope he grovels."

"Me too."

I turn away and walk toward home.

~

"Hi, Mum!" I call as I come through the front door. I kick off my shoes at the shoe rack and walk into the living room. She's reclined on the sofa watching *Countryfile* with a half-finished plate of lasagna next to her. She hits pause on the remote as I walk in.

"Oh, hi, sweetheart! I wasn't expecting you back so early. What happened?"

I sit down in the armchair. "Not very hungry tonight?" I ask, gesturing at the plate. I know I'm putting off telling her.

"Just feeling quite nauseous," she tells me. "It's a delicious dinner! Just a bit too rich for me at the moment."

"Shall I get you a peppermint tea?"

She nods gratefully. "If you would. Then you can tell me what happened to your evening. Did Ryan double-book himself?"

"I'll tell you when I'm back with our tea."

I head down the hallway to the kitchen, fill up the kettle at the sink then put it back on the stand and turn it on. I pull my phone out of my pocket and place it face-up on the counter. No new messages, even after the twenty-minute walk home. I scroll down to Ryan's name in my contacts and delete it, along with his accounts on all the social media apps I have. This is what you're meant to do when you find your boyfriend cheating on you, right? I assume the numb feeling will subside at some point and I'll throw myself on the bed and weep into the pillows, but right now I just feel very tired.

I open my messages, leave the group chat with all of Ryan's friends, then open up my chat with Anna. She's been getting ready to go up to Leeds for university (she's been saving up for uni ever since we started babysitting when we were both fourteen) so I haven't seen her in a couple of weeks.

Ryan cheated on me.

She replies almost immediately.

No!!!!!!!!! What happened??????

I walked in on him with someone from college :(

What a bastard!!! Are you alone???
Want me to come over???

It's okay, I think I'm okay. Just gonna
hang out with Mum tonight.

Say hi to Laura for me. Remember, Emily is doing that girls' night out tomorrow, you're coming, right? Good chance to have a few drinks and say good riddance to the cheating scumbag.

I get two mugs out of the cupboard and put a peppermint teabag in one while I wait for the kettle to finish boiling. I really don't want to go to Emily's girls' night out. Anna stayed at the school we both attended for sixth form while I went to the local college. Emily is part of a group of girls who I never really knew when I was there, but Anna has got closer with them since I left the school. Whenever I go out with them, I always feel a bit like the odd one out. It's much easier when it's just me and Anna. Mum likes to say that I just haven't "found my people" yet, and she tells me off whenever I call myself a hermit. But there's only a month or so until Anna goes off to university so my opportunities to hang out with her are numbered, and I want to take advantage of her being here.

Sure, I'll be there. Just gonna watch some Countryfile tonight lol

A wild night :')

I pour the freshly boiled water into the mug with the teabag, swish it around a bit with a spoon then fish out the teabag and put it in the other mug before pouring water over that one too. I walk back into the living room and give Mum the tea with the bag in, then sit on the armchair and pull my feet up to curl up properly. I cup the mug with my hands and feel a bit calmer as I breathe in the peppermint steam.

"So tell me, what brings you home so early?" Mum asks.

I take a deep breath. "I went round to Ryan's and found him with someone else."

"What?!" She sits up straighter. "You mean ... *with* someone else?"

I nod.

"Oh, love. I'm so sorry."

"It's okay. I mean, it's not. But I feel okay. At the moment, anyway."

"Was it someone you know?"

"Someone from my psychology class. I've never really hung out with her." Imogen was one of those people who floated between social groups, never really sticking in one place. I'd see her in the library from time to time when I was returning books, sitting at a computer by herself. Other times, she'd be sneaking a cigarette by the bike racks with the stoners or laughing with the drama kids in the big hall at lunchtime. She always looked like someone who was fun to be around, but she never hung out with Ryan and the rest of the science nerds so our paths never really crossed.

"And you're sure you feel okay?"

"Yeah. I think so."

"Because it's okay if you don't. It's normal to feel sad about it."

"I know. I'm okay. Let's just watch *Countryfile*."

She smiles at me and presses play on the remote. If it's normal to feel sad when your boyfriend cheats on you, it must be pretty abnormal to feel so ... fine. I pull up a game on my phone to try and get out of my head, shifting around in the chair to get properly comfortable. Maybe the sad will come later.

Chapter 2

The next night, Anna comes round so we can get ready to go out together. I turned eighteen very soon into my second year of sixth-form college but Anna is a May baby so I didn't start going out at night until her birthday had passed. Mum says she used to get into pubs when she was fifteen, but they didn't have bouncers at every entrance back then, with a machine to check if your ID is legit.

"So where is it you're going tonight?" Mum asks Anna as we pop into the living room on our way up to my bedroom.

"It's 80s night at the Railway," Anna tells her. "All the girls from sixth form are going. Lots of us are on holiday in August so it's kinda like our last night out before we go to uni."

"Oh yes, how exciting! Have you got everything you need for student housing?"

"Just about."

"We've got to get ready now," I tell Mum, stepping out of the living room.

"Come and show me your outfits before you leave," she says.

When we get up to my room, Anna puts on an 80s playlist and dumps her bag of stuff out on the floor. She's brought at least five outfit options and what seems like her entire makeup collection.

"You have to help me decide what to wear."

Anna and I always fall into our usual rhythm. She takes up her space sitting cross-legged in front of the full-length mirror and catches me up on all the gossip since we last hung out. Apparently Emily and her boyfriend are determined to make the long-distance thing work even though she's going to Edinburgh when university begins and he's going to Bristol. I give Anna a play-by-play of exactly how last night went down and she's just as outraged that it wasn't Ryan following me down the street to apologize.

"She said he was just sitting there. He didn't even try to follow you?"

I nod. "Didn't even try. What are we doing with my makeup?"

"Go big or go home, Campbell," Anna says to me, brandishing a bright pink eyeshadow. "It's 80s night."

"I'm already home."

"Then you have to go big."

"I don't think that's how it works."

She rolls her eyes at me and I stick my tongue out at her. "Close your eyes," she instructs. She jabs at my eye a bit too enthusiastically and I come away with this amazing pink winged-out eyeshadow that I can't stop staring at in the mirror.

"It's perfect," Anna declares. "You look kickass."

Mum insists on taking photos of us in our outfits.

"It could be the last time you both get ready here!" she says as she gets us to pose in front of the millions of plants in the living room.

"Don't say that," Anna protests.

"I just remember when you were so tiny and going to your first disco …"

"Mum! Come on, let's go," I say to Anna, laughing and pulling her to the front door.

"Have a lovely time! Don't do anything I wouldn't do!" she calls after us.

I deliberately haven't given much time to thinking about what it'll be like to stay here while Anna goes off to university in Leeds. A couple of Ryan's friends are going to the local university, and one is saving up to travel next year, and I just assumed I'd see them from time to time, but I guess that's off the table now. I think Ryan will probably get all of our mutual friends in the breakup; they were all his to start with anyway.

The pub is already busy when we arrive, and Anna quickly locates her friend's table and leaves me there while she goes to get us some drinks.

"Hey, Casey!" Emily kisses me on the cheek as I sit down next to her. "How's it going?"

"Good, thanks! How are you?"

"I'm good!"

We look at each other, and I'm trying to think of something else to ask her when she says, "So, are you excited for uni?"

"I'm not going this year," I remind her. "I'm deferring."

"Oh, okay." There's a short silence. "But you're excited for next year, right?"

Anna arrives back with drinks and I think Emily and I are both relieved that we don't have to think of more things to say to each other. She's perfectly nice, but we just don't have much in common. It had always been me and Anna against the world, but when Dad left and we couldn't afford the school fees any more I had to move to the local sixth-form college to finish my sixteen to eighteen education.

Once we move to the back room of the pub and start dancing, the night starts getting more fun. Any situation where I don't have to make awkward small talk with people I only kind of know is good. The DJ is taking requests and Anna and I mostly forget about the alcohol part of the night and just dance and yell along to our favorite songs. Even though I wasn't looking forward to it, I have to admit that a night out dancing is exactly what I needed to get all the horrible thoughts about Ryan out of my head, at least for a few hours.

A week goes by and I still don't hear anything from Ryan. I find myself wondering what I did wrong to send him straight into the arms of someone else. Sure, we weren't exactly star-crossed lovers, but I thought we were cute together. He could at least have the decency to apologize.

I wake up one August morning to find a rainy, muggy day ahead of me. I roll out of bed, head to the bathroom to brush my teeth, then gently knock on Mum's bedroom door.

"I'm awake," comes the answer, and I push the door open and sit on the side of her bed. It feels so much cozier in here since Dad moved out; Mum has filled the space he left with hobby supplies and the kind of knick-knacks he said made the house look cluttered.

"How are you feeling?" I ask Mum.

She sighs and adjusts the pillows around her. "It's a crash day today, I think."

"Do you want breakfast?"

"Yes please, that would be lovely."

"Sofa or bed?"

"Bed."

I squeeze Mum's hand then head downstairs. I check my phone while the bread toasts and find a message from an unknown number.

Hey Casey. Sorry it's taken me so long to get in touch after last week. I've been thinking about what happened and I really am sorry I hooked up with Imogen, but I just didn't think you were that into me. It was nice to have someone be properly interested in me and it made me realize that I think I need to be in a relationship with someone who actually likes me. Sorry. I'm going to uni in September as well so it's probably for the best.

Part of me has gone straight to outrage; how could he say he thought I wasn't into him? We had been together for nearly eight months! But then my mind turns to the sad resignation in his eyes when I walked into that room, and I reread the text and realize I don't really know how I would define being "into" someone. The kissing was nice, but his wandering hands always inspired more indifference than excitement so we never did more than over-the-clothes groping. My hormones are meant to be raging but I've never really felt the pull toward sex like other people my age seem to. The overwhelming feeling I got when I walked into that room was … relief. Relief that it was over, that I didn't have to worry he was cheating on me at university while I was sitting at home caring for Mum.

"What's on the menu today?" Mum asks, sitting up in bed as I return with our breakfast.

"Only the finest cuisine." I present her plate with a flourish. "Hand-picked peanuts on homemade sourdough."

She laughs and starts eating as I make up an egg cup with all her daily supplements on her side table. "And you'll be pleased to note that overnight, they've discovered a cure for chronic fatigue syndrome," I tell her.

"Oh, wow! So I'll take these pills and I won't feel like a truck has hit me when I wake up every morning?"

"Exactly. A miracle cure."

I sit at the end of her bed and pull my feet up to sit cross-legged, and we eat our breakfasts in companionable silence. It's so much easier to manage our lives together now that I haven't got college to think about. So much nicer to spend some proper time waking up in the mornings and having breakfast rather than chucking some toast at Mum and running out of the door, and I know she feels relieved to know that I'm not completely exhausting myself with caring for her and trying to pass my A-levels at the same time. I scraped enough UCAS points to get into Brunel and study English but I've deferred for a year so we can figure out getting carers for Mum before I leave, and so that I can save up my Carer's Allowance.

"Ryan texted me while I was making breakfast," I tell Mum.

"Oh, wow. What did he say?"

"He apologized."

"It's about time," Mum says. "What's it been, a week? Did he have anything to say for himself?"

"Just that he was sorry. And ..." I don't really know how to say the next part.

"And?"

"That he thought I didn't like him."

Mum furrows her brow. "You didn't like him?"

"Yeah. I mean, yes, I liked him. But maybe ... I don't know. Maybe he had a point."

"What makes you say that?"

"I just ... I don't know if I felt the way I should feel about a boyfriend."

"And how should you feel about a boyfriend?"

"I don't know. Like, wanting to see him all the time. How they are in TV shows and books and stuff."

We each take a bite of toast.

"It doesn't have to be like it is in the movies to be worth pursuing. He was your first boyfriend, and you two were sweet together. But you'll find someone else if you want to, don't worry." She reaches across to me and strokes my arm. "You know it's not your fault, right?"

I pull a face.

"No, really. It's not your fault. What he did, cheating on you, that's all on him. You didn't make him go after someone else because he didn't feel liked enough; he should have had the decency to break up with you first."

At her words, I feel a surge of renewed energy. I had been feeling like it was me not being good enough that had driven him to sleep with Imogen, putting all of the blame on myself for being a boring girlfriend. But really, the decision had been his. No matter if Imogen said she was the one who made the first move, or he said he only did it because he didn't think I liked him very much. It was him who decided to get with someone else while we were still together.

"Yeah. Yeah, it is on him," I agree.

"No one deserves to have that done to them."

"No, I know. I just … I keep wondering if it was really right, us being together."

"Why wouldn't it be?" Mum asks. The answer is on the tip of my tongue, but I can't figure out what it is. It feels like something low buzzing within me, a hum in my whole body that I'm not on the right wavelength for. Like there's more to a relationship than what I've experienced but I don't know where to start looking for it, or even what was missing in the first place.

"I don't know. It just didn't feel right."

"Well, you don't have to think about that now. All you need to focus on is yourself."

"Thanks, Mum," I say, smiling at her. "I'm going to go for a run at the gym, okay?"

"Okay, sweetheart. Enjoy!"

"Do you need anything before I go?" I ask.

"No, you go ahead."

I bound to my room, suddenly filled with a dizzying sense of freedom. I thought that Ryan cheating on me was a mark against my character, proof that I'm not interesting enough to keep his attention. But I just keep recalling that feeling of relief when I walked in on him and Imogen. Maybe this is a good thing.

My walk to the gym feels different today. Same old route, same park cut-through with the same trees, but a different Casey. I listen to my gym playlist and get in a few imaginary kicks and punches at the people I walk past. Bam, trip up that woman. Whomp, hit that boy in the jaw. Kapow, roundhouse kick the slow-walking man in front of me in the back of the head.

I pull down my hood as soon as I get into the gym. Nothing can really replace the feeling of running outside, but on miserable days like this the local leisure center helps a little. I still get that same heavy rhythmic footfall running on a treadmill, and it helps me switch off my brain and be aware of my whole body. I jog up the stairs and put my bag, jacket and keys into a locker. My favorite treadmill is available, the one that looks over the sports hall so I can watch people play badminton, basketball, anything you can play in a sports hall really. As I get onto the treadmill I can see that there are some people roller-skating around it.

I find a good rhythm today. My strides feel longer and more purposeful, and I lose myself in listening to my latest playlist. It's strategically planned so I can increase the speed gradually when the songs change and then do a slow cool-down. As I'm reaching the peak of my speed, my eyes focus a bit more on the roller-skating down in the hall. Everyone is wearing more pads than I would expect for a roller disco, and as I watch, one person cuts across the track drawn on the floor with tape and hits another skater with the side of their body. I gasp and pull my earphones out as the person falls to the floor. I step to the side of the treadmill to get a closer look; I'm sure they must have hurt something falling that hard.

The person laughs, and as they look up I realize it's Imogen. She's wearing a neon green helmet and exchanging friendly chat with the person who knocked her to the floor, offering a high five as she stands up uninjured. They get back into position and start hitting each other again. It definitely doesn't look like any roller disco I went to as a kid. As I look a bit closer, I realize that everyone skating is an adult. There's one person in sneakers in the middle of the track who is using a whistle to run some kind of drill. The skaters are wearing pads on their knees, elbows and wrists, all with helmets, and when a taller woman with a blonde ponytail laughs at something her friend said, I can see that she's wearing a mouthguard.

I realize I've been staring over the side for a while now and get self-conscious, stepping back onto the treadmill to continue my run. But for the entire rest of the playlist, I'm watching what's happening downstairs. The drills they're running mostly seem to be about hitting each other, and a lot of them feature one skater trying to get through three or four others who are trying to hit them out of the way or block their path. I've never seen a sport up close that's so violent, and they're taking such glee in it. I'm amazed by the number of times they get knocked over and still get up with smiles on their faces.

I've just about finished my cool-down when they start taking their safety kit off and gather in the middle of the track to do stretches. Panicked that they'll start leaving before I can get to them, I rip my earphones out and practically sprint to my locker, fumbling the key so bad it falls to the floor. When I eventually get my things out, I rush down the stairs worrying that I've missed them. I have to know what this is.

I'm so caught up in my mission that when I turn the corner toward the sports hall, I collide with someone. I start apologizing immediately.

"Oh my god I'm so sorry—"

"Well, I guess I deserved that."

It's Imogen, and her face is beaming like the sun. Not the reaction I would expect after being shoulder-checked, but I guess she's used to that kind of contact.

"Oh no, Imogen, I'm sorry. I wasn't paying attention." I can feel my face burning pink.

"It's fine, honestly. I'd want to beat me up if I were you," she says, shifting the huge rucksack on her back. She's wearing a loose white t-shirt, through which I can clearly see an acid-green sports bra, and black Capri leggings like mine. "I'd beat up the boyfriend as well while I was at it," she adds, smiling but sounding deadly serious.

I laugh nervously. "I'm not sure I'm the beating-people-up kind to be honest."

"Are you sure? It's a lot of fun. I highly recommend it." She winks at me and moves to carry on walking towards the entrance.

"I saw you from upstairs." She turns back around to face me. "You were roller-skating and hitting people—is it some kind of sport?" I ask.

"Oh yeah, it was derby practice," she says.

I have no idea what she's talking about. We don't live in Derby.

"I don't think I'm tough enough for that." I laugh nervously.

"Sure you are. There's a game up in London tomorrow if you want to come and see what it's about."

Just the word "London" makes me tense up, but I have to admit I'm pretty curious about what this derby thing is—I've never seen anything like it before. I've just never been there without Mum and the thought of being on a train with people I don't know is terrifying. What if we all fall asleep and miss our stop? What if my phone runs out of battery and I lose everyone and get lost in London? What if I catch norovirus and there's only one toilet at the venue and we've all got it and everyone's just throwing up everywhere?

"Casey?" Imogen nudges me and I realize she's still waiting for an answer.

"What ... is it exactly? Derby?"

"Roller derby. Mostly women and nonbinary people, trans-inclusive obviously, but we let the men play with us sometimes." She laughs and punches a guy on the shoulder who's passing by, roller skates hanging from a strap over his shoulder. He grabs his arm in mock pain.

"Yeah, and then the likes of you make me never want to come back," he jokes as he walks past. "You recruiting again?"

Imogen nods and waves goodbye, then turns back to me. "It's a full-contact sport on roller skates, it's full of kickass people, and it's entirely not-for-profit. By the skaters, for the skaters. Are you busy tomorrow? Fancy coming to the game?" she asks.

I still have no idea what she's talking about, but I think about this powerful feeling I've been having, of needing a fresh start. Something new, something I haven't tried before. I can feel my heart flutter in my chest, and Imogen is looking back at me with such hope. The bitterness I was feeling toward her has disappeared, and she seems genuinely interested in trying to help me feel better. It feels like every conversation I have today is a step toward something different. I don't have anything planned for tomorrow. But still, it's *London*.

"Don't worry. I'll look after you in the city. It's the least I can do," she says, winking at me as if she can see me wavering. And that does it.

"Sure, why not," I tell her.

"Amazing," she says, smiling widely at me. "Meet you at the station at eleven?"

I smile back nervously. "See you then." I'm reinventing myself into someone who makes off-the-cuff plans with near strangers.

And she's off, piling into a car with other skaters and giving me a wave goodbye. I don't have any idea what I've signed up for, but it's something new, and that's a start.

Chapter 3

I meet Imogen at the station at eleven and she's brought some teammates along with her. Lucy has pale skin, a shaved head and a distinctive loud, booming laugh. Rae is dressed like a classic hippy stoner with long flowing dyed-red hair.

The last time I went to London was on a school trip in Year 7 that Mum was chaperoning. I was always an anxious kid, and always aware that I needed more reassurance than my sister and her friends did at the same age. When Mum started to get ill, I started getting these spirals of horrible thoughts I couldn't break out of, thinking about all the worst-case scenarios and planning for all of them before I could relax even a little. When Dad left, and later on my sister Billy, I was the only person to run the home and look after Mum, and preparing for those worst-case scenarios started paying off. When thick snow stopped us from getting to the shops for a few days, my stockpile of tins kept us fed. When Mum got the flu and the doctor refused to make a home visit, I was the one who had to hold it together and not panic. Even when her fever stayed really high and paracetamol wouldn't touch it.

Realistically, I know that a trip to London with some new people isn't the end of the world. But I can't stop my mind racing as we get tickets and find the right platform. I don't really know Imogen at all, and Lucy and Rae are completely new. Mum is always able to calm me down when I go into one of my spirals, but I have no idea how my travel-mates would react if I started to panic, especially in a situation that seems completely normal to them.

"Have you seen any roller derby before? Imogen said you were a newbie," Rae interrupts my worries. We've found four seats with a table and Rae is sitting next to me.

"I looked it up last night but I haven't seen it before. I hadn't even heard of it before I saw Imogen skating at the leisure center."

"Oh, a true newbie, that's exciting!" she says. "I won't bore you with all the rules now but feel free to ask me anything when we're there. You'll love it."

I stand pigeon-toed in the queue just inside the doors of an old boxing venue, pulling the sleeves of my jumper over my hands. Everyone around me is chatting and laughing, while people skate by with names on the backs of their t-shirts like "Cunning Stunt," "Ruby Bruiseday," and "Poison Oy Vey."

The queue starts moving and then we're in the main hall. There is a huge track marked out on the floor with people skating around it. I can hear loud, bass-driven music with screaming female vocals over the top. There are a lot of chairs on the ground floor and some mats right up against the track boundaries. I can see a balcony around three of the walls with people crowded onto them, leaning on the railings with pint glasses threatening to fall out of their hands and onto the crowd below. A huge stage at the back of the room has a projection screen cycling through pictures of previous games.

Lots of the photos have people wearing acid green, matching the new streak Imogen has in her hair.

It feels like something is trying to crawl out of my body through my throat. I start to feel panic brewing up inside me as Imogen veers off to go to the bar and I lose Lucy and Rae in the crowd. I sit in the first chair I see and push the pads of two fingers onto the inside of my wrist and breathe. Seven counts in. Hold for four. Eleven counts out. Seven counts in. Hold for four. Eleven counts out. My pulse slows to a more acceptable seventy beats per minute. I'm starting to feel better but I squeeze my tote anyway, and the crunch of the paper bag I keep in there just in case is soothing.

"Casey!" A hand claps down on my shoulder and as I whirl around, I am suffocated by Imogen's hair. She hugs me firmly with one arm, the other hand clutching three bottles of beer. "There you are! We lost you." It's only been a couple of minutes since I lost sight of them all, but the way Imogen grasps me to her you'd think it had been hours.

"Mmph," I mumble as I'm released.

"We've got the best seats in the house." She takes my hand and leads me to the edge of the track where Lucy and Rae are already sitting on the floor next to a sign that states: "Trackside seating. Age 18+ only."

"Hey! She found you!" Rae says, grabbing a beer from Imogen.

"Yup."

"We got suicide seats!" Lucy tells me as she takes her beer from Imogen.

"Lu, you're so 2016, you know we don't call them that anymore," Rae admonishes.

I sit down cross-legged on the floor. Imogen grins at me and nudges my leg with her knee. I can feel nerves bubbling up in me and start rummaging in my bag for some chewing gum to distract myself.

"I can't believe you're not backing the Bullets, they're so much higher ranked than the Angels," Lucy says to Rae, gesturing wildly with a mouthful of crisps.

"But Smack transferred to them a couple of months ago, don't forget," Rae says.

"Psh. A couple of months isn't enough to properly learn how to work together as a team. Smack can't win the game for them."

"Hey," Imogen says softly to me as Rae and Lucy argue, pointing at my bag, "what have you got in there, your whole life?" I'm immediately on the defensive and pull it shut before I see that she's smiling like we have an inside joke.

"Oh … Uh …" I flounder.

"Think you'll be able to fit some skates in there?"

I swallow and think for a second, trying to match Imogen's playful tone. "Well, I haven't decided if it's my thing yet."

"Come on"—she throws her hands up—"hot chicks hitting each other on roller skates? What's not to love?"

"Well, I prefer something with a more subtle art, like badminton."

"You mean the kind of badminton where you knock people over though, right?" Her cheek dimples.

"Obviously. Australian rules."

I'm tonguing the roof of my mouth madly to try and keep from laughing, and Imogen has this wild gleam in her eye.

"You're going to love skating," she says. It doesn't seem like something I have a choice in.

As she turns to talk to Lucy, I can see the back of her vest says "Agatha Frisky."

"Do you all have these names?" I ask. "Is that like … a roller derby thing?"

"Oh yeah!" Lucy says, and she and Rae both turn around so that I can see the names on their backs as well. Lucy is "Lucy Goosey" and Rae is "Death Rae."

"But it doesn't have to be something to do with your actual name, right? Your name isn't secretly Agatha?"

"No," Imogen says, laughing. "They're like our alter egos on the track. When you start playing, you have to come up with a roller derby name and number. Some people just use their last name like football players, but a lot of us have something funny. Usually puns, sometimes nicknames, always fun to shout across the track."

"The best name I've ever seen is Toxic Block Syndrome," Rae tells me, grinning.

"It's about to start, gang," Lucy says, pointing at the track. "You know the rules, right?" she asks me.

I do, kinda, but instead of responding I freeze up and stare blankly at her for a second. The game begins with a rolling whistle blast from a referee on skates in the middle of the track. It bears some resemblance to the sport I researched online last night, but it's much more intense and fast-paced when it's right in front of me. I'm having trouble keeping up.

"The ones with the stars on their helmet covers are the jammers," Imogen says to me, pointing at the track.

"They score the points, right?"

"Yeah. The jammers score a point every time they pass a blocker from the other team. So if you're a blocker, your job is to help your jammer get through the pack and hit the other one out of the way so they can't get past you."

The sound of wheels on the wooden floor cuts all the way through me. It's weirdly energizing, and I feel a surge of pride when I let out a big "oof!" along with the rest of the crowd when Poison Oy Vey comes skidding towards us on her back. She stops centimeters away from me, hops up onto her toe stops and runs back into the action immediately.

"That's why we used to call them suicide seats," Lucy tells me, leaning over but keeping her eyes fixed on the action. "You take your life in your own hands when you sit here." I try and move back from the track boundary without anyone noticing, but over the next few jams I find myself leaning forward with excitement.

"You see how that jammer is tapping their hips?" Rae asks me, pointing towards the track. I nod. The referee following the skater around the track lets off four short whistle-blasts which all the other officials join in with, and everyone on the track goes back to their respective bench to be replaced with a new team of skaters. "That's because they got through the pack first, so they can call off the jam at any time before the other team can score any points."

"Okay, I understand," I say.

A few jams later, I lean over to Imogen. "Why are they getting sent off?" I ask, pointing at a jammer who's skating off the track and over to a set of seats in front of people dressed in black holding stopwatches.

"They just committed a penalty. It's a full contact sport,

but there are limits," Imogen tells me. "You can only hit people in certain places on their body. If you do something blatantly dangerous, you can be ejected from the game, but otherwise each penalty means thirty seconds in the penalty box. You want to avoid getting penalties because you leave your team skating short while you're sitting there. You really don't want to commit a penalty when you're a jammer, because then you create a power jam situation. That's when there's only one jammer on the track and they can just rack up the points."

It's a struggle to keep all the rules in my head and watch the game at the same time. My sister Billy started getting interested in football when she moved in with her boyfriend, but Mum and I never took more than a casual interest in sports. The commercial and celebrity aspects always made it seem very dull to me—there seemed to be more time devoted to advertisements than to playing whatever sport it was. But this … This is a sport I can get behind. I can see so many people working together to put on the game—refs on skates in striped shirts, and people with clipboards and "OFFICIAL" written on the backs of their t-shirts, not to mention the people staffing the merch stands and the door, photographers, people rushing in between jams to repair the track with big rolls of tape—everyone is clearly here for the love of roller derby.

As we near half time I'm actually starting to understand the rules, yelling "Call it off! Call it off!" as Smack Daddy fights their way through the pack. My cry is echoed around the hall and they tap their hips quickly, looking at a referee in the center of the track. He lets off four sharp whistle blasts and the half is over. I can feel a wild energy buzzing beneath my skin, and I can't wait for the second half of the game to start.

"I've got the biggest fear crush on Poison," Rae says to me as we stand at the merch table.

"I just want to *be* her," Imogen says. "You have to buy that, Casey. You'd match with my hair!"

I'm holding a lime-green tank top emblazoned with the words "Bournemouth Bullets" up to my chest to check the sizing.

"I don't know if I can pull off this color. It's so … neon," I stumble.

"Get it. They're a local team, that's why I support them. It'll look great on you," Imogen tells me. She exchanges cash with the person behind the table, pins her new badge on her bag strap and gives me a gentle nudge with her hip before heading to the bar.

I start folding the top to put it back on the table but think better of it and get my purse out of my bag. With my new purchase tucked under my arm, I rush to the toilets and wait patiently in the queue. The sign on the door tells me to let skaters go first, so when I finally get a cubicle the second half is about to start. I hang my bag on the hook behind the door, pull off my top and put the new tank top on. It's more revealing than I'd like, and I curse myself for throwing on my comfy old sports bra this morning. I go to take it off again, but something makes me stop. Me from a few days ago wouldn't even have this decision to make, she'd be at home. I tuck my bra straps nervously under the fabric on my shoulders and pull the neckline up a bit. Maybe it's time for a change. Breathe in for seven, hold for four, out for eleven. I screw up my eyes and shake my head before marching out of the toilets without looking at my reflection.

"Nice!" Rae says when she notices, and Lucy nods approval in my direction.

"Told you," Imogen says, passing me a beer. I put my hand out and open my mouth to say "no thanks," but Imogen misinterprets the gesture and places the bottle in my hand. Maybe the Casey who wears a neon-green tank top is the kind of person who drinks beer while watching sports.

The second half feels much faster than the first. The alcohol in my system gives me a little buzz, and I find myself shouting along with the audience even more. It's a complicated sport, but everyone's patient explanations have really paid off and I'm starting to understand more of the rules. Ruby Bruiseday delivers a particularly ferocious hit to the opposing jammer with her hip, but Rae tells me that the reason she's sent off is because she was stopped on the track when she delivered the hit instead of moving counter-clockwise ("derby direction").

To Lucy's bafflement, the Angels take a pretty sizable lead towards the end of the game, and the final jam has a feeling of friendly competition. Everyone on the track seems to know that whatever they do in the next two minutes won't make a difference to the end result, and they laugh and joke with each other during a time-out as they wait for the officials to finish debating some minutiae about the rules.

At the final whistle, everyone in the crowd gets up and rushes to the edge of the track. Imogen grabs my arm and drags me in so hard I think my shoulder might be dislocated. The players skate around the track and slap our outstretched hands, and it's not until I hear my own hoarse voice whooping that I realize how hard I've been cheering the whole time.

"Right! After-party!" Imogen throws an arm around my shoulders and starts steering me towards the exit. We're both sweating slightly from the excitement and the warm air, and the hair under Imogen's armpit is tickling my shoulder. Of the few friends I've had in the past few years, none of them were very physically affectionate, and none of them would be seen dead with hair anywhere other than their head.

"After-party?" I ask.

"We hit each other, then we drink beer," she explains. I have no choice but to follow.

The first and last time I was properly drunk, I was fourteen and went round to Anna's house while her parents were away. We raided their alcohol cupboard and played "ring of fire" with other people from our class, and downed endless rounds of triple vodka and lemonade. I ended the night with a spectacular display of projectile vomiting all over the bathroom and vowed to myself that I would never drink vodka again. Even the smell of it turns my stomach and makes me feel jittery.

Getting tipsy on beer is a much slower process. Imogen and I are buying each other drinks throughout the evening and I can feel a slow, silly smile spread over my face. Much as I try to suppress it, there's a voice in my head that keeps telling me to stop drinking because I need to get the train home and not end up in Bournemouth because I fell asleep. But when Imogen casually chucks an arm around my shoulders and announces, "Another!" I'm not sure how to say no. Every few minutes I get a shot of anxious adrenaline to the heart when I remember I'm in London with people I don't know very well, but Imogen seems to have a sixth sense for knowing when I'm about to panic. She reaches over and gives me quick squeezes on the leg or arm as we're sat at the pub table. I guess when you spend your free time hitting your friends, sharing touches like this is a normal part of life.

The skaters look so different with their pads and helmets off. It takes me a while before I realize Cunning Stunt, who just got awarded "most feared blocker," is sitting on the other side of me.

"This was your first bout, huh?" she asks.

"Yeah, my first time."

"Did you like it?"

I can't stop the smile cracking my face in two. "I loved it."

Cunning Stunt smiles back at me. "It'll change your life. Welcome to the community!" I get a brief mental image of her standing in a queue for the bank, handing over a bank card with the name "Cunning Stunt" on it. People around me seem to be switching effortlessly from calling people the names on the back of their shirts and more commonplace names I imagine they go by at work or university. I love that everyone has these alter egos, names they use to signify the change that happens when they put on skates. I push aside the thought of myself wobbling around a sports hall and instead imagine transforming into a tough, athletic roller derby skater, with a name like "Brawlipop" or "One Hit Wonder."

We're in the function room of a busy pub, and every way I turn I see team shirts of all colors, with derby names and numbers on the back of them. My instinct is to shy away and tuck myself into a corner somewhere, but Imogen got us seats at a table right in the middle and keeps introducing me to people whose names I have no hope of remembering once I'm out of this chaos.

I last saw Lucy and Rae on a mission to get to the bar, and I recognize Lucy's shouts from near the entrance of the room. When I crane my neck, I can see Rae pulling her long asymmetrical skirt up around her waist in the small amount of floor space available. Imogen and I make our way over to the loose circle that's formed around her.

"Look at this beauty," she declares, pointing at her crotch.

She's wearing pale pink barely-there underwear that contrasts with her tawny skin, and underneath the fabric is a blossoming purple and brown bruise.

"Jeeesus!" exclaims Poison Oy Vey. "How did that happen?"

"I came down awkwardly on a wheel last week," Rae explains, a smug smile flitting about her face. "Full penetration. Seriously uncomfortable. I puked like three times from the pain."

Suddenly there is a flurry of injuries being displayed. Flashed before me are a broken and splinted finger, a shin with a huge bump on it, and a badly bruised rib. My heart rate increases. Sure, I've seen it live now, but I didn't realize roller derby was this dangerous. I was never an adventurous kid; Billy was the one coming home with scrapes and bruises after long days playing outside with her friends. I was always more nervous, never venturing onto the higher play equipment at the park and later, not participating in the ridiculous stunts Ryan and his friends would pull like climbing on top of the roof of the science building to sit and smoke. I've seen how injuries from those kinds of things can put someone out of action for weeks or months on end, and there isn't a backup plan for finding Mum care if I can't move around the house due to a broken leg.

But the way everyone is talking about their bruises and showing them off, it's like they're marks of honor. I try and push my anxiety about being injured to the back of my mind, and the beer helps a lot with that.

"That's nothing, that's fucking nothing!" Imogen cries, fighting her way into the center of the group. "Check this one out." She unbuttons her baggy denim shorts and lets them fall to the ground, displaying simple black underwear and a huge red and purple oval on the side of her right thigh.

"Shit!" exclaims Lucy, "who did that one?"

"Venom," Imogen says proudly. "She knocked me clean off my feet and this was the first part of my body to hit the floor. Sam dragged me to the doctor; they said it was a hematoma and I had to have it drained."

"This is Venom's too," says Lucy, revealing an old yellow bruise on her arm.

"And this," says Rae, pulling up her t-shirt to show a dark brown bruise on her side.

Whoever Venom is, it seems like getting a souvenir from her is some kind of rite of passage.

As the drinks keep coming, I can feel myself getting more and more comfortable in my surroundings. I'm barely even surprised when I find myself in the middle tier of a human pyramid that fails spectacularly just as Poison Oy Vey tries to climb to the top. As I collapse, laughing, crushed between people I've only just met, I get the feeling that maybe it's time for me to do something a bit dangerous and scary. Something unknown. Running is the only exercise-related thing I've done outside of school, and it's not exactly a team sport. Everyone involved in roller derby seems to have this easy, casual physicality about them, and although my nerves prevent me from initiating, I'm enjoying the relaxed touch that seems to come along with the sport. Imogen being constantly by my side is soothing in a way I wasn't expecting.

Not to mention, I can't think of any other situation in which someone accidentally grabbing my boob in an attempt to stand up would result in that person buying me a drink. Ruby Bruiseday insists on "taking me out for dinner first," which means buying me a pint of beer and a packet of crisps, then collecting every candle from the tables around us and placing them on our table. She splits the bag of crisps open and gestures formally towards it.

"Madame."

I giggle.

"Hey! Give me my new friend back!" Imogen tries to hip-check her off the stool but Ruby holds her ground. They keep pushing at each other, nearly upending the table itself.

"Stop flirting with the baby," Lucy admonishes them both, and I flush bright red when I realize she's talking about me. They barely even notice her as they decide arm wrestling is the best way to settle their differences, and soon enough everyone gets involved. I lose spectacularly to at least five people before I wrestle with Imogen, who I'm sure loses on purpose to make me feel better. Note to self: work on arm strength.

"S'nice, isn't it!" she shouts at me as we leave to get the last train home.

A goofy smile spreads over my face. "Yeah, it's nice!"

Rae and I doze through the train journey, only woken to witness Lucy and Imogen's chin-up competition using the handrails, and again a few seconds before our stop. We all grab our bags and run off the train, giggling. My heart is pounding from the last-minute wake-up and the fear of leaving something on the train, but it's impossible to be too anxious with Imogen cackling like a witch beside me as Rae tries to shush her.

As I stumble into bed, I can't stop thinking about the casual hugs from people whose names I didn't even know, and the way my cheeks ache from smiling so much.

Chapter 4

The next morning, getting out of bed is entirely out of the question. Mum knocks quietly on my door around midday.

"Casey? Love, are you okay?"

I groan as I hear the door creak open.

"Are you ill?"

I groan again. My head feels like it's splitting open. "I think I'm dying."

"What's wrong?" Mum hurries into my room and sits on the side of my bed. She places a hand on my forehead. "You're not feverish."

"I think I have a hangover. And I'm dying."

Mum's expression changes from concerned to amused. "I did hear you crashing around a bit as you came in. Did you have a nice time with your friends?"

I smile, but the small movement brings about a wave of nausea and dizziness. I panic, convinced I'm going to throw up all over Mum, then let out a burp and it subsides immediately. She laughs at me.

"Yeah, it was so much fun."

"What was it you went to, a roller hockey game?"

I stifle a laugh. "Roller derby."

"Think you might try it yourself?"

"Yeah, I think so." I surprise myself with how quickly I reply. I'm definitely scared of the violence but thinking about roller derby gives me this all-over frisson I can't quite explain, despite the hangover.

"It sounds like a fun thing to do with your gap year. Anyway, I'll let you get some more sleep. Text me if you want anything. Billy is coming round later with the baby; do you want me to wake you up when she arrives?"

When my older sister had a baby, I decided I wanted to be his cool aunt. Sneaking him cash and taking him to see 15 certificate films is something for later in his life; for now, Harry is only ten months old and all I can really do is try and make him giggle. I'm not sure how it will look to drag myself downstairs hungover, but I feel like that's part of cultivating the cool aunt image.

"Yes please," I say.

Mum nods at the glass of water on my bedside table. "Hydrate." She points at me sternly.

I sit up and take a big glug to show her I'm willing as she walks out of my room, then settle back under the covers to sleep off the worst of my headache.

~

I only get another hour or so of sleep before the doorbell ringing wakes me up. When we realized the door knocker wouldn't cut it any more, given my tendency to listen to music through earphones while I cook, Mum insisted on choosing the most offensively jaunty tune. I hate her a little more each time the postie delivers a parcel, especially because they're never addressed to me. I can't even ignore the doorbell and go back to sleep because it loops twice. I check my phone and realize I shot off an almost unintelligible ramble to Anna last night about roller derby and how great it is. She's just given it a heart reaction so I send her a link to a video, hoping that she'll see how amazing it is as well.

I go across the hall to splash water on my face and hear sounds of greeting and a gurgling baby coming from downstairs. Reflexively, I smile. Billy and I were never best friends as kids, but nothing unites a family like a baby. At least we've got something to talk about now other than our different but similarly absent fathers. She's a few years older than me and we've always had very different ideas of what we want our lives to look like.

I make my way downstairs once I've scrubbed the taste of dead badger out of my mouth. The headache has just about eased off, thankfully.

"Hey, Casey!" my sister says as I walk into the living room.

"Casey was out late last night," Mum tells her, extending a finger to tickle under baby Harry's chin. He giggles and kicks his legs in his bouncer.

"Wow, so you finally gave the Bone Zone a try? What is it on Saturdays—80s night?" Billy asks. The nickname of the local nightclub makes me blush.

"I went up to London."

"Fuck off," my sister says jovially, casting off my statement.

"No, really," I insist. Her mouth drops open and she looks to Mum for confirmation, who nods. "I went to see a roller derby game."

"Is that the thing where lesbians hit each other on roller skates?"

"They're not all lesbians," I protest, ignoring the fact that

60 percent of the people at the after-party wore plaid shirts over their team tops.

"And you went to *London*? Who took you?"

Her disbelief gets my back up. "I've been to London before."

"Yeah, on school trips, and only when Mum was one of the chaperones." Billy laughs but stops short when Mum gives her one of her patented evil glares. "I'm sorry, it's just … It's you. And London. How late were you back?"

I think. "About one in the morning."

She looks surprised and impressed. "Wow, Casey. You've changed."

I want to defend myself against this accusation, but maybe she's right. It was only one day, but I did a ton of stuff that normally makes me panic. Maybe this is all change is—trying new things.

Lunchtime has us all distracted for a while, and Harry manages to get his pureed food all over his clothes rather than in his mouth. Billy leans over every other second to wipe his face clean.

"It's only a bit of food, it won't hurt him. He's allowed to get messy," Mum says.

"But it's gross," she replies, reaching over my shoulder to wipe his mouth even as the spoon is still inside it. I can feel an argument brewing. Billy has never gone quite so far as to ask Mum why she's giving parenting advice when she's too ill to look after a baby, but she's implied it a handful of times. I search around for something to change the subject.

"I'm going to a roller disco with Imogen tomorrow," I tell

them both, suddenly remembering the drunken plans we made getting off the train last night. "I'm going to try it out for myself."

They're both surprised, although Mum has the decency to try and hide it.

"Oh, lovely! Will you be back in time—"

"—for your book group. Yeah, don't worry," I finish for her. I try to ignore the slack-jawed stare Billy is sending my way.

"I'm sorry, *roller disco*?" she asks. "Don't tell me you want to learn how to play this roller race thing."

"Roller derby," I correct.

"Whatever. You could really hurt yourself. Are you tough enough for that?"

I don't give a voice to the whisper in the back of my head, telling me she's right; I'm a wimp and there's no way I'll be able to play it.

"You can get hurt?" Mum asks, looking at me with concern.

"Have you seen it?" Billy asks Mum, ignoring me completely. "They properly chuck themselves at each other. Headbutting, elbow jabs, tripping each other up—"

"Those are penalties. You aren't supposed to do that," I protest.

"Yeah, but it won't stop them trying. Doesn't someone get punched in the face in that film with Elliot Page?"

I ignore Billy and focus on Mum. "It's a full-contact sport, but I'm just trying out roller-skating tomorrow. And they make you wear so many pads and a helmet and mouthguard," I tell her. "I'll be careful."

She looks from me to Billy and back again.

"I bet you'll wimp out at the first hurdle. And all that kit must cost a lot of money," Billy says, focusing her attention back on feeding Harry.

I realize with hot shame that I'm about to cry. I open my mouth to try and protest but feel my chin wobble in a telltale way and shut it.

"Billy," Mum admonishes. "She's trying something new. Give her some credit."

Billy rolls her eyes. "Don't come crying to me when you've broken your leg and can't look after Mum anymore. You knew when I moved that it was too far for me to come and help like I used to."

I stand up suddenly, setting the spoon down on the high chair surface. Harry notices the situation and starts crying, reaching his grabby baby hands out towards my sister.

"I'm going for a run," I announce, willing the tears to not give me away until I'm out of the room.

"Okay, sweetheart, see you later. Film night tonight?" Mum asks brightly, trying to diffuse the tension.

I grunt noncommittally and walk out of the kitchen, feeling more like a surly teenager than I have in a long time. The annoying thing is, I think to myself as I pull on some leggings and an old baggy t-shirt, Billy is voicing all the things I keep catching myself worrying about. This world I've discovered feels like a fantasy, and I'm not ready for it to be over yet.

In my imagination, I'm instantly good at skating. I strap on skates for the first time in my life, and it just comes naturally to me. I'm gliding effortlessly around the hall and everyone is shocked at how talented I am for a total beginner.

"No, I've never skated before," I tell them, easily transitioning into skating backwards and only stumbling slightly on jumping turns. "I'm a runner, I guess that's why I'm so good at it."

The after-school roller disco at the sports hall in the leisure center isn't exactly the perfect venue for the scenario I have in my mind, but I can make it work. Imogen meets me there with Lucy and Rae and another woman called Sam, and they each bring out different items from their bags to lend me. I put on a pair of old-fashioned roller skates, as well as thick, pillow-like pads on my knees and elbows. I have restrictive splint contraptions velcroed around my wrists and a big skate helmet that's been padded out with two borrowed bandannas. Lucy laughs a big, booming laugh at how big the helmet is on me, but Rae comes to my defense and offers me a vegan energy bar that she pulls from somewhere within her many-layered outfit. All the pads have a weird smell, somewhere between cheese and popcorn, and everything is either a bit too big or a bit too small and makes my skin feel really irritated.

When I was a kid, I was always too nervous about hurting myself to go bombing around in Barbie skates like my neighbors. I stand up hesitantly, and instantly realize that my dream of being naturally talented at this is a far-flung fantasy. My feet are shaking underneath me and I've never been more aware of gravity's ability to bring me down to earth.

We're wearing far more protective gear than anyone else at the roller disco. Lucy, Rae, Imogen and Sam put on their pads with ease and for some reason I feel like I need to set off before them so that I can't be intimidated by how good they are. I try and push one foot forward, but as I do the other slides back. The only way I can move is by gripping hard to the brick wall and pulling myself along with my arms. My feet are already aching, and my main thought as I slowly trundle past expert skaters is how to get out of this situation as soon as possible, because it's torture.

"Get lower, Casey!" Lucy yells from behind me. Experimentally, I try and get lower. It just feels like I'm leaning forward. I roll over an uneven bit of floor and instinctively stand straight up, but my legs aren't moving properly and my arms start windmilling and, oh god, this is definitely how I'm going to die.

An arm shoots out in front of me and I grab it, holding on for dear life. Once I'm stable again I realize the arm belongs to Imogen, and she starts gently but firmly adjusting my body without a word. She puts one hand on my sternum and the other on the small of my back, pushing my rounded shoulders back and my hips down. I desperately hope she can't feel how fast my heart is beating; this is the exact opposite of what my instincts are telling me to do. My knees are bent so much my thighs are burning within seconds.

"Are you sure this is right?" I ask, not wishing to seem more ignorant than I've already demonstrated I am. None of the inline skaters here have their knees bent as much as this.

"Roller derby skating is different than regular skating," Imogen tells me. "Keep your knees bent, push outwards from your top inside wheels, and if you think you're going to fall, reach over and touch your toes. It lowers your center of gravity so if you fall, you fall forward onto your pads. You don't have any pads on your bum, or as much natural padding as me"—she winks—"so it'll hurt a hell of a lot more to fall backwards. Fall forward, always."

"I … I …" I stammer.

"I'm going to do a couple of laps to warm up. You've got this, Case," Imogen says, gently punching me on the arm before skating out in front of me and effortlessly joining the crowd of people moving anti-clockwise around the hall.

I don't know whether it's the casual way she called me "Case" or her no-nonsense attitude, but I get as low as I can until my thighs scream for mercy and I push from my top inside wheels and I actually start picking up some speed. The air rushes past me and I start to feel like I might actually be in control of this. The wheels on the polished floor send vibrations through the soles of my feet and right up into my legs. My lower back starts aching, and I realize I'm using muscles I've never really used before, working parts of my body that have been largely ignored until now. I get distracted by all of this, then realize I haven't given myself enough time to slow down before I'll reach the brick wall at the other end of the sports hall and I don't know how to turn yet.

"Um! Imogen!" I say in a high-pitched voice as it gets closer, but she doesn't come to my rescue this time. Remembering her words from earlier, I reach over to try and touch my toes. I'm not too sure how it happens but I find myself skidding forward on my knees at quite a pace and hitting the wall with a dull "thunk."

I do a quick evaluation. All limbs present. Nothing broken. No blood. My heart is still beating faster than I'd like it to be, but I put that down to the exercise/fear combo. I'm surprised at how much the pads cushion my fall. The last time I fell forward like this was when I was running for the bus and it had hurt a *lot* more; I had bruises and scrapes on my knees and palms for ages. I'm getting the same hot wave of embarrassment that happened then, and to my horror I can feel a lump in my throat like I want to cry. I swallow it down and look around, almost expecting a sarcastic laugh or a slow clap, but no one is looking at me. I catch sight of Rae pushing Imogen to collide with Sam, and they fall to the ground in a tangle of limbs and both start laughing.

My instinct is to take the skates off and go home. Realistically, I know that part of learning how to do something involves being very bad at it for a while, but the perfectionist in me refuses to accept this. Outrageous that trial and error involves a lot of error. I drag myself up to sit on a bench in the corner of the hall and tell myself I'll sit down for a minute then try one more time, and if it's still awful I'll go home and accept that I'm never going to be a badass roller derby player. Lucy, Rae, Sam and Imogen are whizzing round the hall, dodging wobbly children and couples holding hands. Imogen spots me sitting on the bench and completes her lap of the track, skating straight at me. I'm convinced she doesn't have enough time to stop, but just before she gets to me she jumps, turns 180 degrees, lands on her wheels then quickly tips up onto her toe stops, gliding smoothly into sitting next to me.

"How did you do that?" I ask, open-mouthed.

"It's called a derby stop," she explains. "You transition into backwards skating however you want, then use your toe stops to brake. Looks cool, huh?"

I nod.

"You'll get there. How are you finding it? I thought I'd leave you to figure out what feels good, but I can stick around and help you out some more if that would be helpful."

I can't imagine a world in which I can do a derby stop. I've never felt so uncoordinated in my life.

I swallow and remind myself that I said I'd try one more time. "Sure, help would be great."

"What are you struggling with?" Imogen asks.

"Well, I don't know how to turn," I tell her.

"Look down at our feet," she tells me. I follow the instruction. "When I press my right foot to the outside, can you see that my wheels turn?" I nod. "You try."

I press down on the outside of my right foot, but my wheels don't turn nearly as much as hers.

"Hmm," she says, "tight trucks. Give me a second." She gets up and skates over to her kit bag, rummaging around for a second before pulling out a purple three-pronged tool and coming back to the bench. She picks up both my feet and swivels me around on the bench so my feet are on her lap in one smooth movement, so quickly I don't have time to protest.

"Um."

"I'll loosen your trucks. Tight trucks are good for stability but you need to learn how to skate a bit more loosey-goosey for roller derby." She frowns at the underside of my skates and sticks the tip of her tongue out of her mouth as she adjusts something on both skates. It feels weird, like they're a part of my body that's gone numb. "Try again."

I put my feet back on the ground, and this time my wheels turn when I put pressure into the outside of my right foot.

"That's it! Try pushing into the inside of your foot. You can see the wheels turn left? So when you want to turn a corner here, you can angle your feet to the left and you'll turn left. Your skates will just do it for you. Angle your shoulders and hips inwards and you'll fly round the corners. Give it a go."

I stand up from the bench and the wobbles take over immediately, but I try and get low how Imogen showed me and push from my inside wheels. The ache that shoots through my thighs feels good. I take a few strides and reach the next corner, angling my feet and body to the left. Miraculously, it works. I feel wobbly, but I'm actually skating. I risk a quick look back over to the bench and Imogen is grinning, giving me a double thumbs-up. I smile back then focus my attention on skating and make it round another corner.

I recognize parts of this from running, from reaching that point where my body stops feeling like it's fighting me with every step and actually starts working with me. It's like that, but faster. A smile creeps over my face.

A whistle blows from the side of the hall and someone yells "Turn around!" as the music changes. Suddenly I'm skating against the tide as people turn around and start skating in the other direction. I bend my knees, take a moment to steady myself then jump a couple of inches in the air and turn around, landing messily on my wheels. I tip up onto my toe-stops but end up over-correcting and land on my hands and knees. Imogen slides towards me on both knees like a rock star during a guitar solo.

"Nice try!" she says, laughing. She offers me an arm to help me get up and I take it, not quite as winded by this fall as I was by the first one. "Let's save the derby stops for your next session, huh?"

I nod and follow behind her as she sets off in front of me. My cheeks are flushed and a riotous energy is flowing through me. I think I like skating.

~

"So you can't actually join the team until our next intake, but that's in the middle of September so you don't have long to wait," Sam explains to me through a mouthful of pancake and maple syrup. We've come to the local American-style diner for something to eat after the roller disco, and it's very welcome as all the falling over and getting back up has made me really hungry. I don't think the portion of fried rice waiting for me at home is going to cut it.

"But until then, you can come to skate with us whenever we rent the hall for ourselves. It's usually once a week and we split the cost between whoever shows up," Rae says.

"And is there somewhere I can buy some kit of my own?" I ask. A few weeks of Carer's Allowance has built up in my bank account, and although I should be saving it for uni, I can't really think about anything except getting back on skates. The thought of putting on the smelly, borrowed kit again makes me feel itchy. I can't stop picturing myself at a game with the star cover on my helmet, dipping and dodging through players to score points.

"The nearest skate shop is only a train ride away. I'm free on Thursday if you want me to come with you?" Imogen offers. I nod enthusiastically, barely thinking about my usual travel nerves now that I've conquered London.

I can't stop gushing to Mum about skating when I get home to push her to and from book club in her wheelchair. So much so that she has to ask me to catch her up the next day because she's too tired to take anything else in. I feel like a small child showing off a new skill or new friends, and when I brush my teeth in front of the bathroom mirror before bed, my eyes are sparkling. All I want to do is get back on skates.

~

"No, look, you've put it on upside down." Imogen takes the wrist guard from me and turns it around. "The hard bit goes under your palm."

True to her word, she has taken me out to get kitted up. The nearest skate shop is a twenty-minute train ride away and is bigger and more intimidating than I thought it would be. The dreams I've been having since the game in London are starting to become a scary reality.

"Okay, well, these fit. And I've got skates, knee pads and elbow pads. What else do I need?"

"A mouthguard. Here." Imogen scans the shelves quickly and wiggles a bright yellow mouthguard at me. "Team colors. And you need a helmet." She looks around. "Excuse me? Could you help us find a helmet that fits please?" she asks the guy behind the counter. He glances at me, then pulls down a selection of helmets for me to try on. I'm trying not to add up the cost as I go along, but surely £49.99 for a helmet is a bit much? That's two-thirds of mine and Mum's weekly food shop.

"You've put it on back to front," Imogen tells me, snapping me out of my thoughts. I feel my face flush, embarrassed that I've already got something wrong, but Imogen is smiling as she helps me. She un-clips the clasp below my chin and lifts it off my head, turns it around and places it back on, wobbling it from side to side on my head. "It's too big anyway." She takes it off and looks to the sales assistant for help.

"That's the smallest size we carry. You could try a children's helmet if you want?" the staff member offers. Imogen erupts into giggles.

"Um … yes please …" I say.

"I'll just get one from the store room." He leaves. Walking into the shop was so intimidating and I can't shake the feeling that I'm not meant to be here. Imogen is a constant reassurance, guiding me through what I need to buy and how it should fit.

"I can't believe you're such a pin-head," Imogen says. I shove her shoulder gently and she pretends to fall over in slow motion. Her arms fly up and she takes a staggered step to the side, letting out an exaggerated "woahhhh" as she crumples. She winks at me from the floor then stands up, but as she does her head clips a display stand of safety pads. The whole display falls, this time not in slow motion but in loud real-time as everyone in the store turns to stare at us. I want the ground to swallow me up.

"Oh, Jesus, fuck, sorry," Imogen apologizes to the shop assistant who's just returned with a purple helmet. I can feel stares on us and my flush deepens as I try not to look at anyone else in the shop. I can't believe we've made such a scene. Imogen seems chastened by this as well and we simultaneously scramble to pick up everything that's fallen to the floor, bumping our heads on the way down.

"Ow!" we exclaim in unison while standing up before bursting into laughter. It's one of those fits of hysteria that's impossible to control, and soon tears are streaming down my face as I struggle to catch my breath. I've never been so embarrassed in my life. I'm mortified at the look the two staff members give each other and our laughter echoes into a short silence. Even the pre-teen boys lusting after the latest electric scooters look embarrassed on our behalf.

"Leave it. Just try on the helmet," I'm told brusquely by the shop assistant, and I obediently take it out of the box and put it on my head. It fits. And it's £20 cheaper than the adult one.

"I'm sorry, I'm so sorry," I say, scrambling in my bag for my debit card.

"Wait, Case. You forgot your helmet." I look behind me and Imogen is holding out a helmet suitable for toddlers. She's laughing silently and mouthing the word "pin-head" in my direction, and I can feel the same wild energy buzzing just beneath my skin that I felt at the game and after-party.

I pay, gather up my goods, and we rush out of the shop, Imogen clutching my arm and quietly crying with laughter. As soon as we get onto the street, we dissolve, gasping for air between laughs.

"I can't believe you knocked over the whole display," I say to her as we pause by a bin. I zip open my new kit bag and take the packaging off everything, shoving it into the bag haphazardly and putting the packaging in the bin.

"It was your fault, you pushed me over," Imogen retorts. She's grinning widely at me even as she wags her finger to tell me off. "Shoving with the hands is unacceptable in roller derby. You can only hit people with your shoulders and your hips."

"How about head-butting?"

"You'll get ejected immediately for a deliberate head-butt. If you're going to hit me, make it legal!"

We manage to regain control of ourselves and start walking towards the train station.

"Case?"

"Mm?" The smell of pastries as we walk past Greggs is distracting, and I'm only half listening.

"I'm sorry about Ryan."

This is unexpected. "What? I mean, we don't have to talk about …" I start.

"We do. I'm sorry. I just … I like you, Casey. You're cool, and I wanna help you learn how to skate. But we started off shitty and I wanted to say I'm sorry for that."

My heart skips at Imogen thinking I'm cool, but I don't know how to respond. We met under such strange circumstances, and even though we've only seen each other a few times, she still wants to hang out more with me. When I'm around Imogen, I feel … different. It feels like a new start, a chance for reinvention. A chance to let go of the quiet, mousey girl too buried in caregiving responsibilities to make proper friends. Roller derby seems like a great place to experiment with an alter ego.

"Look … Imogen …"

"I just … I'm sorry. I haven't seen him since, obviously. I'm in kind of a difficult place at the moment and I thought he was probably lying to me about being single, but I hooked up with him anyway, without checking. There's no excuse."

I'm not really sure how to respond. I'm not used to talking so plainly with anyone except my mum, and Imogen's honesty makes me squirm inside. To tell the truth, I'd almost forgotten about how we met. Ryan seems like a distant spot on the landscape of the new life I'm building for myself without him, and I certainly haven't harbored any hard feelings against Imogen for what happened. The speed at which I've gotten over the betrayal has just confirmed my suspicions that Ryan and I weren't a good match, and I definitely never felt as enthusiastic about our relationship as I am now, learning everything I can about roller derby. I have no idea what to say in response, but I settle on something simple.

"Thank you," I say.

"For what?"

"For, you know, for being honest. It means a lot."

We pause our conversation as we muddle our way through the ticket barriers and fight our way onto a packed train. We've timed the trip badly and have no chance of getting seats at rush hour, so we're pressed up against all the sweaty people making the same journey. I'm painfully aware of my new kit bag taking up too much space, but it also gives me a bit of a barrier from the other passengers. Our conversation has made me feel lighter, more confident. Usually I'm the one saying sorry even if I haven't done anything wrong, so it's a refreshing change to be the one accepting the apology. I look over at Imogen and her eyes crinkle as she smiles at me.

"You kind of did me a massive favor," I say with rising confidence, hanging onto a handrail.

"I did?"

"Yeah. I mean, me and Ryan …" I make a face and Imogen laughs.

"No trophy for perfect couple of the year?"

"We were runners-up."

"After Thunder Bird and Mistress Trix?"

I look at her quizzically. "Who?"

"Roller derby royalty. Don't worry, I'll catch you up."

I smile at her.

She pokes me in the side. "Go on then. Why did I do you a favor?"

I heft my new kit bag more securely onto my shoulder as the train stops at a station, then starts again. One more stop until home.

"I guess … I don't know. It's like I was waiting for something with him. Like I was waiting to feel the way I'm supposed to feel about a boyfriend."

"Supposed to?"

"Yeah. Like the foot-popping moment. It just never happened. We hung out, and we liked the same TV shows and stuff, but I only got together with him because he asked me out."

"I think I get that." She smiles at me and touches my arm. "Regardless of if I did you a favor or not, I hope you can forgive me."

There it is, that stark honesty I'm starting to expect from Imogen. The kind of honesty I don't really know how to respond to.

"Of course I forgive you."

Unexpectedly, Imogen pulls me into a one-armed hug just as the train stops. I stand stiffly for a moment, then put my free arm around her waist and hug her back. We're blocking the entrance and I'm painfully aware of the old lady tutting behind us, but for once I don't care what other people think. We pull away at the same time and Imogen winks at me, then we make our way off the train and out of the station in comfortable silence.

"I'm going this way," I say, as we reach the junction at the bottom of the hill, pointing right.

"I'm this way," Imogen says, pointing straight ahead down the hill. "Wanna hang out tomorrow? We can skate in the park near the sports center, there's some really smooth paths there which are great for practicing on, and that way we don't have to pay for the hall."

I don't even hesitate this time. "Sure. See you tomorrow," I say, pausing before giving Imogen a brief pat on the arm. She chuckles and turns to walk away as I do the same. I wince at how awkward it was and curse myself for not being more natural at physical affection. As I walk away, I try to push down that feeling and start to get excited about learning how to skate properly. Screw the washing up, when I get home I'm trying on my new kit.

Each time I put on my skates, I feel less and less wobbly. The weather stays surprisingly sunny all through August so Imogen and I spend a lot of time skating outdoors in the park as well as the sports hall, and I've started using more than the treadmills at the gym. I even get a trial session with a personal trainer who shows me how to build my abdominal muscles to support my lower back, so it doesn't ache so much after skating. The derby stop that seemed entirely out of reach at that first roller disco ends up being achievable after a couple of sessions practicing transitions, moving from skating forward to backwards in one fluid movement. I order a small book containing all the rules of roller derby and study it at every opportunity: while the shepherd's pie is cooking for dinner, during ad breaks for the trashy reality shows Mum and I are addicted to, in the queue at the chemist to pick up Mum's medication.

At a film night, Mum and Anna both stare at me with happy but confused expressions on their faces as I run them through a situation called a "no earned pass," when a jammer passes a blocker but doesn't earn a point on them.

"I'm talking too much about roller derby, aren't I?" I say. Anna nods at the same time as Mum shakes her head, then they look at each other and laugh.

"It's a bit … weird." Anna makes a face. "You hated netball at school."

"Yeah, but this isn't netball. You can't hit people in netball."

"And since when have you liked violence? I just don't get it," Anna says, shaking her head but smiling at me.

"I think it's brilliant you're picking up a new hobby," Mum tells me, coming to my defense. "You've always loved running, and it's a great way to make new friends."

Anna clasps a hand to her heart. "But we're the only friends Casey could ever need!" she exclaims in mock outrage.

"Let's just watch the rest of the film." I roll my eyes and sigh, hitting play on the remote. Heath Ledger's paused face starts moving again and we settle into our seats to watch. It's part of Mum's ongoing campaign to have Anna and I watch films she deems "classics," and *10 Things I Hate About You* is loaded up tonight. It's our last film night before Anna heads up to Leeds next week, and although I'm going to miss her I'm nowhere near as nervous as I was before I started skating. At least I know I won't be alone for the next year.

~

"How do you feel about trying some laterals today?" Imogen asks as I strap my pads on at the sports hall a few days later. I nod enthusiastically, popping my mouthguard in and smiling at her to show it off. She laughs, "I'll take that as a yes."

There are a few people I don't know here, who Imogen tells me are skaters who joined their "fresh meat" course at the same time as her back in January. I've signed up for the next one which starts next week. I'm a bit nervous to skate in front of people I don't know; most of the sessions here have been with Imogen, Lucy, Rae and Sam. But a lot of them are heading to a mixed scrimmage on Sunday and they want to log a few more hours of skating than they get in their two evening sessions a week. Sam tells me a mixed scrim is where a team hosts anyone who wants to join, splits them into teams and has a friendly game. She travels up and down the country most weekends to be an NSO (non-skating official) at games and is taking a car-load of teammates with her. I jumped at the chance to watch more roller derby, but they don't allow spectators, and after finding out it's a three-and-a-half-hour car journey, my travel sickness is glad I can't go along.

Imogen shows me how to cut smoothly from the inside of the track to the outside, then back to the inside. I've been watching lots of footage of games online and I recognize this is something both blockers and jammers do, either to quickly nip in front of an opponent who thinks they've found a way through, or to dodge a blocker right as they think they've got you trapped. As the others practice techniques they'll be using at the mixed scrim, I head to the end of the hall and use the space to try and get my head around laterals.

I've never been someone who particularly hates monotony; the routine of doing the same thing over and over again feels more soothing than boring, and this continues to be the case with skating. I listen to my body as I attempt the move again and again, with the occasional tip coming in from Rae or Imogen, and when I start getting it right more often than messing it up I try to embed those feelings into my muscle memory. I have to be reminded that the session is coming to an end and hurriedly take off my kit, foregoing my usual post-skate stretching session. The sweat patches on our leggings feel like trophies as Rae, Imogen and I head to a café afterwards.

"Shit, I forgot my shift got moved an hour earlier, I've got to go and shower before work! I'll see you next week!" Rae turns on her heel as we reach the entrance to the café and runs off, leaving Imogen and I to find a table alone.

"I can't stay too long," I tell Imogen as we sit down with iced drinks and cakes. "I've got to go and grab some ingredients for dinner that our online supermarket left out."

"I should probably put in some face time with my mum," she says, grimacing. "You're so lucky to have parents you get along with."

"Parent," I tell her. "But yeah, my mum is pretty great."

"Did you ever have a dad?" she asks me.

"Yeah. My sister's dad buggered off pretty early, on account of being a scumbag, but mine stuck around until I was a teenager."

"Why did he leave? Divorce?"

It's been so long since I've had to explain my home life to someone; Ryan never really asked and Anna was there for the whole thing.

"My mum got pneumonia when I was twelve. She didn't have to go into hospital or anything, but she had to take a lot of time off from her work as a nurse to try and recover. She kept trying to do gradual returns, but every time she went in for more than a day at a time, she had to call in sick for at least a week afterwards because she would just get so exhausted and the viral symptoms would keep coming back. My sister was busy and my dad travelled a lot for work, so I just started picking up more and more household responsibilities—cooking, cleaning. Eventually she just couldn't really leave the house, and whenever my dad was at home he would get frustrated that we couldn't go for outings or act like a 'real family'—whatever that is. He left, like properly left, moved countries and everything, so it's just been us since then. Billy used to come down pretty frequently to help me on the weekends so I could catch up on coursework, but since she got pregnant it's just been me and Mum."

"So has your mum still got pneumonia?" Imogen's eyes are soft as she focuses on me.

"She got diagnosed with post-viral fatigue, and then when the symptoms got worse the specialist said it had progressed into this illness called M.E., or chronic fatigue syndrome. There are different levels of it and her energy fluctuates a lot, but there's no treatment other than resting as much as she needs to."

Imogen reaches out and touches my hand. Hers is soft and warm, and I suddenly worry that mine are clammy and cold. "That sounds really tough."

"We've made it work!" I add brightly. "We found a way for me to get through school and sixth-form college and still support her at home. And this year we need to figure out hiring carers or an agency for when I go to uni."

"Are you worried about that?" She pulls back her hand and breaks off a piece of chocolate brownie on her plate. I take a sip of my iced coffee.

"I guess so," I say, trying to downplay just how much I worry about it. "But she's been slowly doing better over the last year. She goes for walks around the block sometimes, or to the post office round the corner. She spends a lot of her time downstairs, rather than in bed. We can sometimes go to the museums or parks with her wheelchair. She just needs to spend the next day in bed to recover from stuff like that."

"That's really good," Imogen says, smiling at me. "I've never heard of that. I can't imagine getting ill and just … never getting better."

"Yeah, me neither until it happened to her. So you don't get on with your mum?"

Imogen laughs and leans back in her chair. "Oh, it's not so much that. It's just, she's a bit funny about some things. My dad was always the more chilled one, but when he died—"

"Oh my god, I didn't know. I'm so sorry."

She brushes me away with a hand gesture. "It's okay. It happened a long time ago. I only remember bits and bobs of him. But he kind of kept her level, I think. We mostly just keep out of each other's way, then I'm off to Leeds next year for uni, once I've saved up a bit from my café job."

When we leave a little while later, it's with smiles and a hug, and a promise to meet up for at least one more park skating session before I join the team next week. Six weeks ago, I thought my summer was going to be mostly hanging out with Ryan, and I can't believe how much has changed in such a short amount of time. Billy warned me that it's so much more difficult to make friends once you leave school, but I've fallen so easily into these new friendships that I have to believe she's just not looking in the right places. And even though Anna doesn't seem too sure about roller derby itself, she's happy that I'm not going to be spending this coming year at home with just Mum.

I think back to my relationship with Ryan and realize that I never really spoke to him about how the past few years have felt for me. I've been more open with Imogen, who I've barely known for a month, than I was with my boyfriend of eight months. We just went out with his friends or watched films or tv shows together, but never really spoke about our feelings. I never thought that something so unexpected was going to come along, but I'm determined to embrace it while it's here.

~

The weather stays hot and Imogen invites me to watch an impromptu training session at an outdoor basketball court.

"We just couldn't let this weather go to waste," she tells me as we kit up. "We'll be hitting each other so you can't join in with that until you've passed fresh meat, but there's a ton of space for you to play about at the sides."

The tarmac is warm when I put my hand on it, and I love the variety of sounds that our wheels make on different surfaces. It's quieter outside, less echoey. Before I get started on my own practice, I sit and watch Imogen lead some drills. She's a natural leader both on and off the track. She's always telling me about new exercises she's been researching to share with the team, and helping to coach is one of the things she says she enjoys most about roller derby. They're running a drill with multiple jammers trying to get through a pack of blockers all working together, and Imogen's voice is by far the loudest of anyone there. She's constantly communicating—telling her teammates where to move to with her words and her body, sometimes pushing people into position. It's not hard to see how I was so easily convinced to try this new activity—Imogen is the perfect advocate for roller derby. She rejoices in the violence, congratulating her teammates while rubbing bruises they made on her, and there aren't many people who can rival her knowledge of the rules. She's never silent; whenever we're skating together she's always telling me about some minutiae that I haven't understood or encouraging me to think about which muscles in my body are activated when I do different exercises. She's just always, always doing or saying or going, never pausing.

I push up to a kneeling position and up again onto my skates, relishing the way the warm breeze slices past me as I make a wide circle around the other skaters. Fresh meat starts the day after my nineteenth birthday, and I'm quietly optimistic about my own skills. Every spare minute for the past month has been taken up with practicing stops, falls, whips and pushes, and I feel like I can't get enough. Stopping on tarmac feels different than stopping on a polished sports floor, and I practice the different moves, feeling my muscles react to the change in surface. It's usual for my body to be aching, and I've learned to love the feeling.

Imogen comes over to check in with me between drills, giving me tips here and there and cracking jokes, and before I know it the sun has set and it's time to head home.

She nudges me as we're packing up our kit. "Are you excited for fresh meat?"

"I can't wait," I tell her, and I can't stop a smile from spreading across my face.

"You're going to be the best skater there, and I'll take it as a personal failing if you aren't," she says, laughing.

"What am I, your protégé?"

"Absolutely. You're my apprentice."

"You're not a wizard, Imogen."

"I could be." She winks at me. Everything comes so naturally when I'm around her. It's like she's unlocked this easy, free side of me.

Chapter 5

"Smells like fresh meat!" Hands on hips, bright red pigtails coming out of her helmet, and standing about half a foot taller than me, Venom is just as intimidating as her name suggests. Her American accent booms as she stands in skates before the group of about thirty people.

"You're all here because you want to play roller derby, and I'm here because I want to teach you. Here, we learn by doing, so get kitted up and get on the track in five minutes. Put your fuckin' notebooks away."

She skates off onto the track without so much as cracking a smile. There's a stunned silence and then we all rush for our kit bags at once. I hurriedly pull on my now well-used pads, wincing as one of them hits the healing wound just below my left knee. The scab is dark against my skin, the mark of a hot August evening spent skating through the streets without pads. I definitely bit off more than I could chew with the downhill stretch.

As I stand up, I'm mainly just hoping that the lessons with Imogen stick in my mind and I don't make a fool out of myself. Lots of time spent practicing crossovers, stops and hip whips must have had some kind of positive effect, surely. I pop in my mouthguard and skate around the track a few times without any awful consequences. Enthused by this, I decide to stretch out my shoulders as I skate a few more laps, but as I go from my left arm to my right, I have the horrifying thought that everyone else might think I'm brown-nosing the coaches by stretching unprompted. "Hey, look at me, I'm stretching already, I know about *sports*," they'll say as they mock me later at the party I'm not invited to.

I stop stretching and am spared the agony of wondering whether the coaches think I'm so absent-minded that I only stretched out one shoulder. Four sharp whistle blasts signal everyone to come to the middle of the track to join the coaching team. Venom is the clear leader, but there are others helping her, including Rae, Imogen and Lucy. I skate up next to a pale woman with long dark brown hair who towers over me in full showmanship attire: fishnets, knee-high socks, hot pants and a minuscule tank top. I feel weird standing next to her in sports leggings and a loose sleeveless top, like I'm under-dressed. We exchange a quick smile and a nod.

"Okay," Venom starts, "the first thing we're going to do is fall over. You're going to be doing it a lot, and I want you to learn how to do it safely. We're going to start with single knee falls, then we're doing double knee falls and falling small. This is what a single knee fall looks like."

She skates backwards to get a run up, then builds up speed forward and completes a perfect fall, landing on one knee and skidding to a stop right in front of us all.

"So, you lift your leg, bend the other, put your knee down and come to a stop. We'll try it out in groups, then you'll learn a couple more falls."

We get split into four groups to practice. It's repetitive work, but it's not boring. I figure any chance I have to get some feedback on my skating is good, even if it's something

I'm pretty confident in now. I glide up and down the track, performing a single knee fall at the end of each length. I'm in Venom's group, and she gives me a tight nod before moving onto the next person in line. I can see Imogen across the hall demonstrating a double knee fall like she's a rock star, sliding a good few meters on both knees while playing intense air guitar.

I'm on my third length practicing these when I notice the woman in fishnets seems to be having some difficulties, and Venom is busy with other people. I wait for her to reach my side of the track again.

"Hey, I'm Casey," I volunteer.

"Mel." We exchange another nervous smile.

"Sorry," I begin, "I don't want to be overbearing, but it looks like you're having some trouble. Would you like some tips? I learned these a little while ago."

A massive smile breaks across her face and she grabs my arm. "Oh, you sweetheart! I can use all the help I can get. I'm sweating like a bloody pig already," she says in a gravelly Irish voice, tugging at her ponytail as if she could pull it right off. I laugh along with her.

"So knee falls aren't about leg strength, they're about core stability. When I was learning them, I was told to imagine a string going through your belly button to your back and someone is pulling it tight behind you. If you suck in your core like that, you'll be way more stable."

We go up and down a few more times together, and Venom gives us both a nod before blowing a whistle. Mel squeezes my arm and mouths a "thank you" as we move back into the middle of the hall.

Mel and I make a good team. We stick together through the rest of the lesson and keep an eye out for each other, sharing tips about what works and what doesn't. I find that my nervousness has gone, and all I'm thinking about is learning new skills and perfecting old ones.

I'm getting quite a sweat on when we all join together again. Imogen touches my back as she comes past.

"You're doing good. Keep it up."

I smile and take a swig of water from my bottle. "Thanks, Im."

"We're going to do a pace line now," Venom announces, "which means you're going to skate around the track in a line, keeping an arm's length distance between you and the person in front of you, and adjust your speed whenever I adjust mine at the front. If you bump into the person in front of you or leave too large a gap, you'll go into the middle and do ten sit-ups."

This goes on for about twenty minutes, and I begin to notice I'm doing way fewer sit-ups than other people. I lose myself in the skating and stop worrying about being the worst skater there. It turns out a whole summer of lessons from Imogen has paid off, because I'm picking it up a lot faster than the other newbies.

I finish the practice sweaty and smiling and peel off my kit, chatting with the people around me. It's a very liberating feeling to realize that they don't know about the time I peed myself from laughing too much at the age of twelve, or about my crush on one of the science teachers at school, or my awkward rebellious phrase when I wore black lipstick and refused to smile. I'm surprised at myself when I ask Mel if she wants to come skating with me before next week's practice. Surprised that I'm not second-guessing myself, wondering if I'm forcing my company on her or if she secretly hates me. She accepts enthusiastically and we exchange numbers, agreeing to meet up in a few days at the park Imogen and I normally go to.

~

When I get home, I can hear Billy and Mum chatting in the kitchen. I close the front door behind me and walk down the hallway, dropping my kit bag in front of the washing machine.

"And the warrior returns! How was it?" asks Mum, smiling at me.

"It was good! Hey, Billy!"

"Hey! What's in the bag?"

"Just skating kit," I tell her.

"Casey's just been to her first roller derby practice," Mum tells Billy. "What is it they call it … new blood?"

I stifle a laugh. "Fresh meat."

"That sounds a bit intense," Billy remarks, a slice of evening toast halfway into her mouth.

"Casey's tough though. Aren't you, love?"

I make a "grr" face and flex my puny (but growing) bicep, laughing. "Oh, and here's your fiver back, thanks for lending me the cash," I say, passing a five-pound note to Mum from the pocket of my bag.

"So, you have to buy the whole kit AND you have to pay for each session? How much has that set you back?" Billy asks.

I kind of don't want to tell her—it's the most amount of money I've ever spent on myself. "Erm, well, the full kit was about £150—"

"HOW much?!" she interrupts.

"And each session is £5. But when we're full team members we just pay monthly dues, we don't have to pay for each session. And when we have practice sessions in between, we just split the hall cost between all of us who come along, it's only a few quid each." I can feel myself overexplaining as Billy's eyebrows shoot further up her forehead. She looks over at Mum and I can feel the judgement coming.

"I'm sorry," she starts, pointing a finger at Mum, "and you're okay with this?"

"She's eighteen, she can do what she likes with her money," Mum tells her firmly.

"Money she's earning from looking after you! Surely you should have a say in what she does with it? She's meant to be saving for uni. Her dad's the only one who ever had any money, and he's not exactly sending stacks of cash over to help out."

It's all getting a bit loud for me. "Billy, please. I love this. I haven't wanted to do something this badly in a long time." I don't know why I feel like I'm apologizing. I don't have to justify what I spend my Carer's Allowance on. But every time I talk to her, I can feel this dream slipping away from me, like she's the voice of reason in my ear that I'm desperately trying to ignore. I know it's not sensible. I know it costs a lot of money but I can't find the words to tell her that I'm falling in love with this in a way I've never felt before. Skating and being around all these badass people make it feel like my blood is fizzing, like I'm standing on the precipice of something exciting and scary and dangerous. And Billy just keeps reminding me exactly how much of a bad decision it is to get drawn in.

"Like I said before, don't come crying to me when it all falls down around you," Billy says. I roll my eyes at Mum and she gives me a tight smile. I know she hates it when we argue.

"Can we talk about something else now?" I ask. The endorphins from the exercise have thoroughly worn off now, and I'm glad to hear Mum ask about how Harry is getting on. I'm deep in thought as I hang my pads up to air them out and keep them dry. Have I made a huge mistake?

~

I wave enthusiastically at Mel from the bench in the park. It takes her a few seconds to spot me, but when she does she grins and breaks into a slow jog toward me.

"Hey! Sorry I'm late, the cat threw up," she explains, dropping her rucksack with a crash on the bench next to us and ripping it open. "Her water bowl ran dry, so I filled it up for her and she drank basically the whole thing, then threw it up all over the bedroom floor, then went back for more water. I had to distract her with some treats. She's so weird. Anyway, how are you?"

I laugh. "I'm okay! So excited for training next week. I've been skating over the summer but it's not proper training. It's so much fun to have an actual coach."

"You know Imogen, right?"

"Yeah!"

"She seems cool."

"She is," I agree.

Mel and I clip our helmets on and stand up, her more wobbly on her skates than me. I throw my bag over my shoulders and tighten the straps. "Shall we just go round the paths?"

"Sure. This surface looks like it'll grind my knee pads away to nothing if I practice my falls here," she laughs.

We do a couple of laps around the park in silence as Mel gets used to the unevenness of the ground. I'm so glad I ventured outside with my skates early on; Rae refuses to skate outside because she hates how unpredictable it is compared to the polished sports floor we're used to.

"Where did you get your kit from?" I ask Mel on our third time round. Her knee, elbow and wrist guards are all leopard print, and I haven't seen anything like them before.

"I ordered it all online when I moved to the area for my degree," she tells me. "I was determined to join the local team, but I just kept chickening out. And now I've finished my bloody Master's year and I've only just got round to it. It's like, one of those things that you want to do but can't ever really imagine yourself doing, right?"

I nod. "Yeah, it feels like another life, another version of myself."

"Exactly! Rob, my boyfriend, he kept pestering me to join but that just made me want to do it less. We just moved into our first place together last month and I unpacked my kit bag and thought, do you know what, I think it's time for me to be a roller derby girl. I've settled into my new job, we've got a cat, it feels like something I can manage now I haven't got a shit-ton of studying and writing to do in the evenings as well as a basically full-time bar job."

Mel happily rabbits on as we skate around, and I'm questioning Billy's warning even more. It's not necessarily that it's easy to make new friends, but more that I'm putting myself in situations where it's easy to take the first step. It's difficult to ask someone to hang out when you don't have a defined activity to do together, but when you can just say, "hey, do you want to skate together" it becomes so much easier.

"How about you?" Mel asks. "Why did you start skating?"

"I was running on a treadmill at the gym and they were practicing in the sports hall underneath. I bumped into Imogen on the way out and well …" I gesture at myself. "I saw a game and that was it, it was over for me."

Mel laughs with me. "You didn't see *Whip It* like the rest of us and want to be as cool as Elliot Page and Kristen Wiig?"

"I never saw the film."

"Oh wow, that's something we have to do then. It's practically a rite of passage. I've seen it at least ten times. There's some like, eek bits"—she draws a line across her throat, grimacing—"but it was 2009 so I think we can forgive them."

When we finish skating, we promise to set a date to watch it at Mel's flat on the projector screen her boyfriend has set up.

"I don't think it can cope with anything except anime at the moment, so we'll have to see if it works when there are real people on the screen," she tells me, laughing. "Rob is such a weeb."

"And I can meet your cat!" I add.

"Yes, you can meet Sparkle! She's a babe."

I arrive home a lot less nervous than when I left and launch straight into cooking some ramen for dinner. It feels like a good balance: skating and caring. The thought of shaking that up for university brings the nerves back, but I push it to the back of my mind and decide to tackle that beast another day. For now, all I need to think about is getting the food ready so Mum and I can watch *Midsomer Murders*.

Chapter 6

Five weeks into the fresh meat course I have the most painful experience of my life, to date.

It happens while we're learning derby stops. I'm pretty sure I've got them down after having practiced them with Imogen before, so I'm relaxing a bit and just waiting until the drill is over. They were difficult when I first learnt them and I made an effort for the first few tonight, but they're getting sloppier and sloppier as I get more and more relaxed and decide to try something new: hopping straight onto my toe stops from the jump. My left foot is solid, but I don't commit to the jump enough with my right foot and land on my wheels instead of my toe stop. They skid out from underneath me and I must look ridiculous as I windmill my arms to try and stay upright. I fail and fall, sitting down hard onto my left foot.

At first, I'm not sure what's happened or where the noise is coming from, but as people start rushing over to me I realize I'm letting out a constant stream of low, guttural moans. Soon after that comes the pain, and I can hear some restrained laughs coming in my direction as well. Somehow, I've gained the same injury that Rae showed us at the after-party all those months ago—I've come down awkwardly on a wheel.

"That was definitely full penetration," I hear someone mutter near me.

"Well, I hope to god that wasn't her first time," says another voice.

The entire area from the tops of my thighs right up to my belly button is raging with pain, and there's a small focal pinpoint that feels like it's completely on fire. I take off my helmet with the vague thought that it might be useful to be sick into. A moment later, someone hands me an ice pack and I sigh with relief as I push it into my leggings. Someone's taken my skates off and Sam lends me her shoulder to help me hobble off the track so the team can continue practice. I begin panicking as I sit on a bench by the wall. How am I going to get home? Will I still be able to look after Mum? I can feel my skin become cold and wet with sweat. Someone hands me my water bottle but I'm shaking so much I don't want to open it in case I spill it everywhere. I close my eyes and take a deep breath in, trying to calm myself down, but it's not working. I've never hurt myself this badly before, and the thought of not being able to do the things I need to do makes my breath come in short and harsh.

"Shit, Case!" Imogen is stifling a laugh as she crouches down near me. "Are you okay?"

It takes a lot of difficulty for me to actually form words, and I'm almost certain I should spend the effort on something more intelligent than, "Do you think I'll still be able to pee?" but that's what comes out.

Imogen stops stifling the laugh and it comes booming out. She throws her head back and I think I might be a bit high on pain because even though she's sweaty and has makeup everywhere, I'm mesmerized by her face.

"How am I gonna get home if it hurts too much to walk?"

I ask, trying not to let on how worried I am about being hurt.

"Sam will drive you, she's the local taxi service for anyone who gets banged up at practice. Don't worry about it."

Almost instantly, my heart rate drops, and my palms stop feeling quite as clammy. Imogen's calm certainty has a weight to it, which helps me feel a bit more level-headed.

"You're gonna be fine," she says. "Honestly. We'll give you some more ice packs, you'll rest for a while, and you'll be back skating at the next practice. Don't fret."

My breathing returns to normal, and I manage to flash a brief, nervous smile at her.

"I believe you."

~

I'm only walking like John Wayne for a week or so, and it takes another few days to be able to sit down without wincing. I skip telling Anna about my injury in our latest text exchange; she seems a bit freaked out by the possibility of me getting hurt, so I've stopped rambling at her quite so much about roller derby. By the time the bruise heals completely, I'm quickly establishing myself as one of the most competent skaters in fresh meat. I completed the twenty-seven laps of the track in five minutes last week as a test of my endurance, so it surprises me when we move onto hitting and I find it difficult.

"Just hit me, Case!" Mel shouts at me during practice.

I try. I really, really try. I line up beside her and get into derby stance and hold my arms out in front of me for stability. I try so hard to whip my hip to the right like I'm hitting a car door closed with my bum, but as I cut across Mel to hit her on the mid-thigh, our wheels bang together and we end up in a pile on the floor.

"I'm sorry, Mel, I'm really sorry," I apologize as we get up for the thousandth time. She has her usual bright smile on, but I can tell that her patience is running thin. She nods at me, and I interpret this as "try again."

So, I try again. And again. By the time we switch so she's hitting me, I still haven't got it. But if there's one thing I've been really working at, it's my core stability. I can hold a plank position for nearly two minutes before collapsing, and the balance board I bought last month has already got paler patches where I've been balancing on it on one leg for one, two, three minutes at a time. So when Mel hits me, I don't fall. And I don't fall when we swap partners and Lucy starts hitting me harder. In fact, the only time I get floored throughout the rest of the hitting drill is when I get tripped by Venom, who likes to periodically come round and kick our skates out from underneath us to make sure we know how to fall safely.

When the whistle blows I skate to the middle, pop the top on my water bottle and chug. I can feel a line of sweat forming down my back, and we're all breathing heavily. Venom works us hard.

I'm kind of zoned out when the next instructions come—my head is too busy analyzing everything I've been doing wrong—and I join the back of the pace line behind Imogen without a thought.

"Case!"

On hearing my name called, I grab Imogen's hips from behind and swing myself around in front of her, already reaching for Lucy's hips when Imogen pulls me back in line with her.

"No, hit me!" Imogen hisses, and I don't even think about it, just aim my ass at her thigh and swing, scissoring my feet to stay stable. Imogen hits the deck, as does the next person, and the next person. The only one to stay on skates is Venom, who calls out to me: "You call that a hit? I've had mosquito bites worse than that!" I find a rhythm: bam, whap, kapow. I knock people to the floor on my way through the line, managing to not trip anyone and stay upright and this is the moment, *this* is the moment, I start to think I might actually be decent at this.

~

Imogen punches me on the arm as we're putting away our kit after practice. "It's time."

Mel and I look round at her as she shoves her kit haphazardly into her bag.

"Time for what?" Mel asks.

"You need derby names, if you haven't already chosen them. We're ordering scrim tops next week."

My face splits in half, I smile so wide. Everyone on the team has these kickass names printed on the back of the shirts they practice in. I'd be lying if I said I hadn't thought about what I want mine to be, but so far inspiration hasn't struck. We pack up quickly and head to the pub across the road.

"So, you know the deal with roller derby names, right?" Lucy has gathered us newbies around a couple of tables in the smoking garden. I wait impatiently for my bowl of chips—fuel after a tough session.

"They're just like, our alter egos, right?" Mel offers.

"Right," Lucy confirms. "Now you're hitting each other, you're well on your way to being good enough to scrimmage—"

"It's not a test though?" a high voice pipes up from the other table. I look over to see who's asked and recognize Rowan from her spiky dyed-black hair, somehow still intact after two hours sweating in a helmet. She took a lot of big hits tonight and is looking pretty exhausted.

"I mean it's not a test apart from the test bit," Lucy says with a bit of a mean laugh.

"But that's only the rules section and you're all practicing with the app, aren't you?" Imogen pipes up. "We'll judge the rest of the skills as you do them in practice to make sure you're safe enough to scrimmage; we won't have a formal 'test.' Don't worry!"

There are a few nervous laughs.

"And once you've passed those skills you'll officially be able to scrimmage, which means you can order team shirts with your derby names on the back," Lucy says. "So you've gotta make sure you've picked a good one."

Everyone mutters excitedly.

Mel turns to me. "I've known for years that I want my derby name to be Irish Scream," she says decisively.

Imogen grins. "That's brilliant."

"I have no idea what mine's going to be," I admit. "I've been looking at rhymes with Casey but they're all a bit rubbish. Facey, spacey, lacy, racy." I count them off on my fingers.

"Racy is good!" Mel says.

"Yeah, but it's not really me though, is it?" I gesture at my sports leggings and faded black t-shirt.

"What about 'Case' though?" asks Imogen.

"Ooh yeah, that would be good!" says Mel. She pulls her phone out of her bag and her nails click on the screen as she taps. "Okay, what have we got here? Case study, case in point, case sensitive ..."

"Open case, upper case, glasses case," Imogen reads over her shoulder.

"They're all a bit formal," I say.

"Nut case! That's a good one," Mel says.

"Thanks," I reply sarcastically. "Glad to know you think I'm crazy."

"You're onto something there, Mel. Head case?" Imogen adds, ignoring me.

"Basket case?" Mel suggests, laughing.

"Hey! I'm right here!" I protest. "What about ... Justin Case?"

There's a short pause as Mel and Imogen look at each other with smiles.

"That's it. Justin Case," Mel says to me.

"Justin Case!" Imogen exclaims. "That's the one. I can feel it in my jellies."

I roll it around in my head a few times. Justin Case. A slow smile spreads over my face. It's got the right amount of punniness *and* it incorporates my name.

"I think that might be the one," I agree. I can already picture it on the back of a team top. Imogen thumps me on the back.

"Welcome to the team, Timberlake."

Between Mel's packed job schedule and our newly acquired second night a week at training, it's taken us ages to schedule a time for me to come round and watch *Whip It* with her. She's sent Rob for a night out with his friends so we won't be disturbed, and I curl up in a corner of her soft, deep-red sofa, checking my phone while Mel brews us some tea. I send a couple of texts to Anna, carrying on our conversation about the most annoying guy on her course who interrupts her whenever she tries to say something. She still doesn't really get how much I love roller derby. She asked if it was a uni society and why I was joining it at home when I could join the one in London. If she was around I'd drag her to come see it live, but I'm sure she just skipped through the footage of a high-level game I sent her.

"When I grow up, I want to live in a flat like this," I declare, gesturing around me. Mel has fully embraced maximalism and the dark green walls are covered with mismatched ornate picture frames. Off in the corner of the large room is a black desk with two computer screens and tons of gadgets chucked haphazardly over the surface. Mel notices me looking.

"Except for that bit, right? That's Rob's Mojo Dojo Casa House. He said that I can decorate this flat however I want but he has to have a corner for all his bits. It's gonna be a nightmare trying to get the walls back to landlord magnolia when we move out, but it's worth it to me."

The projector is mounted to the ceiling and points at the only white wall in the room. Mel has loaded up the film and brings over two steaming mugs of tea from the kitchen counter. I stroke her cat, Sparkle, who has curled up next to me on the sofa.

She shoots me a wry smile. "I'm only bloody twenty-four as well! The cheek of saying I'm grown up."

I hold my hands up before accepting the tea. "You've got letters after your name and a proper job. I think that qualifies you."

"Shit. I'm turning into my mother." We laugh. "Do you have everything you need?"

I gesture at the snacks surrounding us. "I think if you brought me anything else, I'd pop."

"Nervous host, sorry. I am definitely turning into my mother. Let's watch."

She presses play and I lose myself in the story. So much of it rings true to me, and I unexpectedly feel a few tears make their way down my face during the climactic scene where Bliss declares her love for the sport to her parents. We watch the whole thing without a break, slowly munching on snacks and getting more and more settled in our respective corners of the sofa, Sparkle moving between us for optimum attention and scritches.

"I can't believe I haven't seen that before," I say, as Mel turns the volume down on the end credits.

"Well, it's a bit before your time probably."

"You're the one who was insisting you're not an adult," I tease her.

"Well, it is! You were only little when it came out!" she protests.

"I'm glad she ended up single," I say.

"Yeah, me too. Although …"

I look at Mel as she trails off. "Although?"

"Don't you think … It was supposed to be a queer story, right? I mean, look at our team. Nary a heterosexual in sight throughout roller derby, or so I've come to believe."

"Everyone was straight," I agree. I hadn't really thought about the sexuality of the people on our team before. It's something I just haven't paid attention to, and it feels weird to think about it so objectively. Where do I fit in? Am I the token straight person? "Who would the queer love have been between?"

"Well, the obvious pairing is Pash and Bliss," Mel states, pushing herself around on the sofa so she's facing me, cross-legged. "I've always thought that. The musician was just a distraction. I've seen this film so many times and I still can't remember his name."

"But then she doesn't end up single."

"Well, maybe she does. I just feel like … roller derby and queerness *go* together, you know? Like a warm chocolate brownie and ice cream. It's a grassroots sport, we all run it together, there's no such thing as professional roller derby. It kind of exists outside capitalism in a way that queerness also does."

I mull her words over. "You think queerness exists outside of capitalism?"

"Oh, for sure," she says without hesitation. "Well, when I was presenting as a gay man I guess I bought into the whole gay clubbing scene. But when I came out as trans, I couldn't access any kind of gay bar without getting hate crimed. So, I have to exist in this space outside of it all. I have to seek out communities that won't expel me just for who I am. And roller derby is a home for people like me: people who haven't been able to access sport in more traditional ways."

As we delve into talking deeper about the film and roller derby, I realize I would never have had any kind of conversation like this with Ryan or Anna. We met when we were younger and none of us were really sure who we were. I've never really had my thoughts taken seriously before by anyone other than Mum. Mel has this way of crystallizing and expressing thoughts I've been dancing around for a while, and she really listens when I try to explain what I'm thinking. That roller derby is the missing piece I've been searching for, that I've not felt this way about anything before. That I'm falling in love with it, with how it makes me feel and with the people it surrounds me with. It feels so natural but so new, so right.

Chapter 7

By the time November rolls around, most of us fresh meat are scrimmaging regularly and are training three nights a week (twice with the team and once with whoever wants to at the local sports center). It's hard work, so when a team party rolls around it's a perfect opportunity to have some fun. Officially, the party is to celebrate the end of fresh meat, but privately I feel like it's just an excuse to go to the pub.

Even though I've seen everyone during practice, there are still a few butterflies in my stomach as I paint on black eyeliner and get my bag ready to go out. The party is in the function room of a quirky pub, the kind that sells cups of tea and provides board games on each table.

It's nearly 9 p.m. when I finally set out, my palms sweating slightly despite the cold bite of winter in the air. I keep imagining over and over how I'm going to enter the pub and what I'm going to say. What if everyone's in separate groups and won't talk to me and I have to fight my way into a conversation? What if I get suddenly ill and vomit all over someone and they never let me forget it? What if I say something really embarrassing during a break in the music and everyone hears?

Entering the pub is daunting, but the cheer I get from the crowd of teammates when I enter the function room helps me feel better and seeing Imogen's smiling face among them makes all the nerves go away.

She rushes right over to me, slinging an arm around my waist, and I can smell from her warm breath on my neck that she's had a few drinks already.

"Case! You made it!" she says, beaming at me. "I got you a cider." And there on the table she drags me to is a bottle of cider in front of an empty chair. I grin at Imogen and she sits down, patting the chair.

"Thanks, Im," I say as I sit down, before picking up the cider and taking a long drink of it to warm my belly. I get pulled into a sideways hug by Mel, whose voice is even raspier than normal.

"Babe," she starts, "I'm kind of drunk. What time is it?" She fumbles around in her bag, but I grab my phone out of my pocket faster.

"It's half nine."

"Shit." Her Dublin lilt is even more pronounced than it usually is. "So I asked Rob to come along. I mean, he is my boyfriend, he should be doing stuff with me. Stuff like this, you know what I mean?" I nod encouragingly. "We should totally get you a boyfriend if you want one, they're really good. Anyway, he's not going to be here. Isn't that shit? So you can get me home okay, right?"

"Oh yeah, sure," I say, quietly freaking out about the added responsibility.

Venom comes over with a tray full of shots. I've never done a shot before in my life and I'm worried about it mixing with the cider to form some kind of vomit volcano, but the stern look she gives me makes me more scared of the consequences of not doing the shot, so I throw it back and spend the next few minutes trying to soothe the burn in my throat.

By the time I finish my second bottle of cider, I'm feeling quite drunk and laughing louder than usual. Imogen has leaned right back and thrown an arm across the back of my chair. Her other hand is around her drink and there's a curl she keeps pushing out of her eyes that's kind of mesmerizing. I get distracted by Venom demonstrating correct push-up form on the sticky floor and am amazed when she doesn't stop even when Rae places a half-full pint glass on her back.

"How's the vag, Case?" Lucy shouts from across the table. I can feel my stomach drop out of me.

"What?"

"You know … the fall!" she clarifies.

"Oh! It's alright, thanks. Business as usual, you know." Great. Now she probably thinks I'm some kind of seasoned sex aficionado, or at least experienced beyond the awkward fumbling and groping Ryan and I tried a few times.

I'm jogged out of my freak-out by another round of drinks arriving at the table, but with a drinking game introduced at the same time.

"Never have I ever wiped out on the pavement," Mel declares, pumping her fist in the air. Most people around the table, me included, take a swig of drink.

"Never have I ever kissed a girl," Rae says, waggling her left hand in front of everyone to show off her engagement ring.

"Oh, bullshit!" Imogen yells. "You're a fucking derby girl, of course you've kissed a girl." She takes a glug of her drink, and my heart stops for a couple of seconds but it takes longer for my brain to catch up. Wait … Imogen has kissed a girl? Does that mean … But she was in bed with Ryan. My tipsy brain helpfully provides a full-color HD image of Imogen kissing Kristen Stewart. I screw up my eyes and shake my head slightly, then look around to see what I've missed while my brain has been running in circles.

"Never have I ever puked on the track," Venom declares, lifting her glass to toast at Sam.

"Oh, you fucker," she says, tipping her bottle back to get the final drops out. "I had food poisoning. You think it's funny?"

"Fuckin' hilarious." Venom grins and winks at her. "More drinks! We need more drinks!"

It only takes a couple of minutes for another round and a trayful of shots to arrive at the table, carried by Lucy. She christens the round by lifting a shot and announcing, "Never have I ever had sex with a girl in a moving vehicle." She throws back the shot to a round of applause, then bows at us all.

"Show-off," says Venom, smacking her in the shoulder. "That's not the point of the game." She glances towards my side of the table and widens her eyes at Imogen, who has quietly reached for a shot and downed it.

"What?" she asks as she realizes everyone is staring at her. "If you've done it, you drink, right?"

Kristen Stewart is now wearing only underwear in my brain, and I recognize the neon orange tank top she's pulling over the head of … yes, that's definitely Imogen, and that's definitely imagery I've pulled from the deep recesses of my memory, of walking in on her and Ryan in bed together. I watch Imogen move a bottle towards her lips and something clicks in my mind. Wait, am I having a gay crisis? My eyes widen in alarm and I cast my gaze about for something, anything, to distract me. All I can see is Venom smiling curiously at me.

There's a sharp pain in my shin and I realize Mel has kicked me under the table.

"Ow! What?"

"It's your turn," she explains.

"Oh shit, I …" I cast my mind about for something that isn't going to out me as the kind of person who chickened out of abseiling down a wall on a school trip when I was twelve and had to be rescued by the hot, young, male instructor while my classmates laughed at me. "I've never … I don't know how to drive."

I don't even notice how many people drink because it feels like my throat is held in a vice. I squeeze past everyone to get to the toilets, which are thankfully empty. The fluorescent lights are draining my face of all color, or maybe that's just how I look tonight: drawn and pale with bags under my eyes. My red lipstick suddenly looks clownish instead of sultry, so I wipe it off.

It's only when I sit down on the toilet that I realize I'm actually quite drunk. My head lurches as I reach for the loo roll, and I stumble into the door as I stand up. I take a deep breath in front of the mirror to steady myself, then head back to the table.

To my relief, the game of Never Have I Ever has ended. The music has turned up a notch, and soon we're pushing back the tables and chairs to create a space for dancing. I'm jumping up and down in the middle of a group of people who are fierce and strong and competitive and way, way cooler than me. We scream along to songs and dance until I can't tell whose limbs are whose in our sweaty mob.

Later, we stumble towards one of those greasy kebab shops

I told myself I'd never eat at in case it gave me food poisoning. On the way there, Imogen's arm is around my waist and Mel is leaning on my shoulder. Venom is walking backwards in front of us, hip-checking anyone who gets in her way. We've lost some teammates along the way but there's still a good number of people following behind.

The smell of fried food hits me like I'm being offered a slice of heaven, and I can't eat the kebab fast enough. It energizes me, and I realize I'm sad about the party ending. It feels like my first proper teenage experience, after a haze of exams and school and caring for Mum. When Venom suggests we all go back to her flat, it seems like the perfect continuation of the night.

It doesn't take long to walk there, and it's an even shorter length of time before the first human pyramid is attempted. It fails, as do the second and the third, but on the fourth one I hoist myself right up to the top, grabbing at shorts and leggings and belts and trying not to dislodge anyone else in the process. I reach the top and stay there long enough for a new profile picture, before falling spectacularly to the bottom through everyone else. The chain reaction is inevitable and immediate, and as I lie underneath Mel and on top of Rae, laughing so hard I can barely breathe, I feel a kind of peace. This is what life should be full of, and I can't get enough of it.

Chapter 8

Opening Netflix on my laptop the next day feels like something sinful. I make sure my door is closed and listen for Mum's even snores from across the hallway. At least a couple of hours until she wakes up and we'll have dinner. I take a sip of water and hesitantly type "LGBT" into the search bar, my fingers unfamiliar with the shape of the abbreviation.

It's not like this is entirely a surprise to me. I always knew that I thought women were beautiful, but I've never felt like I do about Imogen before, this need to spend as much time with her as possible. I remember smatterings of PSHE lessons at school and I follow enough queer celebrities to know that what I'm feeling is normal, but it still throws me. I've never really been interested in anyone in this way, regardless of gender. The butterflies in my stomach are completely new to me, and I have no idea what to do with them.

Scrolling through the films, most of them look pretty pornographic. *Blue is the Warmest Color* looks way too sexy. *The Miseducation of Cameron Post* seems intense and sad. And there are quite a few films about couples bringing a woman into their relationship, but that seems too older-married-couple for me. One pops up called *But I'm A Cheerleader*, with a cute cover picture and snappy synopsis telling me it's a "satirical romantic comedy" featuring "a high-school cheerleader whose parents send her to a residential inpatient conversion therapy camp to cure her lesbianism."

I hit play.

~

I've never called anyone just to chat before, other than my dad and my grandma. Both are no longer around, one in a more permanent way than the other, and it's been a few years since I've called anyone other than the doctor's office to book appointments for Mum. I considered calling Anna but our texts have been getting fewer and further between, and I honestly don't know if she could cope with me telling her I think I might be bisexual on the same phone call as telling her I think I have a crush on a woman. It's not that she's homophobic or anything, it's just that we've never talked about this stuff. She just gossips about the latest boy she has a crush on, and I tell her he seems like a nightmare.

I scroll down to Mel's name in my phone book, still wrestling with myself. Of all the people I know, Mel is the one I trust the most to talk about something like this. We haven't had many conversations about the fact that she's trans, but it's not something she ever hides from people. It's just another part of her, like the fact that she adores frogs, or that her voice goes into supersonic ranges whenever she sees a baby animal.

Screwing up my eyes and balling a fist, I hit the "call" button and hold the phone to my ear.

"Hello? Casey?"

"Sorry. Mel, hi. Sorry. Are you alright to chat? You're probably busy, sorry."

"No! Not busy at all, you're fine, love. What's up?"

"I just …" I can't figure out how to say it. I don't even know if we're close enough for me to be calling her with this. Sure, we stick together at practice and met up to skate outside before there was frost on the ground every morning, but this feels like a "best friend" kind of thing. I don't know if we have that place in each other's lives yet.

"Go on …"

"Am I a Megan?"

"What?"

I grab a handful of duvet and twist. "In that film, *But I'm A Cheerleader*. Am I a Megan?"

"I haven't seen it, babe. Who is she?"

"She's this girl who is like, she's a cheerleader."

"Obviously."

"Obviously. And she gets sent to this conversion camp because her parents think she's gay and she's like, I'm not gay. But then she has sex with a girl at the camp and then she actually is gay. And the gay camp has made her gay."

"Back up a second. Are you being sent to a conversion camp? Am I going to have to get the authorities involved?"

I scrunch up my eyes, not sure I'm brave enough to say it. "I think the gay camp is roller derby."

"Wait. What's happening here? Are *you* gay?"

"I don't know. I don't think I'm gay. I mean, I still love Harry Styles."

"Who doesn't?"

"Right? That hair … ugh. I'd bite his entire head off."

"Casey, babe. You're not a praying mantis."

"But you know what I mean. I think I still fancy men … well, men I've never met. And women and nonbinary people are great too, but is there such a thing as being gay for like, one person? I didn't feel like this when I had a boyfriend, I didn't even know people *could* feel like this."

I can hear Mel shifting her position and she breathes out heavily.

"Are you gay for this Megan actor? Wait, I'll google her." I can hear her tapping on her phone. "Okay, got the visual. She's cute! A bit old for you though?"

"I know but …" I take a deep breath. "I think I'm very specifically gay for Imogen."

"Oh, babe."

"I know. It's like having a crush on someone you work with."

"Could get messy."

"Right? I think she's really cool and I love hanging out with her, but recently it's been a bit … charged. She's always so physical. And at first I was like, oh, that's nice, she's a touchy-feely friend. But then I started to really like how she puts her arm round me when we're sitting together, and it feels a little more gay than I originally thought. She's the first person I've really wanted to like, cuddle and kiss and stuff."

"Do you think you want to have sex with her?"

The word sex strikes panic into my heart. I lose hearing for a second and my ears start to ring. "Mel, I'm nineteen years old and I watch *Midsomer Murders* with my mum for fun. Does it seem like I'm experienced with stuff like this?"

She laughs. "Well, I don't know, do I? Look, if you want to bone her, make a move. If you want to be girlfriends, talk to her. Like, it kind of seems like she's pretty open to talking about mostly anything, so just talk to her and don't worry about it."

"But what if I can't help but worry?"

"Don't."

"But …"

"*Don't,*" Mel says firmly. "This is totally normal. When I was your age, I didn't even know what the word transgender meant, just that I really didn't feel like a dude. This is when you're meant to be figuring stuff like this out."

"But Imogen is just so … out there. She's so open and funny and confident and—"

"Love, a lot of that is just straight whiskey."

"You know what I mean."

"Look, Casey, if you're freaked out about kissing girls, just kiss one. Then you won't be freaked out about it anymore. I've got to go and cook some dinner, but you get your rest and I'll see you at training on Monday, okay?"

"Okay. Thanks, Mel."

"No worries, chick. Bye."

"See you later."

Chapter 9

I'm dreading Tuesday practice after my gay crisis. Mel, my total savior, grabs me in an extra-tight hug as soon as I arrive and whispers, "You're grand, chick. Just skate." Despite her soothing words I'm still freaking out, and it's with shaky hands that I'm doing up the Velcro on my knee pads and tightening the laces on my skates.

I'm just checking that my toe stops are tightened properly when the door slams open and Imogen comes charging in.

"Hola, chicas! Ready to hit some bitches?" she yells to no one in particular, chucking down her kit bag next to mine and yanking off her hoodie.

I can't help but grin inanely when she punches me on the arm and says something about a hangover. I don't really take in what she's saying but she's laughing her big booming laugh and pulling on her pads haphazardly and I almost reach out to squeeze her arm but am interrupted by the whistle.

Venom has split the session evenly between endurance and scrimmage, which is basically a practice game. We work ourselves to the bone, repeating two minutes of exercise then thirty seconds of rest for half an hour, then after a short break we do another half-hour of the same thing. I can feel my muscles burning and it brings a smile to my face; all the kettlebell workouts and endurance running sessions are definitely paying off. As the sweat drips off me it's like the droplets are made of my nervousness and awkwardness and all the mixed-up feelings I'm having, so when we start scrimmaging I feel purged, cleansed of anything that would distract me from playing my best.

"Okay, our next game is coming up soon and anyone who's ready for scrimmage is eligible to be picked for the roster. We're going to practice skating in different line-ups and come back into a group every fifteen minutes to discuss what's working and what isn't, and switch those groups up," Venom tells us.

She divides us into groups and hands out fluorescent bibs that smell of sweat, and all I'm doing is focusing on the task ahead of me. I've never played in a full scrimmage before, only short drills, so it's time to keep my brain and reactions sharp and put all the strategies I've learnt over the past couple of months into play.

I'm on the first jam on the inside line, and my job is to stick to that line and not let anyone pass me.

"Jammer on the outside!" I shout, looking back at Imogen on the opposite team with the star cover on her helmet. She sticks her tongue out at me and changes position.

"Five seconds!" shouts the jam timer.

"Jammer on the inside!" I shout, getting as low as I can and preparing for the first hit.

The whistle blows and Imogen explodes like a bullet from a gun, ploughing her shoulder into the space between Venom and me. I push against Venom's shoulder as hard as I can, pointing my feet inwards to slow Imogen's pushing down. She steps back, considering her options, and I'm so focused on her that one of the blockers from her team pushes me out of my inside line position.

"Jammer on the inside!" Venom yells, bowling me into Imogen who has seen the gap and gone for it. My shoulder connects with Imogen's stomach as I almost fall but manage to regain my balance. It's a soft, awkward hit, but it did the trick and she's off the track.

"Recycle her!" I hear the instruction and act without thinking, skating backwards so she has to come in behind me. She gets back onto the track behind me and I dash up beside Venom again. Imogen is grinning, juking from side to side and she goes for the outside of the track.

"Outside, outside! Lane four!" Venom has skated over to help Mel and Rae, and I push on her side to make the defense stronger. Imogen is strong though, and she pushes hard. I have to abandon my post to keep the pack together.

"Bridge!" I shout.

"Bridge!" shouts Mel as she reaches another ten-foot marker.

"Bridging!" Rae reaches the next one and drops out of the fight as well.

It's just Venom left to stop Imogen passing her now, and she has a snarl on her face. Still moving counter-clockwise, she hits Imogen again and again with her shoulder. We're moving forward slowly as the other team's wall gets pushed by our jammer, but not at the same rate as Imogen is pushing against Venom's shoulder, torso, stomach, whatever she can get at.

"Out of play!" comes the call from the referee. Venom curses and falls back. I use this opportunity to hit a blocker from the opposing team off the track, then find Venom and stick to her like glue, re-forming a wall for defense in case our jammer doesn't quite call it off in time.

"Call it! Call it!" Venom shouts, just as Imogen rounds the last turn towards us. There's thirty feet left, then twenty, then ten and I still haven't heard the four sharp whistle blasts that signal the end of the jam. I brace myself, ready for Imogen to hit our wall.

"For fuck's sake, call it, Sam, jammer on!" Venom shouts again. With only a few feet left before Imogen reaches us, our jammer, Sam, calls it off by tapping her hips repeatedly and I relax.

"Get with the picture, folks," Venom says abruptly before skating off ahead of us to the team bench. I exchange a worried look with Mel.

"I thought we did well though," I murmur to her as we skate behind Venom.

"Yeah, it's our first proper scrim. Our jammer got the points," she agrees with me.

Venom's mood doesn't seem to improve all the way through practice. When we switch line-ups, she's on the opposite team to me and hits me with her bony shoulder right into the soft flesh of my underarm, a split-second after the whistle blows for the start of the jam. The pain is so bad my vision goes dark for a second and I fall over, useless, as her team's jammer skips straight past me.

"Pro tip, kid. Often helps if you're standing." Venom chucks this comment my way after the jam is over, nudging Lucy as she does, who laughs. I can feel my blood start to boil, and I'm not sure if I want to cry or scream but I feel like every muscle in my body is stretched to its breaking point.

At the end of practice, I take my kit off facing the wall so I don't have to talk to anyone. I work slowly, putting each item methodically back in my bag so it fits perfectly. Roller derby is a place where I've started to believe in myself, like I know what I'm doing and am improving consistently, but one evening of grumpy Venom has my confidence shot.

"Hey." A warm hand touches my arm as I zip up my bag and I instantly feel self-conscious about how sweaty I am. "You alright?"

I look up and it's Imogen, and to my horror I can feel scalding tears pool in my eyes. I open my mouth to try and vocalize some off-the-cuff response that I'm fine, thanks very much, and I'll see her at practice on Thursday, but no words come out and I end up sitting there like a goldfish. I close my mouth, squeeze my eyes shut, humiliated, and just shake my head. A couple of hot tears streak down my cheeks.

"She can be such an arsehole sometimes," Imogen says bluntly. "I don't know what her problem is, but nothing is ever good enough. She's got some kind of weird complex. Just ignore her."

I wipe my eyes and look at Imogen.

"Really?"

"Truly. Mel was in a state as well. I just walked her out."

I manage a weak smile. "Well, then I don't feel like so much of a dick."

"You're not a dick. Seriously, you did so well for your first scrimmage. I think I've gotta step up my game!"

I shove her gently on the shoulder. "Shut up."

"Seriously. You're good. Like, really good."

I can't quite find the words to express how valuable her approval of my skating is, so I manage to squeeze out a "thanks" and stand up, hauling my bag onto my shoulder.

"Hey, Case," Imogen says as we walk towards the door.

"Yeah?"

"Do you want to go for a drink?"

Every muscle in my body clenches.

"What ... now?"

"Well ... yeah, we could go now," she says. "I just thought, you know, you're not feeling great and when I'm not feeling great a beer does wonders."

I'm tempted, I'm so tempted, but I feel absolutely gross and all I can think about is getting home and getting in the shower. I can feel my skin itching from the salt in my sweat.

"Could we do it tomorrow maybe? I just ..." I gesture at my body. "I'm stinky. I need to shower."

"Tomorrow. Cool. See you at the Buttercross at six o'clock?"

"Yeah, sure."

We've reached the point where I need to turn right and Imogen needs to turn left. I risk catching her eye for the first time since she asked me for a drink, and she looks almost ... shy? But only for a split second, before she grins widely.

"See you tomorrow," she says, chucking me under the chin and walking away.

Chapter 10

My phone tells me the time is 6.07 and I'm telling myself to stay calm, that she'll be here any moment now. It's not like Imogen to be on time for anything anyway. I pull my coat around me a little tighter, keeping out the chill of the brisk winter air. I shift from foot to foot and check my phone again. 6.09. It feels later than it actually is, and I worry about Mum at home by herself, even though she's got leftover stew from last night and an entire season of *Outlander* to watch.

I glance around, trying not to seem like I'm looking for someone, and suddenly there she is in front of me, her hair twisted up into a red bobble hat. As our eyes meet, she smiles wide and grabs me for a hug. Her warm breath gives me a pleasant shiver down my neck.

"I'm so glad we're doing this. Come on, let's go."

She grabs my gloved hand and pulls me down the alleyway between two pasty shops, giggling as we imagine the turf war between them. Imogen does her best impression of a warrior armed with only pasties and gestures so wildly she nearly upturns a small table outside a pub further down the road. We skitter away from disapproving looks, giggling madly to ourselves.

"Where are we going?" I ask.

"You'll see."

We reach the edge of the cathedral grounds and come to a tall metal structure lit up in green.

"What's your favorite color?" she asks me.

"Oh, come on."

"What?"

"That's so touristy," I say, nodding at the sculpture in front of us. It was installed years ago, but it's one of those things that you never do in your own hometown. Like living in Brighton but never exploring the Palace Pier. "You're going to waste 50p on that?"

"What's your favorite color?" she asks again, and I know from the steely look in her eyes that I'm going to have to answer. I shove my hands in my pockets.

"I don't know. Purple?"

"Purple. Done." She looks at the instructions printed at the foot of the sculpture, carefully typing on her phone then putting it back in the pocket of her brown bomber jacket. She stands next to me and offers me her arm. I thread mine through hers and resist the urge to put my head on her shoulder as the lights change from green to purple. We spend a couple of minutes just watching the lights skip up and down, and I feel her turn her head slightly towards me. Everything in me wants to mirror her, but I can't bring myself to move.

"So where now?" I ask.

"This way!" Imogen calls as she unlinks arms and skips down the path towards the cathedral. I have to take a couple of running steps to catch up to her. The gravel crunches beneath our feet as Imogen grabs my arm again.

"Are we going to the Christmas market?"

"Ding ding ding! You're correct!" Imogen smiles at me as we join the line to get in. It moves quickly, and once we're in she leads me through the crowds. She dodges between people expertly, and even to my relatively inexperienced eye she is a natural-born jammer. She gets through throngs of people with such ease that it's barely thirty seconds before she's pushing me toward a picnic bench and heading for the stand that smells of Christmas.

I never even think about visiting the market until Mum and I put up our Christmas tree and we come to pick out the next decoration for it. It's set up on the grounds behind the cathedral, with small German-style huts on the walkway surrounding an ice rink that covers what, in warmer months, is usually a green. I pull my hat down over my ears a little further and sit on my hands to try and stop myself nervously fidgeting.

"It's just Imogen. Stop freaking out," I tell myself sternly.

"What are you frowning about?" Imogen asks as she sets down two full polystyrene cups and a plastic container with chips in it next to us on the table. She straddles the long bench facing toward me and pushes one of the cups in my direction.

"Nothing! Mmm, thank you," I say, cupping the mulled wine between my hands and feeling the warmth soak through the fabric of my gloves. I blow on the surface gently and take my first scalding but delicious sip.

"You're welcome. How are you feeling today?"

"Hmm?"

"About practice and Venom being a mega-bitch."

"Oh." I frown. "Fine, I guess." I take another sip.

"Because you seemed pretty upset yesterday."

"Yeah, I just … I really want to get on the roster, you know?"

"I know." Imogen smiles at me and pushes the tray of chips toward me. "Eat." I take a chip and we sit in comfortable silence, sipping mulled wine between mouthfuls of food. "You're going to get on the roster, you know," she tells me, matter-of-fact.

"What?"

"You're the kind of person Venom likes," she elaborates. "You show up, do the work, do the homework, and don't complain. It's like, there's no fuss with you."

"No *outward* fuss," I add, thinking of the butterflies in my stomach any time I try something new.

"Exactly. No matter what's going on inside your head, you just get on with it. And you're a really good skater. Like, you definitely shouldn't underestimate yourself."

The compliments make me feel a strange mixture of proud and embarrassed, like I want to curl in on myself just because Imogen noticed these things about me, but I'm also blooming with joy that she did.

"So are you. You're an amazing skater," I say.

"I'm alright. But I don't come to every practice, and when I am there, I let my emotions get in the way. I go for revenge hits and I lose my confidence if someone knocks me over or I have a bad jam. You just dust yourself off and get back out there."

I drink more wine, feeling the warmth in my stomach gather. "I hope you get rostered."

"Me too. Have you managed to scrub the numbers off your arms yet?"

"No!" I exclaim. "Is there a secret way of doing it?" Last night Imogen grabbed my arm just before the scrimmage and scrawled "04" in Sharpie black just below my shoulder before turning me round and doing the other arm as well. I remember feeling a sense of belonging I thought only existed in films, and part of me is happy I couldn't get the numbers completely off.

Imogen shakes her head. "Not until you invest in arm bands with your derby number on them. Until then, it's fresh Sharpie twice a week and you spend the rest of the time rubbing your skin raw trying to get it off in the shower. An exfoliating net helps a lot. Come on, let's look around."

We drink the rest of our wine then start weaving through the crowds of people milling around the stalls. We wander about, eating chips and browsing, giggling at the more ridiculous things on sale. We stamp our feet to keep warm and nudge each other's shoulders, and I barely even register which queue we're in until we get to the entrance of the ice-skating area.

"I don't even know how to ice skate!" I protest. Imogen hip checks me gently.

"Don't be a baby. It's fun. Plus, you know how to roller-skate now."

"I did it once when I was eight. And I did the splits, unintentionally. I ripped my jeans."

"So don't do the splits. Come on! She'll have a size five," she adds to the uninterested person manning the booth.

All of a sudden I'm making my way cautiously out onto the ice and trying to remember how it felt ten years ago. It seemed easy … up until I did the splits, that is. But wow is it more slippery than I remember. Imogen has my left hand in an iron grip, and I've got the railing firmly grasped in my other hand.

I'm sliding my feet along slowly; left foot, stop, right foot up to meet it, stop, and I carry on like this until we reach a group of people hanging out by the railing and taking selfies.

"Come on, we'll just go around them," Imogen says, gently tugging on my hand.

"But I'll die," I tell her, somewhat facetiously.

"No you won't," she laughs.

"Yes I will. I'm going to fall over in front of everyone and die of embarrassment. Tell my mum I love her."

"Shut up."

"Play something atmospheric."

"Stop being an arsehole. Come on."

I automatically take derby stance, transferring the hand on the railing to Imogen's other outstretched hand as she skates backwards in front of me. I briefly wonder where she learnt to ice skate so well. It occurs to me that I don't really know much about Imogen. I know that she lives with her mum and loves roller derby, and that she would much rather stay in bed until midday and stay up until 4 a.m. than keep waking hours society would deem "normal." I know that even the evilest of hangovers isn't enough to deter her from skating—she calls it "sweating the stink out." But I don't know many real things about her, not really.

I've been thinking too much and not concentrating on keeping my feet underneath me and now I'm paying for it. My right foot slips and I'm falling and I automatically go to do a double knee slide. But no, I haven't got any knee pads on so I desperately try to right myself but it's not working.

"Get low, Case. I've got you." Imogen's arms are under my shoulders and her voice is hot in my ear. "I've got you." I bend my knees and pull back, shaking, still gripping her forearms tightly. I smile and we somehow make it back to the railing without disaster.

It takes a good ten minutes until I feel confident enough to let go of the railing again, but still keep my hand hovering above it just in case. Imogen stays with me the entire time even though I can see her shooting envious looks at the people flying around the ice five times for every one lap of ours. But she stays and goes at the painstakingly slow pace I'm setting, and we eventually get a bit faster and I let go of Imogen's hand and skate all by myself for the first time.

"This is actually mildly pleasant," I say.

"Only mildly?"

"Yeah. Like, it's not as horrifying as I thought it would be."

"Horrifying. There's a nice word for your expectations of this evening."

"No, I love surprises!"

"Just not surprises that involve balancing on ice for an hour?"

"They're more difficult."

"But doable?"

I turn my head and beam at Imogen. "Definitely doable." I reach out and take her hand again, even though I don't need it any more.

~

As she drags me through the winding streets of the old town, Imogen gets more and more jittery.

"Do you like tea? I can make you some tea when we get in. Mum will still be out."

"Tea would be lovely."

"I don't know if we've got any biscuits though. And if we do, they'll just be the boring ones."

"Unacceptable. I demand interesting biscuits," I joke, nudging Imogen's elbow. She looks back, alarmed for a second but then her face smooths and she gives me a small smile. I've never seen her like this before, so unsure of herself.

"Here we are." She fumbles at the lock of a very old door on a small, terraced house. I've always wanted to live in this area of the city. As we walk through the hallway I notice trinkets covering every surface. There are dozens of them, set out so neatly and without a speck of dust. They seem at odds with Imogen's chaotic nature.

"I'll put the kettle on," Imogen says, putting her keys down in the dish by the door. They clatter loudly.

"Imogen? Are you home?"

Imogen curses under her breath as a short Black woman with neat cornrow braids and a matronly manner comes bustling down the stairs and into the hallway.

"Hi, Mum."

"Imogen! And this must be your friend Catherine?"

I step forward and hold out my hand. "It's Casey, actually."

"Casey! What a wonderful nickname. I'm Grace. It's so lovely to meet you." She has a soft Jamaican accent.

"Your home is beautiful."

"Thank you, thank you. Well, aren't we going to welcome our guest properly, Imogen? Come on, coat off, shoes off, into the front room, and I'll make us all some tea."

I take my coat and shoes off, then follow Imogen and we

both sink down onto a yellow sofa with doilies draped over the back. It's covered in plastic wrap, but much softer than I expected.

"I'm so sorry," she murmurs. "I just wanted to get you warmed up a bit after ice skating. I thought she would still be out at her group."

"It's fine! I'm fine," I say, "really. Your mum seems lovely."

Imogen rolls her eyes at me.

"She's quite …"

"Nice?"

"Yes, but …"

"Welcoming?"

Imogen sighs. "Conservative. So don't … I hate asking this, but no politics or religion?"

"Conservative?"

"It could get very awkward very quickly."

Before I can ask Imogen what she means by this, her mum comes back in with a tray laden with mugs of steaming hot tea and a plate of chocolate biscuits.

"See, you do have exciting biscuits," I say, nudging Imogen. She tenses up. It's like she's a completely different person: turned into herself instead of open, quiet and unassuming instead of bold and outgoing.

"Thanks, Mum."

"Yes, thank you, Grace. This is really lovely."

"Well, it's cold out there. I want you girls to get nice and warm. Now then, Catherine, Imogen tells me you're on a gap year as well. Do you have a job like her?"

"No, but I care for my Mum. And I'm going to university next year."

"Imogen is going next year as well," Grace tells me. "Do you want sugar in your tea?"

"Oh, yes please, two please."

"And for me, Mum."

"You will have one, Imogen."

I'm feeling more and more uncomfortable sitting between them. There's some kind of tension that I can't quite figure out.

"So, you do roller-skating as well, Catherine?"

"Yeah, I love it. I'm so glad Imogen introduced me to it."

"Well, you can do what you like, but Imogen knows how I feel about it. Of course, the exercise is good, which is why Imogen does it. But the kinds of people it attracts …" She kisses her teeth. "I know that you're not like those other girls."

"What girls would those be, Mum?"

I can feel something bubbling under the surface here. I gulp my tea, scalding the roof of my mouth.

"You know those girls."

"My friends?"

"Not now, Imogen. We have a guest."

"They're my friends, Mum."

"I see them going around kissing each other on the mouth. I know that my good girl would not be like that, she just does roller-skating for exercise."

It suddenly sinks in. Imogen is keeping a secret from her mum. The big secret. I look from Grace to Imogen and back again, and I can see the disapproval and concern on Grace's face, but where I expected defiance in Imogen is a sad resignation.

"Come on, Case, I'll walk you home." It's so awkward.

Everything in me is screaming to be as polite as possible and avoid conflict, but it feels inevitable here. Grace tuts as I put down my mug.

"Thank you for the tea, Grace, it was lovely to meet you."

Her expression softens when she looks at me. "You too, Catherine. Have a safe walk home."

I leave the living room and pull on my coat and shoes while Imogen does the same. Her face is thunder and we walk to the end of her street in silence.

"Look." I touch her arm as we pass the bookshop at the end of the road. "They've clearly caught on." I point out a book called *Roller Girl* in the window as part of a display of suggested Christmas presents.

"Well, someone had to."

We carry on walking in silence, bypassing the Christmas fair and walking through the cathedral grounds again.

"You don't have to walk me home."

"Believe me, it's better than the alternative."

"Im, wait."

She turns and folds her arms, glaring at me.

"What?" she demands.

"I just … I'm sorry."

"What have you got to be sorry for? Sorry my mum is a homophobic arsehole?"

"I'm sorry that's how you grew up. Like, I'm sure your mum is lovely"—Imogen makes an impatient, condescending sound—"but to have those views? That really sucks."

"Tell me about it."

"But it just makes you even more …" I take a deep breath. "Even more amazing."

She takes a break from tapping her foot and I can hear her breath catch.

I continue, "I mean, look where you came from and where you are now. I feel like, I dunno, if I was brought up with those views I might have just swallowed them."

We're in between lampposts and I can just about make out Imogen's face. She's not looking at me, she's looking at the red gravel below us. I'm just about to reach out and take her hand when a large group of boys comes around the corner, bellowing like they're on a stag do. My hand jerks like I've been electrocuted, and the moment is gone. We walk on a little further.

"My mum wasn't always like this. Her and my dad were religious, but not fire and brimstone. I don't think you would have done that if the same thing happened to you," Imogen says after a while.

"I don't know. You've got some serious guts. It's just … You're so open to things. You totally accept the things that are happening, and you're so spontaneous and nice to people you barely even know. You didn't have to do this today, try and cheer me up because I had a bad practice yesterday, but you did. You just put yourself out there all the time." I don't know where I've mustered the confidence to be spilling all of this to Imogen. I just know that since she came barreling into my life, things have been different. My world has slowly been getting bigger than the little sphere I'd put around me and Mum. I feel like I'm part of something bigger, like I'm discovering new things about myself every day and am less anxious about things going wrong and disturbing the peace I've worked so hard to build.

"Put myself out there?"

I'm desperate to bring us back to a place of connection but Imogen asks me this like I'm saying it's a bad thing. "Like ... you're just all out, all the time. I'm like a snail or something, I've got my shell and I just come out for a look every now and then."

"So I'm a slug in this analogy?"

"Obviously," I smile at her, joking, and she flashes me a quick, fake smile, not quite catching my eye.

"Look at my fucking shell though, Case. You don't know what it's like. You act like it's this great gift that I can be open with people, but the fact is, I have to be so closed off at home. I'm an open fucking book because I have to take every second of being myself that I can possibly get."

"I'm sorry." I reach out to her and she brushes my hand away.

"I know, I know. I just ... I'm out of here soon anyway. Nine more months and I'm gone. Forever." She seems to be talking more to herself than to me. "And today ... Look, it doesn't even matter. You're probably better off without ... I have to go." I can feel the moment slipping away from us already. She hasn't moved an inch, but I can feel this huge distance open up between us. What does she mean, gone forever? That I'm better off without ... What? Is she saying that she feels the same way about me that I do about her?

"Imogen ... please ..."

"Are you okay getting home from here?"

"Yeah, but don't you want some company?"

"No. I'm going to have a wander. Clear my head. Have a drink, maybe."

"Alone?"

"I'll see you at practice, okay?"

"Okay," I reply. She catches my eye for the briefest second then drops her gaze.

"Text me when you get home, yeah?" Imogen says. Her hand twitches at her side, and she makes a fist.

"I will."

She gives me a tight smile and walks off, hands in pockets.

Chapter 11

"Outside, outside!" I shout. "Jammer on the outside!" I scissor my feet and swerve towards the outside of the track, trying to stop Imogen from getting through. I think I'm too late but I aim my hip at her thigh and swing as hard as I can anyway. I only just clip her leg and her wheels touch outside of the track boundary for a split second but it's enough. Imogen has to skate backwards to come back in and then I'm on her the whole time, making sure she's behind me for as long as possible.

"Case!" Venom shouts a warning at me and I turn left just in time to see a blocker from the other team try to cut in front of me to get Imogen through. I juke around them and keep Imogen behind me, and now that Venom is opposite me and providing her body for me to brace against, it's getting easier. Imogen is darting around, but I can tell she's getting tired. She tries for the outside line again and I hit her out of the track boundaries again. She takes a couple of seconds to get back up and I see the jam timer lift the whistle to his lips to signal the end of the two-minute jam, so I relax. There's no way she can get past me in the few seconds of the jam we have left.

My mind is already analyzing how I did when the end-of-jam whistle blasts sound out. I lift a foot to cross my skates over and circle round to my bench when I feel something, or someone, hit me from the right. I'm fully upright and have let go of Venom, so I twist awkwardly to avoid landing on my tailbone, and I look over to see Imogen skating off in the opposite direction. The fall knocks the breath out of me and I sit on the floor, dazed, trying to figure out why she's hit me when we're not even in play.

"Hey, chick, what are you doing on the floor now?" Mel offers me a hand, which I take, hopping up onto my toe stops with her help.

No one else seems to have noticed what's happened. Maybe Imogen had already committed to the hit when the first whistle blast went off and she couldn't back out. But my gut instinct tells me something isn't right. It's been a week or so and we've exchanged a few texts since our chat in the cathedral grounds. Aside from being a little short, there's been nothing to indicate she's angry at me. I can't keep myself from wondering though. I try to shake it off, giving her the benefit of the doubt.

Four illegal hits later, I'm done. I've got a swollen lip from an "accidental" head-butt, a bump coming up on my shin from an over-exaggerated trip, and a couple of bruises blooming on my ribs from elbow jabs. I find myself hitting even harder than usual, no matter who it is. I'm giving as good as I'm getting, and I can hear the grunts of pain as I hit my way to the front of the pack during a particularly intense jam.

By the end of practice, I'm fuming. I never normally let my feelings get involved when I skate, but no one's ever been as consistently on my case as Imogen is at the moment. It gives me a kind of fiery energy and my mind is just focused on the task at hand—skating. I stop trying to analyze what Imogen must be thinking to go off on me like this; my mind crystallizes and becomes one with my body, powering me through practice with an energy I didn't know I had.

Venom is waving the jammer helmet cover at me, and I can see the stars in the opposing color on Imogen's helmet cover, so I grab it from Venom and pull it on, lining up beside Imogen. I can sense her, stony-faced, beside me as I skate to the inside and get on my toe stops, bending down so low my knuckles drag on the ground. I sway back and forth, sizing up the blockers in front of me. Mel is quite spry and very bony when she hits, so I'm going to aim far away from her. The five-second shout goes up and I poise, then explode like a spring from a box on the whistle. I can't see where I'm going to get through so I just skate straight up to the wall of yellow bibs and hit with my shoulders, hips, thighs, anything I can use to make a gap. I've jammed a few times before and I love having nothing else to think about other than getting through my opponents and skating as fast as I can.

I keep hitting until I finally get through and I'm lead jammer, but Imogen is hot on my tail. I can see her bowed-over stance in the left side of my vision and she's pumping her arms to catch up with me.

I round the second turn, then turn three and I'm coming up to the back of the pack again. I point my toes inwards in a plow to make my wheels screech on the floor, slowing me down. I can see Imogen coming up and she's skating so fast I don't think she's going to be able to stop. I focus my attention on her movement and angle my hips to cut in front of her at the last second, so her legs go out from under her. I skate through the pack, scoring four points, and call the jam off by tapping my hips.

I'm used to the vibe between us being playful—we normally celebrate good hits on each other with high fives—but when I look back at Imogen with a grin on my face she's still sitting on the floor. Her face is full of such resignation that my smile fades immediately. I swallow hard, and I'm glad when Venom announces the end of practice.

After stretching, I take my pads off quickly and chuck everything haphazardly in my bag, and then get frustrated when it won't zip up. I take a deep breath, get everything back out and slowly stick all the Velcro down and re-stack it neatly like I normally do. I barely even notice Mel saying goodbye to me because I'm so intensely aware of Imogen sitting nearby, radiating anger. I swear I can see her hands shake as she aggressively zips her bag up and stalks out the door.

"Kid." I look up and Venom claps me on the shoulder. "It's beer o'clock. Come on."

Venom? Asking me out for a drink? Alone? We're the only ones left and I mutely follow her out of the sports hall and across the road to the local pub. No one else is here. We choose a table, and she goes to the bar, then slams a beer down in front of me, drinking some of her own while standing. She puts her beer down then sits and looks at me sternly.

"Drink."

We sit in silence for a little while, until my beer is halfway empty. I still have no idea why she's asked me here.

"Okay, I need to see more of what I saw from you tonight."

I look up, confused.

"What?"

"Whatever was kicking you tonight, you need to let it kick you some more. Your energy was intense and your skating was good."

I can't think of anything to say back to this. I had intense energy? I thought it was mostly chaotic.

Another silence, and a bit more of my beer goes down.

"I don't feel good about it." I say, truthfully.

"Huh?"

"Usually I come away from practice feeling good. But tonight I feel like shit." But as I say this, I start to question myself. Do I feel like shit because of practice, or because Imogen was weird? Do I even feel shit at all, or am I just focused? I think back to my skating this evening and realize that maybe intense was the right word. I was single-minded, focused on doing everything I could to help my team win. Imogen was the only one who reacted badly to my intensity; everyone else was all smiles. Roller derby is strange: you celebrate your friends when they hurt you. "I don't know," I continue, "I just feel like something was wrong tonight."

"Oh, hon." Somehow she's found time to reapply the red lipstick that matches her hair. She tugs on one of her pigtails and smirks at me. "I bet the sex is good though, right?"

I splutter on a sip of beer.

"What?!"

"I mean, you were really giving each other a hard time tonight, and I know tension like that can be amazing but it can make it trickier on the track."

"I …" I'm starting to realize what she means. She thinks Imogen and I are … I can't get my head around it.

"Teammate relationships," Venom continues, "I mean, shit.

They're tough at the best of times but when you're on opposing teams for a scrimmage, it can get competitive."

"Imogen?" I ask. Venom nods. "There's no sex!" I exclaim, loud enough that I can hear a glass clatter behind the bar in the short silence that follows.

"Oh shit. I just assumed …"

"There's no sex," I reiterate more quietly. "There's no relationship. We're just friends."

There's a silence as I take another gulp of my beer.

"So you're not …?"

"Me? Gay?" She nods. "I don't know. Maybe bi?"

"I mean if you were wavering on that, roller derby is the thing that will push you the rest of the way there." Venom laughs.

"Really?"

"Yup. Roller derby makes you queer. I can't even count on both fingers and toes how many people have joined our team then realized they have same-sex tendencies."

"Really?" I repeat. Venom nods sagely.

"Truly," she confirms. "Me included. I was married to a dude back across the pond when I discovered roller derby. Turns out being around a ton of kickass people who are comfortable in their own sexuality makes you realize some things you might have been trying to bury deep down inside of you. He was a bit of a scumbag anyhow, but it was my derby sisters and siblings who got me out of there. The sport does powerful things. Not just sexuality, gender as well. Have you noticed how many nonbinary people we have on the team?"

She smiles at me and I let out a giggle. "It's not exactly representative of the general public," I agree.

"It's because we're all so fucking cool," she jokes, punching me on the shoulder. She downs the rest of her beer and pushes the glass away from her slightly.

"Thanks, Venom."

"No problem, kid. I've gotta run. But you should talk to Imogen. And keep skating as hard as you did tonight. Keep that up and you're on the roster."

My heart sings at this. I had no idea Venom would think I was good enough, I thought I was too much of a newbie. I beam up at her.

"Thanks. See you Thursday."

"Thursday."

Chapter 12

"Beer?" Mel asks, turning around from the fridge. "Anyone?"

"Beer me," Imogen says from the armchair in the corner. Mel throws one her way and she catches it without taking her eyes off the projector screen, where Soul City is playing The Bay Brawlers in a game that happened yesterday but we've decided not to look up the final score for.

"Rae? Case?"

"Yeah, one for me as well," Rae says.

I pick at a hangnail. "I'm fine with my lemonade, Mel."

Mel nods, then walks back over and hands beers out before settling on the huge floor cushion opposite the armchair. "What's happened then?"

"It's the Brawlers. What do you think?" Imogen says, snorting a sarcastic laugh.

"Yeah, but Soul have really upped their game recently."

"It's the Brawlers," Imogen repeats. "No one can ever beat them."

We all pick up on the sharp edge in Imogen's voice and back off. I pick up my feet and tuck them underneath me on the sofa, pulling my long sleeves down over my hands to soothe the icy chill of the can of lemonade in my hand. Sparkle purring next to me is soothing.

"Look, guys, I know we're all nervous …" Rae begins.

"Shhhh … Thunder Bird. Mother of Mary would you look at her?" Mel exclaims, waving a hand distractedly at Rae.

"Against Grim though? Really?" Imogen interjects.

"Look! Look at her shoulders. She is a majestic beast, no one's getting past her in a million years," Mel asserts. "I would leave Rob for her in an instant."

We watch as the agile Grim Reever comes up against Thunder Bird, fighting to make it past her. Eventually, though, she gets through.

"See?" Imogen says to Mel with a smug smile.

"Oh come on, she couldn't hold her forever. She held her for a long time, though."

"Yeah, but she could have held her for longer. She screwed up when she—"

"GUYS! Come on." Rae is standing up now, brandishing her beer in the air. "Look. We're all nervous. We all want to be rostered. But the team list will come out when it comes out and I suggest we all just watch in peace instead of getting on each other's nerves."

A short, stunned silence follows, and Imogen jumps up from the armchair, slings her empty beer bottle into the recycling bin and grabs another one from the fridge, before collapsing back down into her seat.

"When is it? Do we know when Venom is posting it?" Mel asks, tugging nervously at a braid.

"I think she said seven?" I offer.

"What's the time now?"

"6.55."

"Okay."

We pass three more jams in near silence, everyone checking their phones. I'm just about to unlock my phone when I get a beep and a notification on my lock screen: "Ve Nom has tagged you in a post." I can hear other phones buzzing in the room, and everyone scrambles to check the team group.

"Oh, wow. Oh, wow," Mel mutters under her breath. "Holy crap, I'm on the roster."

"Me too!" Rae exclaims, and they high five. I'm frantically tapping the right icons to get to the post and scan down the list, not quite believing it when I see my name up there. I made it. I'm playing in two weeks' time.

"Well done, guys!" Imogen holds up her beer towards us all and downs the rest. "Sorry, I have to go. Enjoy the rest of the footage!" A bright smile is plastered on her face as she grabs her coat and heads out of the flat. I quickly look at the list again and notice that Imogen's name isn't on there.

"Shit," I say.

"Shit," Mel agrees. "Look, love, you should probably just let her go …"

I barely even hear Mel as I haphazardly stuff my feet into my shoes and rush out of her flat, running down the stairs and out onto the street.

"Im!" I shout as I see she's halfway down the street, but she doesn't look back. "Imogen!" As I get closer, I begin to suspect she's not answering on purpose. I finally catch up with her, my heavy breath clouding in the air. I touch her shoulder then collapse in half, my hands on my knees as she turns around.

"Hey, Case," she says in a tight voice, waiting as I catch my breath.

"Look, Imogen, it doesn't matter. Just because you didn't make the roster this time, doesn't mean you won't ever again."

"This is the speech I practiced for you," she says. I look up and see her eyes glisten.

"I just don't think you should take this personally," I continue. "Venom's probably trying to give the newbies a chance, and she's been really hot on missing practices recently and maybe we've just shown up more than you."

"Case, Case. Slow down." She grabs my shoulders and looks me dead in the eye, her gaze soft and warm. "Slow down. It's fine. I get it." She takes a step closer. "It's fine. I'll play the next one."

"It's not fine. It should have been you." I blink angrily as tears flood my eyes without warning.

"You're shivering," Imogen says, rubbing my arms a few times before opening up her coat and gathering me into a hug. I tense, not allowing myself to relax into it. It feels like she's ending our conversation prematurely, placating me when I should be apologizing more for stealing her place on the roster, which is exactly what I feel like I've done.

"Sshh," she says, "it's okay."

"It's not okay," I mumble into her hair as I feel my last defenses crumble. I relax, put my arms around her and she pulls her coat tight around my back. She's only a couple of inches taller than me, but I still feel gathered up, protected from the world. Tentatively, I rest my chin on her shoulder and she makes a noise of encouragement, so I lean my head against hers. For the first time, I let myself imagine it. Walking down a snowy street sipping hot chocolate, stopping to rub noses and lace our gloved fingers together. I allow myself to really feel what I've been trying to deny ever since the disastrous end to our date. I really like Imogen.

When she pulls away, I'm not ready for it. I manage to stop an indignant mewl before it leaves my throat, and I immediately start to feel the cold air bite at me. I clamp my hands under my armpits, looking up at Imogen.

"What are you going to do now?" I ask.

"Go home. Chill. Wrap my mum's presents. It is nearly Christmas after all!" She laughs, but it sounds forced. "Look, Case, have a good time with your family, I'll see you soon, okay?"

It feels like there's a promise in that, one that's much more than seeing me at the next roller derby practice. I start to let myself believe it.

"I'll see you soon," I say. I hesitate, then reach for her hand and squeeze it gently. She looks from her hand to me, surprise written on every part of her face. Her smile softens, she cups the side of my face with her other hand and winks at me, before turning around and walking down the street. I watch her leave for longer than I'd like to, before returning to Mel's flat and ringing the doorbell.

I must look dazed as I walk in because Mel sits me down and gives me a cup of tea.

"Chick, you're freezing. What happened? Are you okay?"

I give them both a brief rundown of what happened, leaving out the part about my big lesbian crush coming out to play.

When Rae leaves, I tuck my feet underneath me on the sofa and take out my phone, clicking the cover on and off absentmindedly. I can't stop thinking about what happened with Imogen. It's been like there's this brick wall between us that she's put up; she hasn't been her normal jokey self recently, ever since I met her mum. But this evening, just for a moment, it felt like she had taken it down and I could see her again. The real Imogen. The one who is brave and sensitive and fierce. I feel like I'm getting her back.

"Okay." Mel comes back and sits beside me. "What really happened out there?"

"What do you mean? I told you what happened."

"Don't give me that shit, babe." Mel is matter-of-fact, and I crack immediately.

"I don't know. I just ... I don't know. It seemed like maybe she was ... reciprocating?"

"Are you serious?" Mel's tone is excited and she's smiling.

I struggle for what to say to adequately describe what happened between Imogen and me on the street. Finally, I settle on: "We had a moment."

Mel makes some kind of strangled noise between a shout of glee and what I imagine a baby dinosaur would sound like.

"Tell me more, woman!"

I laugh. "I really don't know, we just connected. I felt my defenses lower, you know?"

"Did you kiss?"

"No."

"Hold hands? Rub noses?"

"Shut up." I shove Mel on the shoulder.

"So what do you mean by a moment then?" She makes air quotes when she says the word "moment."

"We hugged." Unwittingly, a smile creeps across my face and I can feel red flooding my cheeks.

"You hugged? What are you, twelve years old?"

"Shut up!"

"Okay, okay. So you hugged. What now?"

I click my phone cover on and off with a little more vigor. "I don't know."

"When are you seeing her next?"

"I don't know."

"Well, find out then," Mel says, giving my phone a nudge. "Text her."

"What should I say?"

"Whatever you want. Will I make us a cup of tea while you think?"

"Yes please."

While Mel busies herself making me a cup of tea, I tap my thumbs lightly on the screen, typing and deleting over and over again. Eventually, I type out a three-word message and dither over the send button. I screw my eyes closed and press it. Immediately, I'm freaking out but Mel comes back and hands me a hot mug of tea.

"So? What did you say?"

Wordlessly, I show her my screen, the sent text sitting unread in our ongoing text log.

Can we talk?

~

The next few days pass in a blur and suddenly it's Christmas, and I've still heard nothing from Imogen.

"Casey?"

"What? Oh— sorry, Mum. Here you go." I pass the gravy

boat to her while she looks at me concerned. She raises her eyebrows at me in a question. I give her a tight smile and thumbs-up before tuning back to the current conversation topic of choice being discussed by the rest of my family. Mum's sister Gail and her husband Liam are here, along with their son Paul, and Billy and her partner Mark take up the rest of the space around the table in our small dining room, while baby Harry is asleep in his travel cot. There's barely enough room to use cutlery but since Mum's fatigue started getting worse, we can't travel to Aunt Gail's bigger house in Essex like we normally do for Christmas.

"So I said to Stu, right, I said to him that if he thought I was going to help him out he could bloody forget it," Mark says, brandishing a fork at my cousin Paul.

"Too right, he never gave you a leg-up when you needed it."

"My point exactly, Paul, he never gave me a leg-up, so now that the shoe's on the other foot, why should I?"

"To be a decent human being," I mutter under my breath, pushing some potatoes around my plate.

"What's that?" Suddenly I have the undivided attention of everyone in the room.

"Oh, I just said I'm going to the loo," I say brightly. I don't need to go, but I could use a break from everyone constantly talking over each other. I palm my phone, warm from being sat on during Christmas dinner, and silently curse women's clothing for not having pockets as I head to the bathroom. I bet if men wore dresses they'd have pockets. I leave the seat down and sit on the top of the toilet, idly unlocking my phone to check my messages.

Babe im so wasted come save me!!!!!!!
My dad is singing sex bomb on karaoke
and I want to die!!!!!!!

That's Mel, and I check the timestamp. 3.30 p.m. I laugh and send her back a wine glass emoji.

Is practice on 28th at the normal time?

That one I've already replied to: Rae, being pragmatic as usual.

Can we talk?

My unanswered message to Imogen. It tells me she's read it but not replied, and I'm just about to lock my phone again when I see a bubble appear on the left of the screen, with three flashing dots. She's typing? I don't even realize I'm holding my breath until I let it all out in a dramatic sigh when the bubble disappears. I close down the app and reopen it hoping it's a technological fault, but no, the bubble has gone and there's no reply. I even wait another couple of minutes to make sure but nothing else happens.

I sigh, flush the toilet and wash my hands. My phone goes back up my sleeve and I head out to the dining room. Mum passes me in the doorway, looking at me apologetically.

"Just going for a little nap, sweetheart," she tells me. "You'll be okay?"

I nod and head back into the kitchen. When I sit back down, my aunt pokes me in the side.

"So, Casey, are you still with that Ryan boy?" she asks. Wow, it's really been a long time since we've seen each other.

"Um no, we broke up in the summer," I tell her.

"Oh no! What happened?" She claps a hand over her mouth in shock.

"He … uh … he cheated on me?" It comes out like a question, and I'm not sure why. Almost like I'm apologizing for his indiscretion.

"No!" she gasps, appalled. "How terrible! Well, it sounds like you're better off without him. Any other nice boys in the pipeline?"

Liam nudges Gail. "Or girls, ey! Ey!" He breaks into loud guffaws which are matched around the table.

I feel like I've been punched in the stomach. My cheeks flush red as I realize it's literally laughable for me to possibly be in a relationship with someone who isn't a boy. I fix my eyes on my plate, not wanting to look up and praying someone says something to validate that it would be perfectly normal for me to have a girlfriend. But no one does.

"No, no one at the moment," I say, more to my unfinished dinner than to anyone around the table. I always knew Gail and Liam were more … old-fashioned when it came to gender and sexuality stuff, but I expected better from Billy. We were raised by our hippy mum who always instilled ideals of openness and equality in us in every way she could. If Mum were here, I know she'd say something, but I can't bring myself to be the one to challenge them today.

"Any ideas on universities?" Gail asks.

"I've deferred a year at the London one but I'm not sure if I'll go this year or defer another year."

"Why would you defer another year?" Billy asks. "I thought you were settled on going this year?"

"Well, we haven't got anything sorted for Mum yet, and I don't want to leave her without enough help at home," I say.

"You're sure it's got nothing to do with this roller derby thing? You can't give up even more of your life to that game."

"Billy, please. Let's not talk about it now."

"Wait, you're deferring *another* year?" Mark gets involved in our conversation as well. "For this stupid game?"

I automatically look at the end of the table to catch Mum's eye and beg for her to interrupt, to tell Billy and Mark it's none of their business what I do in my free time, forgetting that she's gone to have a nap upstairs. There's no one here to save me this time.

"It's not stupid," I say bitterly, "and that's got nothing to do with it. I just know it's probably going to take a while to find a carer for Mum, and—"

"How hard can it be?" Mark interrupts. "All they've got to do is cook and clean. Piece of piss."

"She needs—" I start again.

"And don't you be putting pressure on Billy to come down and look after her. She's got enough on her plate looking after the little one. When she got pregnant, she made it very clear that she didn't have the time to come down here constantly and check up on you both." He's simplifying that time in our lives dramatically. Billy was always the one who went out playing more when we were kids, who had loads of friends and hit the clubs as soon as she turned eighteen. When Mum got ill, Billy took it incredibly personally. She would much rather have been out with her friends than stay at home to help Mum in and out of the bath. She softened as the years went on and it became clear that M.E. was going to be a long-term thing, but I remember lots of long intense phone calls between Mum and Billy when she got pregnant. Mum being ill didn't fit with her image of the family she was growing.

"We don't *need* checking up on," I protest.

"I can't believe you're throwing away your life for this," Billy continues.

"I'm not—"

"It's just a bloody game," she says. I give up trying to protest and just let their criticisms wash over me. It doesn't seem like I even need to be a part of this conversation; they're just discussing my life between themselves and don't need my input. I wish I hadn't mentioned deferring another year. Although as much as I deny it to myself, I can't help but privately admit that part of it is because I feel like I've finally found a community I fit into and leaving that is just adding to my fears of being lost and alone in London. Part of me is hoping Imogen decides to defer another year as well.

"Look at all the opportunities you've got," Mark tells me, looking at Billy even as he does, and she nods along with a smug smile. "Highest marks for English in your fancy private school. Billy tells me you were meant to be saving money for uni but instead you've decided to blow it all, along with a load of time and energy, on this rollerblading thing. Billy never had half the opportunities you had. Left state school with five GCSEs. You could make so much more of yourself. You could be the first person in this family to go to university, but instead you're deferring another year for what, exactly?"

"I'm going to go and check on Mum," I say, avoiding everyone's gaze as I push my chair back and stand up. I'm well aware she's just napping and doesn't need checking on, but I can't cope with the constant questioning. I head upstairs and walk straight into my room, sitting on the edge of my bed. Just one conversation has left me doubting roller derby entirely. Sure, I enjoy it, but there's no such thing as being a professional jammer. Everything about the sport is grassroots—by the skaters, for the skaters. We volunteer our time and energy because we've all fallen in love with it—the people, the sport, the camaraderie. A lot of people on the team travel most weekends to skate, officiate, photograph and announce games in sports halls up and down the country. But it's not a career. I walk into the corridor and look at Mum sleeping soundly in her room through the cracked-open door and think about how much I want to provide for her as she gets older, how much I don't want her to have to be scrimping and saving on benefits for the rest of her life. I wish there was a handbook for this kind of thing.

Chapter 13

Anna and I manage to grab an evening together to watch films with Mum while she's home from uni, but I don't get a chance to talk to her alone because she heads straight back up to Leeds after Boxing Day to work overtime at the pet shop she's picked up a job at. We have a great time watching *The Craft* and *She's All That*, but we don't really get much time to talk other than for her to catch me up on the latest dramas in her life.

In an uncharacteristically festive display, Venom has brought us all Santa hats to wear over our helmets on our first practice back after Christmas. The thought is certainly there, but it makes scrimmaging difficult as it's tricky to put helmet covers on over them.

Imogen doesn't show up, heightening my anxiety, and I have almost managed to convince myself she hates me so much she's moved away when she walks in right at the end of practice with a stranger. She's hanging onto the arm of a tall, impossibly handsome Black guy who she introduces as Nathan.

While everyone rushes to fawn over the new arrival, Mel stays behind and squeezes my arm.

"We're going to the pub, right? For our secret Santa thing? Let's just stay for the presents then we can get the fuck out of there and chat about it."

I nod wordlessly and zip up my bag, slinging it over my

back as I go to greet Imogen.

"Case!" she shouts and starts towards me, one arm raised to chuck over my shoulder as usual, when she stops. It's almost as if she checks herself, then slaps me on the side of the arm instead. "Good Christmas?"

"Lovely thanks," I lie. "Yours?"

"Bloody awful, but it's done now, hey?" She smiles, but there's something cold behind her eyes that doesn't quite reveal the whole picture.

"Oh wow, is this the famous Casey?" Nathan's gorgeousness is even more intimidating up close. He's got a shaved head, impressively buff shoulders and the longest eyelashes I've ever seen on a boy … Wait, famous?

"I'm famous?" I say without thinking. Imogen shoves Nathan.

"She wouldn't shut up about you," he says, looking me dead in the eye and winking.

"What." Why wouldn't she shut up about me? What is this?

"Come on, Nath, you've got to meet Venom. She's our coach and she's terrifying." Imogen pulls him away and we all troop across the road to the pub.

As soon as we get in there, Mel announces that she's going to the toilet and stamps on my foot so hard I almost see stars.

"Jesus fucking … Oh, okay." I realize what she's telling me. I follow her and we crowd into the smallest and smelliest toilet known to humanity. Mel sits on the closed lid and points a finger at me.

"Who is he?" she demands.

"I don't know."

"Like, is he a cousin? A boyfriend? Who is he?"

"I don't know."

"Are they dating? When did she meet him?"

"I don't know, Mel." I don't know how many more times I can tell Mel I don't know anything about him, that this has shocked me just as much as it has shocked her.

"Okay, sorry. I'm sorry. I'm just … blindsided. I'm totally blindsided, chick."

"Yeah, me too."

Anxious thoughts start to creep in, and I recognize these spiraling patterns from pre-roller derby times. Things like, I'm such an idiot for believing anything could happen between Imogen and me. For thinking that a hug was more than a hug, and that a friendly trip to the Christmas market was a date.

"Oh, babe." It's only when Mel pulls me into a hug I realize I'm crying. Big, sloppy sobs that have me reaching for the scratchy toilet roll on offer and leaving a healthy mixture of drool and tears on Mel's jumper. "Shh, Casey, it's okay. It's okay."

"I'm s-so stupid," I cry.

"It's okay. You're alright."

"I can't believe I actually— Oh god, I'm s-such an idiot."

"You're not an idiot, love."

Eventually I manage to pull myself together and look at my reflection. I wish I was one of those dignified criers like in the films where a single tear rolls down their unblemished face. I'm an ugly crier: my nose and top lip are bright red and swollen, and my eyes are pink from the tears. I blot my face with cold water compresses made from toilet roll until the red has calmed down a bit.

"You can do this," Mel says as she cajoles me out of the toilet. "One drink, then Secret Santa, then we'll go. I'll walk you home."

I cling to her hand as we make our way back to the table. Imogen is practically draped across Nathan's lap when I sit down. I look at her and she catches my eye then looks away immediately; the expression on her face is unreadable.

Mel puts a beer in front of me and I'm halfway down the glass before I risk a look upwards again. The beer has put warmth in my belly but that all drains away when I see the way Nathan and Imogen are laughing together as Imogen gestures wildly, stopping to nudge him in the side with her elbow and giggle. I can't bear the thoughts that follow.

"Shall we do Secret Santa?" I offer, much too loudly.

"Good idea, Case, let's do it," Rae says.

Everyone rummages around in their kit bags for their gift. I got Mel, and she squeals in ecstasy when she unwraps the unicorn toe guards I got her.

"They're so *purple*! I love them! Thank you, babe!" She throws her arms around my neck and squeezes me tightly.

Venom reaches across the table and hands me a large, flat gift wrapped in brown paper. I look at her quizzically and she shrugs at me. "Go on. Open it."

I open it carefully, almost forgetting about Imogen and Nathan in my curiosity about what Venom got me. It's a picture frame. I turn it over and it's this gorgeous, stylized print with "Cut yourself some fucking slack, kid" written on it and decorated like the night sky.

"Oh my god. Thank you, Venom!" I beam at her, and I can tell she's struggling not to smile back. She shrugs again.

"I thought it was cool."

"I love it."

She raises her glass to me and we clink pints of beer. I can never get a proper read on Venom. Sometimes she's the meanest coach ever, with zero humor, and sometimes I see a kind of softness in her.

Mel has given Imogen a selection of colorful scarves to wear under her helmet. She selects one and pulls it over her hair immediately. It's black and has a pink glittery skull and crossbones design dotted all over it. Nathan plucks it from her head and models it on his own, pouting and posing. They laugh together and the pit in my stomach opens up again. I smile at a point somewhere over Imogen's shoulder before setting my gaze firmly on my nearly empty pint glass. Mel gets up to go to the toilet and I suddenly realize I can't take another second here.

"Right, I'm off," I announce to no one in particular, slapping my knee like a middle-aged dad and standing up.

"Already?" asks Rae. "Are you sure?"

"Yep." I give her a quick one-armed hug and stride out before anyone can make any kind of protest.

It's only a short walk home, but the exercise and the cold December air clear my head as I set out. I'm questioning everything I thought I knew. Little hints that I thought Imogen had given me now look more like bones she threw to a mistakenly devoted dog. I just can't see a scenario where things work out the way I thought they might just before Christmas. My crush on Imogen felt fun before. I had a few nerves, sure, but it was mostly excitement, all wrapped in with the discovery of roller derby and this new life I never thought I could have. Even the thought of going to university has been starting to feel a little bit less scary. But these feelings are definitely not fun.

A few minutes into my walk, Mel texts me.

Did you want me to walk you home love?

I reply:

No thanks, I'm okay. Just need to think.

My brain is a mess of images: ice skating with Imogen, the look she gave me after I met her mum, Imogen and Nathan together, the long hug just before Christmas, and this distance that she seems to have put between us. I can't figure any of it out. I fumble with my key in the front door, my eyes suddenly blurred with tears, and as I walk in I can see the flickering light in the living room that means Mum is still up.

"Hi, sweetheart! Did you have a nice time?" she shouts out to me.

I go into the living room, ready to paste a smile on my face but as soon as Mum looks at me I can't keep it up. My face crumples and I sit on the sofa next to her with my head in my hands.

"Oh no! What's wrong?" she asks. But I can't even begin to think how I would tell her. The laughs at the Christmas table keep going round in my mind along with all the different memories of Imogen, and I realize I've never really spoken to my mum about anything to do with this. So I just cry, and she leans over and holds me until I'm all cried out. I never cried like this when Ryan and I broke up.

Eventually I surface, hiccupping and wiping my face with a tissue Mum passes me.

"What is it, darling? What's got you so upset?"

I shake my head and scrunch up my eyes.

"You know you can talk to me about anything, don't you?" she asks. I look up at her.

"Mum, would you still love me even if there was something … different about me?"

"Of course!" There's no hesitation there at all. "You're my daughter and I'll love you no matter what. I promise."

But I still can't bring myself to tell her. Instead, I just lean my head onto her shoulder and let her stroke my hair. Maybe another day I'll say something.

Chapter 14

I don't have butterflies in my stomach, they're more like bats. Another two weeks have passed with no word from Imogen, and now it's the day of my first game. I'm sitting on a bench in the changing room, carefully lining up the Velcro straps on all of my protective gear.

"Okay, guys, gals, nonbinary pals, everyone got their kit on? We're going out for a warm-up in ten minutes," Fi, our line-up manager, announces, moving smoothly around the changing room in her wheelchair as she checks on everyone. "Bash, you got your mouthguard this time? Okay, good. Gem, have you eaten something? Get that banana down. I know you feel sick but it'll do you a world of good. We can't have you fainting on the track. Casey. Casey?"

I snap out of my reverie. "Yes?"

"You okay? You look pale."

I make fists with my clammy hands. "I'm scared."

"I know. Everyone is before their first game. You'll be okay."

Her words have done nothing to calm me down, and neither do Mel's well-intentioned breathing exercises when she notices me panicking. I just can't stop thinking about the crowd out there, watching everything on the track, and I can't stop imagining various embarrassing situations. I could trip and fall as I skate onto the track for the first time. Something could come over me and I could act on an intrusive thought to do something completely against the rules, like head-butting someone in the stomach, and getting sent off. I could forget all of my training and be such a hindrance to the team that they keep me sitting on the bench for the rest of the game, or even send me to take my kit off because they don't want to be associated with me at all. I start to get dizzy and my breath comes in shorter and shorter as my vision tunnels.

"Case. Look at me." I look up, and straight into Imogen's face. She must have come into the changing room to say good luck before the game started.

"Hey, Im," I say, flashing her a nervous smile.

"Drink some water." She pushes a water bottle into my hands and watches as I take small sips. "Good. That's it."

"I don't feel good," I tell her.

"I know, babe. Just keep sipping that water, you're doing fine. Tell me what you had for breakfast."

I look up in confusion. "I don't know— toast, I think?"

"Oooh tasty. What did you have on it? Marmite?"

I make a face. "Eww, gross. No, I had jam."

"Heathen."

I giggle weakly. "Just because you're wrong."

"If you were a real Brit, you'd like Marmite. Go on, what else did you have? A cup of tea?"

My breathing starts to slow a bit. I'm confused why Imogen is asking about my breakfast, but thinking about something other than the impending game is helping, it's grounding me. I screw up my eyes and try and remember. "Yeah, I had some tea."

"Two sugars? Come on, Case, the more you think about little stuff like this, the less you'll panic. I've got you."

"Yeah, two sugars."

"That's it. What are you gonna have for dinner?"

"I dunno. We've got some leftover quiche in the freezer."

"Yeah? What with?"

"Maybe some potatoes and salad." Thinking about small things like this is helping. I'm getting distracted from imagining worst-case scenarios on the track.

"You're doing well, Case. I'm here. You're okay," Imogen says.

"I'm just scared," I admit.

"Hey, what's the worst that could happen?"

"I could break my leg and throw up on the track in front of everyone."

"Yeah, and?"

I don't understand the question. "I can't imagine anything worse. My life would end."

"But your life wouldn't end. You know what would happen? I'd be over there with you in a flash, help clean you up and stay in the ambulance with you on the way to hospital. And in a little while it would just be a funny story to tell the newbies and scare them."

"You'd go with me to the hospital?"

"Of course. Case, you don't have to worry about anything. I'd look after you. I promise. We all look after each other here. When Sam broke her ankle, we brought her food and walked her dogs for her. You're not alone when you're on a roller derby team."

I can feel her taking the weight of my worry from me. This is the Imogen I know, and I don't know what's brought her back but I'm thankful she's here. My hands are dry, my breathing is back to normal, and I've stopped feeling dizzy. I look around and the changing room is empty apart from Imogen and me at one end of a long row of benches.

"Where is everyone?" I ask.

"They went out for warm-up a couple of minutes ago. You can go and catch up."

"Shit. Okay."

"Stop. Breathe. You're okay." Imogen chucks me under the chin and smiles at me. "You're going to kick ass out there."

I can't help but smile back. I pop in my mouthguard and stand up. We leave the changing room together, and I skate into the sports hall. Imogen peels off to sit with some other teammates who aren't skating, and I think I spot Nathan amongst them. I gulp, then remind myself what Imogen said to me. She promised I wouldn't have to worry about anything, because she would be there if anything bad happened. And she left Nathan to come and see me in the changing room. Buoyed by that thought, I meet my teammates on the track and join in the warm-up.

I'm on track for the first jam of the game, and I've been given the inside line. My job is to stick to this line no matter what and stop any Hellfire opponents getting past me. As soon as the whistle blows, a blocker from the other team knocks me over. Bad start. Before I can start hating myself for messing up so early on, I get back up and skate fast to catch up to the pack, touching Venom on the back as I reach my teammates.

"Okay, re-form people," she instructs us, and I position

myself between the track boundary and Gem. We're opposite each other and have a hand on each other's shoulder, bracing ourselves against the powerful jammer we'll be trying to stop getting past us. I always find it difficult to tell people apart when they're in their derby gear, but the bright pink leggings the jammer wears really help to spot her skating towards us. Her teammates are confident enough in her abilities to let her tackle us by herself and have stayed back to try and stop our jammer getting through for her initial pass. I center myself and wait for the hit.

Pink leggings, otherwise known as Jam Slam, launches herself into Gem and me, leading with her hips and pushing against our legs. We automatically rotate 180 degrees, so my back is against her and Gem is in front of me providing support. I grab both her shoulders and push back as hard as I can, letting my skates creep forward as slowly as possible. Jam Slam is relentless and I yell wordlessly, causing Venom to come over from where she was helping our jammer get through and provide her body as another obstacle in Jam Slam's way. We push our hips together, hard, and I'm so focused on keeping my body in contact with Venom's that I forget to guard the inside line. All of a sudden, an opposing blocker comes up on my left and pushes me out of the way, giving Jam Slam an opportunity to skip around me. She delivers a solid hit with her shoulder to Gem, who crumples to the floor, and hops around her, her legs and arms pumping as she skates the diamond around the track.

But finally, our jammer has got through and is catching up to her. I hear the four short whistle blasts that signal the jam is over and sigh with relief, skating back to our bench.

"How did we do?" I ask Yasmin, our bench manager.

"*Nil points*," she says, pointing at the scoreboard, "but we're just getting started. Have a drink," she tells me. I pop the top on my water bottle and take a long drink from it.

The next few times I'm on the track, I feel like I can't quite keep up with what's happening. I manage to get a few hits in, but mostly I feel like my job is to get in the way of as many opponents as possible. But slowly, it starts to feel more manageable. It's just a scrimmage, I tell myself. I'm doing exactly the same things as I normally do at practice, but this time I'm skating against people I don't know and there's a crowd watching us. The thrumming bass of the music system moves through my body and pumps me up, and I get a thrill every time I hear the announcers call me "Justin Case 04."

Half time arrives much sooner than I expected.

"Okay everyone, make sure you have a snack or at least drink a bit of water. And go and pee NOW," Venom tells us all sternly.

The score is 86-74 to them; we keep falling behind then closing the gap a bit then falling behind again. I'm too nervous to eat anything so I just stand up to go to the toilets. Skating on the carpet in the hallways is much harder than I expect, though, and before I really know what's happening, I'm arse over tit in front of a whole line of people outside the toilets.

"Oh honey, do you need any help?"

I look in the direction of the voice and it's Nathan, still looking impossibly handsome.

"No, don't worry, I'm fine. I'm just an idiot."

He laughs and offers me a hand anyway, which I take gratefully as I can hear people still sniggering behind me.

"You look so great out there. Imogen is so proud of you," he says to me.

"She is?"

"Hell yeah! You're like her little protégé. Over Christmas, she wouldn't stop bragging about how she recruited you and taught you how to skate."

"Oh, so you spent Christmas with her? That's nice. How did you guys meet?"

"Our mums were in the same baby group and we grew up together, so we're basically family," he explains. "Look, I've gotta go and grab some beers but good luck out there, alright? You're kicking ass."

"I … yeah, thanks. Enjoy!" My mind is stuck on that word "family," and my brain is scanning back through everything I've seen of his interactions with Imogen. The inside jokes, the natural physicality, how relaxed they are with each other. As I glide not-so-effortlessly past the line outside the toilets I try to keep myself in check. This doesn't mean anything. Even if Nathan isn't her boyfriend, that doesn't mean Imogen is interested in me. But I can't help feeling uplifted a bit by this news.

Back at the bench, Yasmin is giving everyone a pep talk.

"So, this isn't a championship game, but that doesn't mean we should relax. We're doing well in holding off their jammer as long as possible. Blockers, you're doing a fantastic job, I want you to keep going. Jammers, I'm going to need you to be more aggressive, deliver more hits. Take advantage of the fact that our blockers are holding them back and try to overtake them on points."

I nod seriously, clicking my mouthguard on and off my teeth with my tongue. Mel touches my shoulder.

"You alright, chick?" she asks, looking concerned. "Still panicking?"

I take a deep, slow breath and smile at her. "I'm okay. I'm good."

It's a couple of jams into the second half before I'm on track again. I skate up just in front of the jammer line on the inside track boundary, keeping my head turned to the right so I can see what's coming up behind me. The whistle blows and I shove my shoulder, hard, against Mel's. The opposing jammer, Rack n Roll, tries to wedge their shoulder between our bodies and delivers some powerful hits, but Mel and I are solid and they soon give up and head for the outer reaches of the track. I skate forward and cast an eye about for our jammer, Cillit Bang, who is having some trouble with the Hellfire blockers up ahead. I head straight for them and without thinking too hard about it, deliver a well-timed body check that causes a minuscule gap to open up in the previously impenetrable wall. That's enough for Cillit Bang to get out of the pack and be called lead jammer. Mel and Gem are still holding back Rack n Roll. Cillit Bang manages to get round the track and skips down the inside line as I shove a blocker out of the way. Four points. All the other opposing skaters are too busy concentrating on getting their own jammer out of the pack for their initial pass to pay attention to Cillit Bang, and before they know it she scores four more points on them. Rack n Roll finally gets out of the pack and chases Cillit Bang down, causing her to call off the jam, but not before scoring an extra two points. I skate back towards the team bench feeling confident.

The next few jams take much the same structure, but the Hellfire Harlots are becoming wise to our tactics of helping our jammers through and are combating this by putting in their strongest blockers, the ones who can weather our hits more effectively. The score is 115-96 with the Harlots in the lead, and Yasmin calls a team time-out for a huddle at the bench.

"Our tactics were working, but not anymore. Our nippiest jammers aren't getting past them, so we're going to have to try and out-hit them this time. They're strong, but we can be stronger. We can't just outrun these ones; we're going to have to plough straight through them."

Everyone is nodding in agreement.

"Fi and I have had a chat, and we'd like Casey to jam."

Everyone keeps nodding in agreement. I stop and stare.

"What? But … I'm not a jammer. I'm a blocker. I'm not fast."

"We don't need fast. We need strong. We've built our team around having fast jammers and strong blockers, and right now that's not scoring any points. You've been working on jamming at practice. What I want you to do is to try it out for one jam. Keep it penalty-free, and if you tire out then pass the star to Venom. She'll back you up. The only way this can be a bad thing is if you commit a penalty and make it a power jam, so keep it clean. We can close this gap. One good jam is all we need."

I'm passed the jammer helmet cover and line it up with the stars on my helmet in a daze. I screw my eyes up and take a deep breath, then open my eyes with renewed clarity. Our new tactic is for my teammates to ignore me completely and hold back their jammer, then I just hit my way through the pack. I place myself evenly between the inside and outside lines on the track. The whistle goes and I skip past my teammates, who already have their eyes on the Harlots' jammer. As I pass Mel, I swear I can hear her whisper, "Bring it on, bitches."

I don't hesitate at the back; I just aim my shoulders at the gap between two of the blockers' bodies and hit and hit and hit. I get my shoulder through. I give one of them a good bash with my hip, get my hip through and sit on the other blocker's leg. It kind of feels like I'm being birthed, and the thought almost makes me laugh but I focus, hop over their legs, and come shoulder-to-shoulder with another blocker. I duck down, spring up and deliver a hit to the solar plexus with my shoulder. I can hear the "oof" as the wind is knocked out of her. I get past the last blocker by lowering my shoulder and skating straight into their side, then I'm home free. The open space in front of me seems vast and I'm pushing and pushing to be the fastest I possibly can. One lap, and on the second lap I catch up to the back of the pack again.

They're wiser this time. My team are still keeping Hellfire's jammer back, but Hellfire are using all of their energy to strengthen the wall I'm trying to get through. Their two strongest blockers are glued together at the hip, waist and shoulder, and the other two blockers are pushing on them from either side to make the bond stronger. I go in hip-first this time which blindsides them a little, just long enough for me to deliver a body check apiece and plough through. The other blockers run into the middle to stop me but Venom and Gem have my back and deal with them before they can get to me, and before I know it I've scored four points, and then four more. I'm about to attempt my fourth pass through the pack when Hellfire's jammer finally gets out and makes it around the track towards me. I look over to the bench where Yasmin is furiously hitting her hips, and I tap my hips to call the jam off. My first ever time jamming in a bout, and I scored an 8-point jam. Not bad.

I skate back to the bench smiling. The claps on the back are gratifying and I feel pride not just for myself, but for my team. I wouldn't have been able to score so many points if they hadn't kept the other jammer back for so long.

We catch up over the next 20 minutes; our new strategy is working well and I'm focused throughout. There's thirty seconds left on the clock and I'm up to jam. The score is 143-140 to the Hellfire Harlots so it's still anybody's game.

I skip through the pack almost instantaneously and am called as lead jammer. I risk a glance back as I skate and my team is holding back the other jammer. I speed round the track, coming up towards the back of the pack again, head towards the inside and jump the apex, only just making the jump and zooming past Hellfire's skaters. Four points. The screams from the crowd are urging me on and I slow down just behind the pack for my second scoring pass. My team is still keeping the other jammer back and a grin is spreading across my face. We've totally got this. I'm so happy about the idea of winning that I take a hard hit from a Hellfire blocker and step off the track, then step back on and hit her back without even thinking. I realize with a horrified "oh shiii—" what I've done. That's a cut track penalty which equals thirty seconds in the penalty box. I look left and see the referee signaling me off with his arms making an X then pointing off the track, and I want to cry. That means a power jam for the other team, and our blockers are good but they can't hold back the jammer indefinitely. My only hope is that I get let out before the jam ends and even the score.

When I sit down in the penalty box I don't even look at the team bench for fear of the scowls that might be coming my way. If I could scowl at myself, I definitely would. What an idiot. I should have just called off the jam while we were winning, but I had to try for more points. So frustrating.

Thirty seconds is a long time when you're watching your team lose because of you. Miraculously, I only have ten seconds left in my penalty when the Hellfire jammer finally gets through the pack for her initial pass and starts coming around again for her first scoring pass. When I hear "black oh-four, done" from the penalty timer behind me, I sprint to get to her and try to hit her off. Just three points would be a disaster. I succeed with a well-timed hip check and skate backwards briefly to make sure she has to come back in behind me. As I head for the pack again I think everything might be okay. But their jammer is just too fast and it's only a couple of seconds before she hits the pack as well and gets past one blocker. I can see the jam timer lift the whistle to their lips out of the corner of my eye, and I skate as fast as I can to earn as many points as possible, but the whistle goes to signal the end of the jam, and the game. I cross everything as the scores are checked by the officials, then the final score is updated on the projector for everyone to see—146-147 to us.

I scream with joy and am immediately knocked to the floor by Mel, who has launched herself at me, followed immediately by the rest of the team. I can barely tell whose limbs are whose and I think I might be crying as I get the life hugged out of me. We disentangle and stand up, and I see

Imogen running ahead of the rest of the crowd to get to the track boundary, but she doesn't stop there, just carries on running straight towards me. She's got this wild smile on her face and something else I can't read, and as she comes towards me I hold my hands out, about to tell her I'm too sweaty to hug. She pushes my hands aside, goes up onto her tiptoes, throws her arms around my neck and kisses me.

Imogen. Is kissing me. My brain can't process this. There are shouts from my team and far too soon, way before I manage to start kissing back, I'm wrenched away for a victory lap around the track. I can feel her bright pink lipstick smeared across my mouth, and I grin wider than I've ever done before as I'm dragged around the track, slapping the outstretched hands reaching towards me. I'm definitely crying now, but not those ugly sobs that make my face swollen and red, just happy streams of tears that feel like they're washing away all the horrible confusing feelings I've been having, all these worries that I've been moving backward instead of forward.

I stop back at the bench, and Imogen is there. She grabs my hand immediately, lacing her fingers into mine despite my sweaty wrist guards. We just stare at each other, smiling wide, until she breaks away to go and pull up some track tape. The cheers dissipate and we all get to work turning the sports hall from a roller derby venue back into badminton courts. The kiss stays vivid in my mind the entire time.

Chapter 15

The after-party is at the pub just across the road from the sports center; the one where Venom took me after practice that one time. Once the sports hall is clear, we all walk over in a big crowd. I'm still flying high from a combination of the last-minute win and the kiss with Imogen. I smile as I take a drink, focusing my attention on Mel, who's sitting next to me. She leans in and whispers loudly, "What's happening with Imogen, babe?"

"I don't know," I murmur through clenched teeth, casting my eyes to the right to see if Imogen has noticed our conversation.

"Did she just kiss you?"

"Yeah, she did."

Imogen leans over from my other side and touches my wrist. "You okay, Case?"

"Oh yeah!" I say brightly.

"Are you sure?" She shifts her body slightly towards me and takes my hand in hers. "Come with me," she says. She laces her fingers through mine and stands, before leading me through the crowded pub to the quiet, cold beer garden.

"What's wrong?" she asks.

"I just ..." I take a deep breath, considering whether I'm actually going to say it or not. "What happened, back there? At the end of the game?" I ask her.

She looks down towards the floor, and my breath catches.

But then she looks up at me and her expression is shy and excited and nervous all at the same time. I've never seen her look anything like this.

"I don't know. I mean, what happened for you?"

"You kissed me," I say, slowly, seriously, and I can almost see a wall come down in front of her eyes. She unlaces her fingers from mine and takes a long drink from her glass.

"I'm sorry. I shouldn't have."

"No … Im …"

"I misread things; it shouldn't have happened. Don't worry, it won't happen again."

"Imogen—"

"Let's just go back inside, okay? We can pretend it never happened."

I'm shocked at what I do next. I reach out, faltering slightly, towards Imogen's hand, the one that's currently clenched in a fist. As soon as my hand touches hers, she softens and looks up at me. I lace our fingers together and look up at her, nervously licking my lips and leaning my face towards hers.

"Case …" she whispers just before our lips meet, and it's everything I wanted it to be. It's exciting and safe and grounded and buoying, and I hear her make a sound of encouragement, so I take a shuffling step forward and let my other hand rest on her waist. She fumbles slightly, putting down her drink on the table near us while trying not to break the kiss, and we giggle, our teeth clashing. She tastes like beer and chewing gum.

"So you …?" she asks.

I respond by kissing her again, and she moans and pushes her hand into my hair, stepping forward. I feel a frisson of electricity at all the places we're touching, as well as a hot lump in the back of my throat. As our lips open and tongues touch, a few scalding hot tears make their way down my face to join our kiss. We pull away from each other.

"Are you crying?" she asks.

I smile and nod, blinking a couple more tears out and rubbing my face with my hand. "Sorry."

"No, don't be sorry, I just … I didn't realize."

"*You* didn't realize? I thought Nathan was your boyfriend!"

She bursts out laughing. "Case, Nathan is a flaming homosexual. He's also basically my cousin."

I laugh as well, and she winds her arm further around my waist and pulls me in.

"Believe me, the only person I want to be kissing is you," she says softly, leaning in to kiss me again. This time I make sure to lock the feeling in my brain for good. The way her top lip feels between mine, how our cold noses push past each other, the moment when she tugs on my bottom lip gently with her teeth—

A clatter at the door makes us jump apart from each other and look back at the noise. Venom and Fi are at the door, both with cigarettes in their hands. Venom raises one eyebrow at us.

"Finally. Jeez."

I bite my lip, and I can't stop a schoolgirl giggle from emerging. Imogen holds my hand more firmly, looks at me and says, "Finally, yeah."

Chapter 16

It's a cold bright day the next Saturday and Sam texts the team group chat and suggests a trip down to the nearest beach to skate along the seafront cycle path. We pile into four different cars (Mel and I with Sam, Imogen with Venom), kit bags squashed in wherever we can find space, and face the January chill in our skating gear. The padding helps to keep the bite away from my skin, which I can feel turning red wherever the wind is whipping me. There are fifteen of us in our helmets and mouthguards, rucksacks strapped to our backs, and we've taken over the seafront. We go slow and chat, then race to a bollard, then whip through a pace line, laughing and chatting the whole time. My eyes stream as we skate east, towards the sun. Every now and then we go silent, battling the oncoming wind. I can barely hear the sea over the sound of our wheels on tarmac, but it's always there to the right of me. It's frothy and green today, with even the strongest windsurfers struggling to stay upright.

We're headed to a café about five miles down the coast that I vaguely remember going to with Mum, Dad and Billy when I was much younger. The pancakes taste like food from the gods after our long skate here, and we devour our food in near silence before decamping to an empty tennis court opposite the café and putting our skates back on. Our full bellies slow us down as we play games, and eventually we all collapse, giggling, onto the ground. Imogen pulls me off to a corner and wraps her hoodie around my shoulders when I start shivering.

"Let's hang out next week," Imogen says decisively as we sit cross-legged facing each other, eyes twinkling.

"Okay! When?"

"Do you want to meet me after I finish work on Tuesday? We could go and get some food, have a drink, maybe go to the cinema or something?"

"I have to help my mum get to her book group on Tuesdays," I explain. "Maybe Wednesday daytime?"

"Sure. That's cool that she's in a book group."

"It's only a ten-minute walk away," I tell her. "But I have to push her there in a wheelchair, then I come home, and I go and get her after it finishes."

"How's she gonna get there when you go to uni in London?" Imogen asks innocently, not realizing that this is the one thing, other than her, that has been plaguing me for months.

"Well, we need to hire some carers for her."

"I'm sure you'll find some great people."

Her face is friendly, open, unconcerned. I take a deep breath, about to voice the thing I've been trying not to think about. "What if I can't do it?"

"Do what?"

I gesture broadly. "Life. I'm just …"

"Scared?" Imogen asks.

I nod.

"Me too."

The sea is rough, but the sound of it is calming, and I open up. As we talk about our histories, our fears, I can feel these things spilling out of me like the sea onto the shore. Her intense scrutiny sometimes makes me want to curl in on myself but I keep going until she stops me, pressing her mouth to mine. But even though we're not talking anymore, she's coaxing the details from me. Her lips are rough and chapped, and she tugs at my mouth and takes from me in tiny portions. I forget the cold tarmac we're sitting on and lean closer on my skates, pushing as she pulls like the sea behind us. We don't need words for what this is, other than a beginning.

~

I'm immediately flushed when I get home, hot from what I have to say to Mum and Billy, who are having a cup of tea at the kitchen table. The conversation around the dinner table at Christmas is echoing in my mind, and I try to think about how Billy reacted to the joke about me having a girlfriend. Did she laugh along with everyone? Was it a genuine laugh, or one of those ones you do when you want to fit in and not rock the boat? And then there was last week when Mum said she would love me no matter what. Maybe I should talk to them separately, but I don't feel like I can keep it inside any longer. I feel like Mum, at least, will be able to see it on me. Like she'll somehow know that I swapped cars with Gem and we spent the whole car ride home holding hands in the back seat with Imogen, smiling at each other with the newness of it all.

I haven't even told Anna yet. I've tried implying a couple of times by text but she keeps barreling right past the hints and asking if there are any hot guys on my team. The life I'm living now feels so different to the one we lived before she moved away, and I just can't find the right words to tell her about how much I've changed. More and more time is going by between our texts but I don't feel the loss of her presence in my life as much as I thought I would; I've found a community here that surrounds me with support. I resign myself to telling her about Imogen the next time I see her.

I make us all some tea and get the biscuit tin out of the top cupboard. I tell Mum and Billy about the team outing, and I can feel my eyes sparkle every time I talk about Imogen. Billy doesn't even make too many snide comments about skating. Finally, when I take a deep breath and sit on my hands, Mum looks at me like she knows what I'm about to say.

"Me and Imogen …" I start.

She opens her mouth and closes it again, smiling at me instead.

"We … I think we're girlfriends now."

Her smile widens. I look over at Billy, nervous to catch her eye.

"So this is why you've been doing the whole roller derby thing?" she asks after a short silence.

I'm torn between being offended that she thinks I started a whole new hobby to chase a girl and being touched that she said the name of the sport correctly.

"Billy," Mum admonishes her gently.

"What? Okay, okay. I'm happy for you. But you know the same rules apply as with Ryan. If she breaks your heart, I'm gonna beat her up." She smiles at me, and I can see a gentleness within her that she hardly ever lets out.

"Thanks, sis," I say, smiling at her. She winks at me.

"Gotta keep the family safe, right?"

Chapter 17

Imogen and I have a plan to meet at the cinema for a midday showing of the new horror film that's out, but I wake up in the morning to a bright light behind my curtains that suggests something other than the horrible rain we've been having. I open them and gasp.

"Snow!" I shout.

"I know!" Mum shouts back. She comes into my room and we look out at our back garden covered in a thick layer of snow. Her energy levels aren't doing their usual crash over winter, and it almost feels like old times with her coming into my room as soon as I wake up to talk about our day ahead. I love how the snow muffles everything, how the world just seems like a quieter place. I grab my phone and scroll through texts from the rest of the team excited about the weather. I navigate to my contacts and hover over Imogen's name, debating whether or not to call or text, when a call from her comes through.

"Hey! I was just about to call you," I say after answering the phone. Mum smiles at me and walks out of my room.

"So, I don't know how you feel about the snow," Imogen goes straight in, "but I love it."

"Me too."

"Let's scrap the cinema plan. It's too pretty to spend hours in a big room watching a screen."

"Sounds good."

"Wear warm clothes. I'll be at yours in half an hour."

The line goes dead before I can ask what we're doing instead. I rifle through my wardrobe, picking out lots of thin layers to wear.

"What are you doing today then?" Mum asks as I'm preparing some breakfast in the kitchen.

"I don't know. Imogen just said she'd be here in half an hour."

"Did you hear the schools are closed today? Looks like it's a snow day for a lot of people."

"What are you going to do?" I ask.

Mum holds up her latest crime thriller with a bookmark about a third of the way through.

"There's been a murder," she says, in a terrible imitation of a Scottish accent. I laugh as she walks through to the living room with a cup of tea.

I crunch my toast slowly, savoring the taste of the honey spreading over my tongue. I knew that coming out could be difficult, as well as exciting and validating. I never knew that it could be so … freeing. So amazing to speak the truth of who I am and to have those I love accept it. The sun is slicing through the blinds and I can hear Mum gasp at something in her book. I can't imagine feeling anything but happy about this. Feeling anything except joy at finding myself in a place where I am safe and accepted and loved.

The doorbell rings.

"I'll get it!" I shout up the hallway as I go to open the door. Imogen is standing there in a bright red bobble hat and a huge black puffa jacket, but I barely register those before she throws a snowball at me.

"Imogen!" I yell, looking down at my jumper which has a huge wet patch on it. She giggles as I pull on my brown boots and use them to push the snow out of the front door. She's already making another snowball from the snow on the wall outside.

"Ready or not," she says, pulling her arm back, a glint in her eye. I put my hands in the air.

"Just let me put my coat and gloves on," I say while laughing.

The streets are empty of cars and only a couple of buses are braving their way through the snow on the main road. We walk slowly, holding gloved hands on our way into town.

"I love the snow," she tells me as we reach the high street. "I remember the first time I saw proper snow when I was little. I must have been about seven, and Mum was fussing over me being too cold but I just couldn't get enough of it. Whenever she turned her back, I was out in the garden without shoes or gloves on, throwing snowballs at the kitchen window."

I laugh. "Didn't you get into trouble?"

"Loads. But it was much better once my toes and fingers weren't freezing. I remember we went up to the top of St Catherine's Hill and sledded down on tea trays. She used to be so much fun."

"Sounds amazing."

We make our way down to the cathedral gardens chatting about our favorite memories of the snow. There are so many people out on the grass, building snowmen and having snowball fights. Imogen grins mischievously, then bends down and scoops some snow into her hands, forming it into a ball.

"Come on, Timberlake, let's show them how it's done."

I bend down and start making a snowball of my own as she runs off, pelting random people and hiding behind trees. I run after her and we end up in a huge snowball fight with what feels like an entire army of people. I've never done anything like this before, just connected with random people on the street in this way. Imogen is a natural, going easy on the smaller kids and getting super competitive with a big pack of teenage boys who decide it's their mission to take us down. After a heated fight, we collapse onto a nearby bench and Imogen holds her hands up.

"We surrender!" she shouts. "You win!"

"It's over!" I add. She turns her head and smiles at me, just as a snowball hits me in the face. I whip my head around to see one of the teenage boys running away and shake my fist in his direction.

"Don't you love it like this?" Imogen says, gesturing around us.

"Only if I'm prepared."

"Oh, come on, it's romantic."

"Having teenage boys throw things at me isn't my idea of romance," I tell her sternly, but I can't stop a smile creeping through.

"I'm sure that last one was a mistake."

"Sure, sure."

"Hey, at least you'll have a really cool bruise."

I break my mood and wipe what's left on my glove all over her face. Her shock lasts just long enough for me to get a head start and form some weapons of my own.

∞

I've never really been one for horror films. When I'm feeling particularly anxious I get bad nightmares that I don't want to fuel. But when the snow melts, Imogen insists that we make up for our failed cinema date by going to see the latest monster movie. I fail in my attempt to get her to go to the perfectly good rom-com on at the same time.

"Films are always scarier when you don't see the bad guy," Imogen tells me as we walk to the cinema together. "Once you see it, it's fine. They're not scary anymore."

I raise an eyebrow at her. "Are you sure about that?"

"Yes! You can always tell when it's special effects or puppets. And then you can sit back and enjoy it because you can see that it's not real. And this one is just a big shark."

"So it's not scary at all that they're trapped in a submarine and there's a monster shark on the loose … because you can see the shark?"

"Exactly."

Imogen insists on getting my ticket for me and splurges on the biggest box of popcorn I've ever seen in my life. I stand back a little at the counter and watch how she brightens the dullest of days for anyone she comes into contact with. She does a bit about drowning in popcorn and the person behind the counter grins, surprised.

"We should have gone splits on that," I tell her as we walk into the screen together. "Why did we get popcorn here when we could have gotten it so much cheaper at the supermarket?"

"It's romantic," Imogen says, in a way that suggests she's already won an argument. "And besides, you can get the next one." She nudges me and winks.

We find seats next to each other near the back and Imogen immediately puts the armrest between us up out of the way and puts a hand on my thigh. Even though we've been friends for a while and I'm getting used to her high levels of physical affection, nothing could have prepared me for what it's like to be dating her. Imogen's love language is definitely touch. She wedges the popcorn box between her knees and I take a handful and slowly eat my way through it.

I don't really know what to do with my hands. I toy with the idea of putting my hand on her thigh as well, but something about it feels ridiculous. Her hand is hot on my leg and she gives it a squeeze as the trailers end. I summon some confidence and thread my arm through Imogen's and put my hand on top of hers. She shuffles in closer and I hear her make a sound of approval.

I can't really focus on what's happening on the screen because I'm suddenly uncomfortably aware of the amount of saliva in my mouth. I swallow once, which only seems to up the production. Why is my body like this? I can't swallow again because then Imogen will notice that I seem to be some kind of saliva-producing machine and will be forever disgusted by me, ending our relationship on the spot.

"Are you okay?" she whispers to me.

Oh god, she's noticed. This is it. "I'm fine. Why?"

"You're holding my hand quite tightly." She motions down to our hands and to my horror I can see that I'm gripping onto hers much more tightly than I meant to. "It's not even the scary part yet."

"Sorry."

"It's okay." She pushes our palms together and entwines

her fingers with mine. She smiles at me and turns her head back to the screen.

I've done this before with Ryan. We used to sit right at the back row and kiss during films, all initiated by him. I was very much a passive participant in these make-out sessions. To be honest, I didn't really understand why people wanted to kiss so much—it was a fun activity, but I got bored of it after a few minutes. Ryan was all push, moving into my space and kissing me without breaks. In TV shows make-out scenes always had moments of pause, where their lips are only just touching and they seem suspended in the moment together. There were no pauses with Ryan.

But I never felt this chasm opening in my stomach with him. I'm acutely aware of how my arm is pressing into Imogen's side and how my palm is sweating slightly and my breath is coming in a bit short. I have no idea who any of the characters in the film are because the only thing I can hear is my heart beating. Is it supposed to be beating that loudly? Can Imogen hear it?

She takes a breath in and settles even more when she lets it out, letting go of my hand and reaching further over my thigh, squeezing my inner leg gently. I feel like I'm about to have a heart attack. I rest my head on her shoulder and hold onto her wrist, and she makes a sound in her throat and turns her head, planting a kiss on my temple. Her head stays turned and I can feel us poised in zero gravity as she waits for me to look up. When I do, her face is framed by the light from the screen and I swear I've never seen anything so beautiful in my life. She brushes her nose against mine, her eyes half-closing. And I realize that the things I'm feeling aren't fear, they're want. I push towards her and our lips meet and … there. She smiles in surprise and laughs a little and I pull back, worried. But she's there again, wetting her lips with her tongue and moving in to kiss me again.

There's a sudden screech of violins from the screen and I jump, turning to look at the screen and regretting it immediately as I see a shark ripping a human body in half. I reflexively move my hands up to my eyes, turning back to Imogen.

"It's CGI," she whispers to me.

"Doesn't look like it."

"It's not real blood."

"It looks real enough."

I move my hands away to see that she's laughing at me, but only gently. She moves her free hand to the side of my face and gently strokes my cheek. "I promise, it's not real."

We move in at the same time, and I can't believe that I get to do this whenever I want. Imogen pushes her hand back towards my ear and pulls me in close with her other arm and the rush of feelings I get make me go temporarily deaf. My whole body is shimmering and I take a shaky breath in and push back towards her, reaching out a cautious hand to the dip of her waist. Imogen makes a sound in her throat and catches my lower lip gently with her teeth and if I thought I was having a heart attack before, I must have multiple hearts that are all having attacks now. Liquid tingles run from my head right down my neck and all over my back. Is this what it's supposed to feel like?

There's a significant cough from a few rows behind us. Imogen pulls away, planting a soft kiss on the tip of my nose before settling back into her seat, and I turn round to face the screen again. I let my eyes blur the screen and all I can focus on is Imogen's hand, replaced on my thigh and drawing small circles with her finger just above my knee.

I feel like I'm floating on my walk home after Imogen has to run to a shift at the café. I finally understand what it is that everyone's been obsessing over. Maybe this is what it was supposed to be like the whole time.

~

At practice the next evening, we're working on default strategy as a team—the things we do automatically on the track, unless the bench manager tells us otherwise. I'm trying to keep it all in my head but it's difficult when Imogen is whispering innuendos after every third thing Yasmin is telling us. It's hard to have a single-minded focus on playing roller derby when your girlfriend is pinching your bum as you line up on track.

"You two are so cute," Mel says to me as we have a water break at our team bench. Imogen is jamming on the track and has turned to skate backwards and wink at me as she whizzes past.

"Head in the game, Frisky!" Venom shouts at her from their team bench. Imogen salutes her and turns around again as she approaches the back of the pack. Mel and I laugh and she nudges me.

"Things going good with you two?"

I can't stop a smile cracking my face in two. "Yeah, they really are. We just … fit. You know?"

"Yeah, I remember the heady days of NRE."

"NRE?"

"New Relationship Energy. When you just can't get enough of each other. Before you start farting in front of each other."

"Mel! Do you and Rob fart in front of each other?" I gasp in mock outrage.

She looks shifty. "Well, I try not to let him hear me. But sometimes they sneak out."

We're still giggling as we line up on the track for the next jam. We're both blocking and Imogen is jamming for the other team, starting from the penalty box for a sloppy back block on her final attempt through the pack. The "five seconds" shout comes from newbie Charlie who is helping out at practice, and we focus on the task at hand. Mel turns 180 degrees and we slide into natural positioning with each other, one arm each bracing against the other's shoulder. She's definitely a natural blocker, eyes everywhere on the track and loud shouts to communicate what's happening to the rest of us. I still get flustered during my first jam of practice and forget everything I've learned, so it's really helpful to have Mel yelling at me to get into a specific position on the track so I can just follow her instructions.

Imogen dodges around behind me as Mel guides me into different positions to block her. We move together as one, and I love how roller derby moves my friendships onto another level, one where we're practically reading each other's minds and know just how hard to push against each other to make the strongest bond between us. Sam and Rae join us in blocking Imogen's path. If Mel's a born blocker, Imogen is a born jammer. She hops around on her toe stops like she hasn't even got skates on, testing our wall and tiring us out before making a run on the outside line and being called lead jammer by one of our refs. I know rosters are formed with so many considerations, but it's mad to me that she wasn't rostered for our last game. Luckily she's on for the next one; I think missing one shocked her into turning up to practice enough to satisfy attendance requirements.

As Imogen dashes around the track, we move into five seconds of offense to help get our own jammer through. It always goes by faster than I can count in my head, and the call of "jammer on!" from Yasmin at the bench comes just as I've pushed a blocker out of the way so that Gem can skip through on the inside. We re-form and hold Imogen for long enough that she's forced to call off the jam without scoring any points as Gem comes speeding up behind her.

Back on the team bench, Yasmin has called a time-out and gathers us round to talk tactics. I take a moment to look at my team around me and realize how different my life looks to last year. I never could have thought I would have this level of intimacy with so many new people, but roller derby has a way of bringing you together for a single purpose. There's such a mixture of different people, but we all really care about this one thing and so the other things don't seem to matter as much.

I finish the practice happy and tired, and Imogen plants a sweaty kiss on my forehead as she rushes out to get a lift home with Sam. It's only a twenty-minute walk from the gym to Imogen's place, but twenty minutes at 10 p.m. on a winter's night with a heavy kit bag after two hours of hitting each other is very different to a twenty-minute stroll through the park in the summer.

Mum is still awake when I get home, and I make us both a cup of chamomile tea.

"How was practice?" she asks.

"It was good! I felt like I was really contributing to the team and pulling my weight."

"Well, of course you are, you're brilliant at everything you put your mind to." Mum smiles at me.

"That's not true, I never took to hula-hooping."

"And I had such great hopes of you becoming a professional hula-hooper." She sighs and we sip our tea in companionable silence for a few moments.

"I've been meaning to talk to you actually," Mum says, putting her mug down on the side table by the sofa. I instantly cycle through all the worst possible reasons for this—she's ill, Billy is ill, Harry is ill, maybe *I'm* ill? "It's about Imogen." Imogen's ill?

"What's wrong?"

"Nothing's wrong. I just wanted to make sure you're being … well … safe, with her."

Oh god. "Mum, you don't have to—"

"Because even if she can't get you pregnant, you know you can still get—"

"Mum!"

"No, I'm doing this. There are these things called dental dams that—"

"Mother!"

"Or maybe she *can* get you pregnant, I don't know."

"She can't get me pregnant."

"I just want you to know about your options."

We're both turning bright red and I want the floor to

swallow me whole. "I really appreciate it, but honestly, I'm fine."

"And you know you don't have to do anything you don't want to do?"

"I know."

"I just don't want you to feel pressured to move faster than you'd like to. Your body is your own and you get to decide on things like that when you're ready. And I know it's cringey to talk about it with your mum but you really can. We might find it embarrassing but it's important you know that."

Mum tried to have The Talk with me when I started going out with Ryan, but I completely shut it down. I don't think I was ready to even think about having sex, let alone talk about it. She pushed a little envelope full of condoms under my bedroom door and I hid them in my sock drawer (where they still are) and that was that. But the way I'm feeling about Imogen, I don't know … Even thinking that sends hot tendrils into my stomach and I blink hard, back in the room with Mum.

"Thanks, Mum. I know I can come to you with anything."

"I love you. Your comfort and safety are the most important things in my life."

"I love you too."

"Well, and Billy's obviously."

"No, you've said it now. I'm the favorite child!" I tease her. Mum pokes me in the side and we start giggling. "I'm going to head up to bed. Do you need anything before I do?"

"No thanks. Night, love."

"Night."

Chapter 18

Going to parties with Imogen was always an experience, but going to parties as Imogen's girlfriend is something else entirely. When I arrive at Mel's flat, she throws her arms around me and kisses me sloppily in front of everyone, before holding up my hand like I've just won a boxing match and whooping.

"Hello, lovely Case," she declares, grinning widely at me. "Help me convince everyone to do a human pyramid."

I giggle at her enthusiasm. "Im, I don't think anyone is ready to do a human pyramid at the moment, it's only half nine."

"But we have to! S'a derby tradition!" I can detect a bit of a slur in her words, but before I have a chance to do or say anything Sam arrives, which Imogen is also incredibly excited about. I grab a can of lemonade, then go and find Mel.

"How much has Imogen had to drink?" I ask her quietly.

"Babe, she arrived half-cut," Mel tells me. "Is everything okay with her? I mean, I know she goes a bit hard on the booze sometimes, but it's pretty constant at the moment." The niggling worry at the back of my mind is getting bigger by the second. I start filing through my memories of Imogen, noting all the times she's got drunk and realizing how frequent they are.

"I think she's okay. She hasn't mentioned anything to me about having a hard time at the moment," I say to Mel. "I mean, there's her mum, who is pretty strict. Maybe she's just fed up with living at home and can't wait to move away for uni." The thought of what will happen in September when we both move away has my heart in a vice. I try and push it to the back of my thoughts.

"Oh sure, I understand that. We'll keep an eye on her together, won't we?" Mel says.

"Yeah of course," I reply.

This is a "welcome to the team" party for the new class of fresh meat, who started coming to practice the week after our last game. Mel insisted that we introduce it as a tradition, since we'd spent weeks too scared to talk to the veterans on the team when we first started. It's nice to not be one of the newest people around, and I can see last year's me in the sparkling eyes of the new members as the obligatory bruise sharing starts. I remember the fear and awe and the butterflies in my stomach when I thought, "Is this going to be a thing I do? Is this my sport?"

"Has anyone ever gotten seriously hurt?" One of the newbies, Charlie, asks as Gem shows off the gnarly-looking scars from her ankle surgery.

"No," I say. "I mean, yes," I clarify. "People have broken bones and stuff, but nothing serious as in life-threatening. Unless you count concussions."

They stare at me, wide-eyed.

"But those are people who wear shitty helmets and don't replace them after falls," I add, hoping I'm not scaring them off.

"Lesson one: buy a good helmet," they say, pretending to write it down in a notebook.

"And good knee pads. Venom is always going on about how fucked her knees are," I add. "And if you do get injured, you really don't need to worry. We'll look after you until you're better."

"Really?"

"Of course. We're a team." I smile at them. "That's what we do. We look after each other."

Speaking on behalf of the team makes my heart sing. It's felt like just Mum and I against the world for a while now, and it feels incredible now to have this whole team of badass people on my side—well, except when we're scrimmaging, and I curse Mel's bony shoulders for dotting my torso with bruises. Charlie has talked about how roller derby is the first place they've felt confident enough to ask people to use they/them pronouns and I'm so proud to be a part of this safe place, this haven of acceptance. Venom once told us that roller derby attracts all the weirdos, and I think that's only partly true—it attracts people who haven't felt like part of anything before and teaches them how to be a team.

Next on the agenda is the traditional human pyramid—much to Imogen's delight—and after that the music gets cranked up a bit more. We move the furniture to the edges of Mel's small living room and make an impromptu dance floor, and I'm reminded of my first team party. I remember looking around while dancing and being struck by how happy I was to be surrounded by such kickass people. Any worry about Imogen drinking too much gets pushed to the back of my thoughts.

Imogen pulls me to the side and pushes me quite roughly against a wall. I'm not expecting it and I bump my head.

"Ouch! What was that for?" I ask, rubbing the back of my head and frowning.

"Oh, I'm sorry!" she exclaims. "Here, let me kiss it better." She leans in and kisses me slowly, pushing one hand into my hair and the other hooked round my waist. "See? All better!"

"That's not where it hurts."

"It's a multi-purpose kiss. Like those painkillers that work especially for period pain."

"It's expensive, pink and useless?" I tease.

"You know what I mean."

"And keeps trying to convince people it's way better than the cheap stuff, even though it's exactly the same thing?"

"Are you calling me cheap?" Imogen asks, mock outraged, but she's smiling. She leans in for another kiss, and I relax into it this time, ignoring the drunken whoops from our teammates. Imogen pulls her face away, smiling at me.

"Come with me," she says, grabbing my hand and leading me into Mel's bedroom. She takes me to the bed, which is piled with coats, and dramatically sweeps them onto the floor with her arm. Sparkle lets out a disgruntled meow from her spot under the bed.

"Come here," she says. She sits down and pats the space next to her. I sit on the bed with her. "You're great, you know that?" She's looking at me like she's won a prize, and I feel suddenly shy, like I'm under bright stage lights.

"I'm alright." I shrug.

"No, you're more than alright."

Imogen rains kisses onto my face, little light ones on my hairline and eyelids and cheeks. The sparks in my stomach come back as she deepens the kiss. Our tongues touch as our lips open and she moans encouragingly, pulling me closer with both hands on my waist. It never felt like this with Ryan.

Our awkward fumbling felt more like something to be endured than enjoyed. I once ghosted my hand over the bulge in his jeans out of curiosity and immediately regretted it; his enthusiasm grew while mine shrank. But this feels … right. We're breathing more heavily now, and Imogen hooks a leg up onto the bed to get even closer. Our chests and stomachs press together, and I have one hand tangled in her hair and the other on her waist. I can feel sounds build in my throat but I'm still too nervous to let them out, scared that if I show any signs of enjoying myself, that means it has to go further.

While I'm wrestling with myself, Imogen is pulling my top up a few inches and sighing as her hands find the warm skin on my back. My breath catches, and I pull away slightly.

"Not here," I say.

"Hmm?" She's busied herself with kissing my neck, and the warmth inside me builds as she drags her tongue up behind my ear. Her teeth graze my earlobe.

"Not here," I say, more loudly this time, and she pulls away from what she's doing but stays close, her face right next to mine and her hands holding me tenderly.

"What's wrong?" she asks.

"Just … Not here."

"Is it me?"

"Im." I cup her face in my hand. "Of course it's not you. I just don't want to fool around in Mel's bedroom while anyone could walk in at any time."

She smiles mischievously. "Isn't that half the fun?" But her hands are still, her fingers resting firmly on my skin but not moving any further. "Not here. I get it."

"Is that okay?" I check with her.

"Yeah. Another time."

I feel like I've swallowed sunshine. My whole body lights up at the thought, and unthinkingly I pinch Imogen's t-shirt between my finger and thumb and take a deep breath in. "Another time," I promise quietly.

But she hasn't heard me and her t-shirt is ripped away from my hand as she yells, "I love this song!" and runs from the room.

I stand up, straighten my clothes, and start picking up all the coats and placing them carefully back on the bed. Then I take a deep breath to steady myself and walk out of the room.

The dance floor is still going, and Imogen is bringing over a tray of shots, filled to the brim with a clear liquid that I assume is vodka. One of them nearly tips over, but she grabs it with her other hand and downs it, handing out shots to anyone who wants one and grabbing two more for herself. I make my way over to her as fast as I can but by the time I reach her, they're gone.

"Hey! Do you want a glass of water? I'm going to go and get one, good to stay hydrated, right?" I say brightly. Mel and I flash concerned eyes at each other.

"I don't want water," Imogen states firmly.

"Just one glass, babe. You gotta keep hydrated, right?" Mel chimes in.

"I told you I don't want water." Imogen makes a motion with her arms like she's trying to push us away and stumbles back over to the dance floor. Mel grabs a chair and drags it forward just in time for Imogen to fall onto it. I squat down in front of her as she slumps backwards in it.

"Im, maybe it's time to go home," I say gently.

"'M not having a good time anymore," she slurs.

"I know, chick, I know," Mel says, rubbing her shoulder. "Let's get you in a taxi."

"I'll take her, make sure she gets in okay," I tell Mel. I extricate my and Imogen's coats from the pile in the bedroom, then order a taxi and say a quick goodbye to those on the outskirts of the dancing, trying to get Imogen out of the flat with the least attention on her as possible.

"You're so nice to me, Case," she says, leaning heavily on me with her arm slung around my shoulders as we slowly descend the stairs down to the street.

"Hey, we look after each other, right?" I tell her.

"Yeah. Always be there for you."

"And I'll always be there for you."

"Anything. I'd do anything."

"I know, Im. Me too."

We make it to the ground floor and into the taxi without too much hassle. It's only a five-minute journey, and I crank both windows open and keep an eye on Imogen, making sure she doesn't look like she's going to be sick in the car. She slumps onto my side, and I put my arm around her waist and kiss her on the side of the head. Sure, Imogen likes to drink, but I've never seen her like this before. It worries me. I try to push it to the back of my head, focusing on getting her home safely for the time being.

"Home! I'm home!" she yells as we drive slowly down her street.

"Just here is fine," I say to the driver, "I'll be back out in a minute," while trying to keep Imogen from waking up the whole street as we get out.

"You're coming in?" she asks me.

"I can make sure you get to bed okay, but then I've got to go home so I'm around for Mum in the morning."

"No, that's not fair. I want cuddles with you."

She lurches at me outside her front door and kisses me sloppily. I smile against her and kiss her back gently, tucking a stray piece of hair behind her ear.

"Let's get you inside," I say.

Out of the corner of my eye, I can see the curtains twitch in the living room, then a few seconds later the door flies open and Imogen's mum is standing in the doorway with her arms crossed in a purple dressing gown.

"What's wrong with her?" she demands of me. I have no idea what to say to get Imogen in the least trouble possible, but I decide the truth is probably the best option.

"She's had a bit too much to drink," I say. I can't quite tell if her stern expression is solely due to Imogen being drunk, or if she saw us kissing.

"Get inside, Imogen."

"Want Casey," she mumbles back.

"Just you. Inside now." She grabs Imogen by the arm and pulls her inside roughly, shutting the door behind them both. I stand there shocked for a few seconds and consider whether knocking on the door to offer my apologies again would be welcome or not. I decide not to, and after a pause I turn around and get back into the taxi.

I'm driven home through the old town, and the cold air streaming in through the windows is welcome as I try and process what happened tonight. It started out so well, with my teammates and my girlfriend having a great time together, but I don't know why Imogen was hit so hard by the alcohol this time. I've never seen her not be able to hold her alcohol. By the time I arrive home and put my key in the door, I still haven't figured it out. Mum is already in bed, and I pad up the stairs quietly and into my room. After a lot of deliberation, I decide to send Imogen a text.

I'm here if you need anything.

I can't think of what else to say and I don't know if anything else would be useful, so I leave it at that and go to sleep hoping that she'll be at practice in a couple of days' time.

Chapter 19

My text log with Imogen stays empty, and she doesn't show up at our usual practice start time at the sports hall on Monday. We're just about finished with the warm-up when she shows up, dumps her gear in the corner and starts getting changed without a word to any of us. I catch Mel's eye and she shrugs at me. I look over at Imogen and try to get her attention, but she steadfastly keeps her eyes on her kit, matching up the Velcro on her pads in her usual haphazard manner. She skates over to us all gathered in the middle of the track.

"Hey," I say quietly to her, "are you okay? What happened with your mum?"

"I don't wanna talk about it." The way she says this is so stern and final that I don't even attempt any other questions.

"Okay, make a pace line, people!" Venom barks the instruction at us and we obey, lining up one behind the other an arm length away from each other. I'm just behind Imogen and about halfway down the line. We start by hitting each other, practicing our lateral movement when paired with a hip check. I start to notice that Imogen isn't quite as agile as she normally is. She's taking a while to stand up again when she's being knocked over, which is happening way more frequently than usual. I hit her gently when it's my turn to go through the pace line, and she stumbles but rights herself pretty quickly.

It's Imogen's turn through the line next, and I look behind me at her. Her movements seem delayed and sloppy. She's executing the hits on everyone else but with a wider arc than necessary, and it's taking her quite a bit of time to reset in time for hitting the next person. As she comes up the line towards me, I engage my core and loosen my knees, ready for the impact, but she sails across in front of me without making contact at all.

"Lemme try again," she says, sticking out her tongue in concentration and coming round for another hit. I steady myself again, bending my knees more so I'm nearer to the ground should I fall over.

Her hip doesn't make contact with me, but her skate does. She cuts in front of me far too late and kicks my foot out from underneath me. I always thought that breaking a bone would happen in slow motion, but when I land face-first and crack my nose on the floor, the blood spurts out a lot quicker than I expect it to. It doesn't hurt yet, just feels warm, and I look up to see Imogen staring in shock down at me. She drops quickly to the floor and paws ineffectively at my face, getting blood all over her wrist guards in the process.

"Oh my god. Oh my god, Casey. I'm so sorry. I didn't mean ..." In amongst the smell of the blood I can smell something sharper coming from her, something familiar.

"First aider coming through," Yasmin calls, and her face appears next to Imogen's.

"What's happened? Is everyone okay?" Venom's face appears now.

"Casey ..." Imogen says, looking at me with fear and despair written all over her face. She stands up and faces

Venom. "I don't know what happened, I went in to hit her and—"

"Jesus, what's that smell?" Venom's voice booms over the chatter I can hear, and the hall is suddenly silent except for the slow dripping of my blood onto the polished floor. "Have you been drinking?" She looks straight at Imogen.

"Im—" I start, but she cuts me off.

"I'm sorry, I'm so sorry," she repeats over and over again, and now I recognize the way her eyes don't quite focus on me, and the slur in her speech. She slips over on her skates, falling straight onto her bum.

"Imogen." Venom is stern and, honestly, kind of terrifying. "Are you drunk?"

"I didn't have much."

"You signed the team agreement, right? The one that says you won't skate if you're under the influence of alcohol?"

"Yes, but—"

I'm just looking from one of them to the other. My instinct is to defend Imogen, but she's the reason I'm sitting here on the floor with blood all over my face.

"You agreed to this. You knew that skating drunk is dangerous, especially if you're doing contact."

"Venom, my mum—"

"Get out, Imogen."

"I'm sorry."

"You do not get to come in here and hurt people and get away with it. Get the fuck out of my practice."

"But—"

"Right now."

Imogen takes off her skates while sitting down, then picks

them up by the laces and walks over to her kit bag in silence. She grabs it and walks quickly out of the sports hall, the door crashing shut behind her.

"I should go after her," I say, taking off my skates and standing up, far too quickly. The world lurches and I stumble right a few steps.

"Kid, I think you need to look after yourself right now. Go after her tomorrow, okay?" Venom says, dragging a plastic chair over to me and sitting me down firmly on it.

"But—"

"No. You're bleeding. That's number one, okay?"

"I'm just going to see if she's okay," I insist. I grab the thick wad of blue paper towel Yasmin has been holding to my face. I press it against my nose and stand up more carefully, only breaking into a fast walk when I'm sure the world isn't going to throw me to the floor again.

Imogen is already halfway across the car park when I get out of the front door of the gym. I shout after her and she turns around. We walk towards each other and I can see she's been crying. I want to be gentle and caring but I think that went out the door as soon as my nose hit the floor.

"What are you doing?" I demand.

"I don't know."

"What's happened with your mum?"

"It's complicated."

"Try me."

"I can't."

We stare at each other and I can feel that brick wall come down again, the one I thought we had got rid of after she kissed me for the first time.

"You know you can tell me anything," I say to her, but even my own voice sounds far away to me right now. It sounds more like an accusation than a gesture of kindness.

Imogen laughs and then her face crumples and she's crying. I reach out toward her but she takes a step back.

"I'm sorry. I can't," she says, and then she turns away and is gone.

~

Mum insists on coming with me to the urgent care unit the next day, and I have to talk her down from going to A&E straight after I get home. I don't know where I'm drawing such a state of relaxation about injury from, but everything feels quite far away and unreal. I keep seeing the moment before I hit the ground and my brain is cycling between that and a picture of Imogen's face, crying, before she turned away and left. It almost feels like I've been floating ever since; I sat for what felt like hours on my bed just staring into space before getting ready to sleep. And when I slept, eight hours went past like I'd just blinked. My body wasn't refreshed like normal and my thoughts just launched straight into images of the previous night.

The bleeding had stopped before I even got home from practice and I thought I'd be able to sneak upstairs to bed so Mum couldn't see and worry about me, but she was up late watching the latest reality TV series she's hooked on and called me into the living room as soon as I opened the front door, so I had to fill her in. Having been a nurse in A&E herself, the only time I've seen her panic about injuries and illnesses was after she got ill. Since developing M.E., she's done a huge amount of reading on post-viral conditions. She gets quite twitchy if Billy or I get a bad cold or the flu, encouraging us to rest for weeks afterwards. Although she's never said so, I suspect she partly blames herself for falling ill because she pushed so hard to go back to work before she was really ready. She was always such an active person, constantly dragging the whole family on endless country walks and insisting that the proper cure for illness was to blast it with fresh air. She applied the same method when she first got pneumonia, with a very different outcome than what she was used to.

The urgent care unit confirms for me what we all knew: my nose is broken and I have two black eyes to go with it. Mouth breathing makes me feel anxious because it's what I do whenever I start to panic, so I feel like I'm on the verge of freaking out constantly.

That afternoon, I tell Mum I'm going to the shops to get some popcorn for when we watch a film later tonight. I put on my long grey coat, bobble hat and gloves, and wrap a huge scarf around my neck and the bottom half of my face, trying to hide myself and the huge bruises blooming around my eyes and nose as much as possible. The cold air hurts as I speed-walk down the high street before I can change my mind. I make my way through the old cobbled streets and stop outside Imogen's front door.

Im, can you call me?

What happened with your mum?

Please talk to me. I don't blame you.
I just want to know you're okay.

The last texts sitting in our message log confirm for me that she's read them and definitely not replied. I steady myself, take a deep breath in (through my mouth, though it's not quite as steadying as breathing in through my nose) and clench and unclench my fists a couple of times, still unsure if I'm about to do this or not. I knock on the door.

Imogen's mum opens the door with a hopeful look that quickly turns into anger, and I can tell immediately that things aren't good. There are shoes all over the floor in front of the shoe rack in the hallway. Half her hair is in braids and the other half is sectioned out into three large twists. The other night, her dressing gown was the mark of a homely woman, one who stayed up waiting for her daughter to come home to have a stern talk with her about being late. This time, the dressing gown is lopsided and loosely bound, and I would guess she hasn't changed out of it yet today even though the sun is already setting.

"What do you want?" she demands impatiently.

"I'd like to talk to Imogen please." My voice comes out soft and high, not at all the firm calmness I wanted to give off.

"She's not here," she tells me.

"Do you know when she's coming back?"

At this, Imogen's mum lets out a rough sob, then claps her hand over her mouth and slams the door shut in my face.

I'm stunned. The wind picks up, whistling in my ears, and I pull the hat more firmly over them. My hand hovers next to the door, hand in a fist, ready to knock again. Panic rises up in me, and I remind myself that Imogen said she wouldn't leave me, that she would always make sure I was okay, and that she would always be there for me. I hold these words close to my heart and cling onto them, taking a couple more deep breaths before lowering my hand and walking away decisively.

The walk home seems much longer than the walk there, and it's only when I get out my keys to open the door that I realize I didn't get any popcorn.

Chapter 20

The next day Mel gets a text from Imogen saying not to worry, that she's safe, but she's not in town anymore and isn't coming back to practice for the time being. Rather than soothing me, it just worries me more. Why would she text Mel and not me? Where has she gone? What happened with her mum? What's happened that she doesn't feel she can talk to me about?

I'm a complete mess. Mum starts coming to check on me in the mornings and it's rare that she finds me well-rested. My eyes are constantly swollen and bloodshot from crying so much. I've kept up with the things that absolutely have to be done at home, but the freezer is empty and I've given up on my usual gym routine and missed a derby practice. Mum eventually convinces me to at least come downstairs (although I bring my duvet with me) and have something to eat, but everything tastes like ash in my mouth. I can't stop staring at the messages I've sent to Imogen that have gone unanswered.

I'm on my third day of wearing the same pajamas when there's a knock at the door. I trudge down the hallway to answer it and Mel appears behind the door, bearing the biggest bar of chocolate I've ever seen in my life.

"Oh my love." She gathers me up in her arms and holds me tight to her. "Your mum called me. How are you doing? Wait, stupid question. Come on, let's go and sit down. I've brought the big guns."

We go back into the living room. Mel kicks her shoes off and climbs onto the sofa with me.

"Okay, so we've got the obvious." She pulls a bottle of red wine and two plastic wine glasses out of her rucksack and sets them on the coffee table along with the chocolate. "Some little luxuries." Two face masks and a bath bomb come out of the bag along with a scented candle, which she puts on the table and lights. "And I know it's retro, but I can't risk this not being on any streaming services." A DVD of *Legally Blonde* goes on top of the chocolate.

I smile weakly at her. "Thanks, Mel." My voice comes out hoarse.

"Now go and wash your face and we'll get these face masks on."

Watching Elle Woods obliterate the awful men in her life is just the tonic I need, and I think it's the first time I've laughed since I broke my nose. The bruising and swelling has started to go down and I don't feel like such a hideous monster every time I look in the mirror.

Mel turns to me. "Do you want to talk about it?"

I start to shake my head but realize quickly that actually, it would probably be good to talk about it. "Have you heard from her since she texted you?" I ask her.

"No. I've even tried calling her but she won't pick up. It's good to know she's safe, but I can't believe she just bailed like that."

"I can't either. You don't think … Could it be because of me?" I've been trying not to think too hard about this possibility, and voicing it brings tears.

"Oh, love. Of course it's not because of you. You're a

wonderful girlfriend and you've done nothing to make this happen."

"Why do you think she left?"

"You said she had a difficult relationship with her mum, maybe it's to do with that. Honestly, I have no idea."

"I just … I don't really know what to do without her. She introduced me to roller derby and she's always been there. We were just getting started. I don't even know if we're still together, she didn't even break up with me. She just left."

"I know, babe. She at the very least owes you an explanation."

"But she won't talk to me. I don't get it. She knew she could talk to me about anything."

We're silent for a moment.

"Maybe she knew that, but she just needed to deal with something by herself," Mel says.

"It sucks."

"I know. But it will get better. And you can't let everything else go to shit. Have a wallow, and I'm always here if you want to talk about it, but you've gotta come back to practice when your nose is okay. Otherwise it'll be this big thing that you need to overcome."

It feels weird to think about going to roller derby practice without Imogen being there. Sure, she missed it sometimes, but I always knew she was coming back.

"I'll try my best."

Slower than seems possible, the days without Imogen eventually turn into weeks. When the weather is good enough, I adjust my daily runs to go past her house and slow down as much as I dare to peek in the windows. Nothing ever seems to change, apart from the one time I thought I saw her mum standing by the upstairs window with her head in her hands. I feel the loss of her keenly, like a hole in my stomach.

Just as the bruises disappear from my face, Venom reminds us about the away game we have coming up.

"Our next away game is soon, and preliminary line-ups are going to be the same as our last home game. We're playing to win, so we're going to train to win. I'm afraid you're all going to be aching until then, so suck it up."

"And don't forget to figure out whose car you're going in," Yasmin tells us all sternly. "I'm not dealing with last-minute panics about your train being cancelled, sort out a car to go in."

The thought of travelling and skating on the same day makes me feel sick, and that's not even considering the fact that Imogen is gone. After I told Mum what happened with Mark at Christmas, she'd had a chat with Billy and the outcome was my sister agreeing to come to the game. I have no idea what to think about this, no sense whether she's coming as a sisterly show of support or to add ammo to her argument that it's too dangerous and not the right thing for me to be focusing on. I try to swallow down my anxiety about it and tell myself it'll be fine on the day, but I'm not sure I believe myself.

~

It's not fine on the day. The roads are full of traffic so the whole journey is stopping and starting, and I feel nauseous from the moment I get into Sam's car. I have a constantly dry mouth, and it seems like all the moisture that should be in my mouth is instead on my palms. No matter how many times I wipe them dry, little beads of sweat start appearing almost immediately afterwards.

I try to distract myself by applying my makeup with shaky hands, but my heart won't stop fluttering and staring in a mirror while we're in traffic makes me feel even more queasy.

When we eventually arrive, my nerves are frayed. I'm shaking like a leaf, and when I catch a glimpse of myself in the changing room mirrors, my face is white and clammy underneath the makeup. I'm glad Billy said she was going to be a bit late so I've got a chance to calm down before I see her. The pressure of her watching me skate for the first time is really getting to me.

"Case! How's it going?" Venom asks, clapping me so hard on the back I think I might puke.

"Tip top," I force out, grimacing.

"Good stuff. You're on the first line-up. Just go slow, you'll be fine."

"Yep. Okay," I say, trying to open my mouth as little as possible to try and remove the possibility of throwing up.

I kit up slowly, then stand without my skates on. The butterflies in my stomach had turned into bats a long time ago. I swallow, hard, and try to keep down the protein bar I scarfed in the car. The sudden urge to pee distracts me for a couple minutes, and afterwards I stand in front of the mirrors, glad I've got the toilets to myself for a moment. Breathing in for ten and out for ten doesn't work, even after I've counted to a hundred. Tensing and relaxing my body doesn't work. The bats in my stomach get more and more frantic.

When I go back into the changing room, I'm stunned that everyone seems so relaxed. Excited and pumped up, sure, but not actively panicking like me. As if they don't even care that within the hour, there will be hundreds of people watching us play roller derby against our toughest team yet.

"Casey, are you okay, babe?" Mel comes over, strapping on her elbow pads as she walks. I try and reply, but only manage to shake my head and open and close my mouth as my breath comes far too quickly. My heart is pounding and I feel all weak and clammy. All I can do is wish Imogen was here. She would know how to make everything better, how to say and do the right things that would get me to calm down.

"Come with me." Mel takes me by the arm and leads me quickly out of the changing rooms and right out of the building, straight to a wall we can sit down on. Cool rain mists onto my face, and I take a deep breath in.

"I don't know what to do," I tell Mel. My mind is racing, all I can do is repeat I-don't-know-what-to-do I-don't-know-what-to-do in my head to myself over and over. It's like my brain hasn't got space for any other thoughts, and even if I could access calming thoughts the "I-don't-know-what-to-do" is shouting over them.

"You're fine. Look, we're both fine. We're just sitting outside, we've got our kit on, we'll get our skates on and skate about for a couple of hours. It's no different than at practice. And you've played in a game before." Mel takes both of my hands and squeezes them. I can't quite look at her in the eye, and I can't get anywhere past "sitting outside" because if I think about that then I'll think about how I'll probably fall over and get loads of penalties and injure someone and break all the bones in my body and everyone will be watching and laughing and I'll lie on the floor all broken bones and tears and snot and then I will die right there and it will be my own fault—

At some point I forget about the deep breathing and now the breaths I'm taking are too shallow to fill up my lungs properly. I'm starting to feel a little light-headed and I can't really hear the words coming out of Mel's mouth. There's a bottle of water in my hand. I lift it to my lips and try to take a sip, but my body just won't let me do it. I picture the water going into my mouth and down my throat, and the thought of it makes me feel sick. Black spots start to appear in my vision. There's a paper bag being held to my face, but I can't hear the crackling that should come with it. My vision tunnels, my eyes roll back, and I'm not aware of anything else.

I drift in and out of consciousness and am vaguely aware of being carried somewhere by a few different people. By the time the world stops shifting around, I'm back, and everything is a bit blurry. I open my eyes then blink, hard, a few times. I'm in the changing rooms lying on a bench with a hoodie under my head, and someone is holding my wrist.

"Hey, Casey, how are you feeling?" She's looking down at her wristwatch and I realize she must be taking my pulse. The dark green uniform tells me she's a medic.

"Hey. Um … What's happening?"

"You passed out. It started raining pretty hard, so your teammates helped carry you inside, and we're in the changing rooms now. Do you remember what happened?"

"I … uh …"

"It's okay, take your time. Just stay there for a bit." She hands me a bottle of water and I sit up slowly. I open it and pause right at my mouth, remembering how it felt to be so certain that drinking even a tiny bit of water would make me throw up. I take a small sip and can feel the cold water travel down my throat. It makes me shiver.

"Has the game started?" I ask.

"Your team is just warming up at the moment." She looks at me with kind eyes. "How are you feeling?"

"I'm okay."

"That was a nasty panic attack. Do you get them a lot?"

"Uh … panic attack? I don't know."

"Was it your first one?"

I pull up a vague memory of hearing a teacher at school talk about panic attacks and what to do if you experience them during an exam.

"I don't know … maybe."

"Your heart rate is back to normal and you seem to be breathing okay now."

"Yeah, I just couldn't …" I put my hand to my chest and breathe in, slowly, noticing with relief that my lungs fill all the way up and empty just as easily.

"They're very common. It's a little rarer to lose consciousness from a panic attack, but it can definitely happen if you're hyperventilating and not getting enough air into your lungs."

My mind is racing, and I can't keep hold of everything she's saying to me. I always knew I was an anxious person, but I didn't realize it could have such a physical effect on me. I shift and lean my back against the wall, swinging my feet down onto the floor. The medic gets up from the floor and sits opposite me on another bench.

"I need to get out onto the track," I tell her.

"It's okay, take your time."

"But we're skating short today anyway, they need me."

"They can cope without you. We just need to focus on getting you feeling better, okay?"

I know I'm letting my team down. A chesty cough wiped out a few of our best players, so we only had twelve today to start with and now that's down to eleven. That's one jam on, one jam off for almost everyone. I stand up, but instantly my vision starts to darken at the edges and I sit back down.

"I would recommend you don't skate for the time being, okay?"

I nod, not really sure what I'm agreeing to. I can hear the game start, and the crowd starts cheering. Billy said she was going to be late, but that she'd arrive during the first half. She's going to arrive and be looking for me, and I won't be there.

"I need to skate," I tell her.

"I'd really prefer it if you managed to drink some water and eat some food first," the medic says firmly. "Do you think you can do that?" She passes me a breakfast bar, and I try to focus on taking sips of water and small bites of the bar. Everything tastes like cardboard, and I'm incredibly aware of my stomach making growling noises. It's so difficult to swallow each mouthful. Every time I do I'm convinced this is the one that's going to reappear when I projectile vomit all over the changing room. I move the oat-mush around in my mouth and almost gag a few times at the thought of swallowing it, only managing it when I take tiny sips of water at the same time. It feels like my throat has almost entirely closed over. The mental block is even more powerful. It reminds me of that feeling when you're in bed in the morning and you know you need to get up to do something scary, and the snooze keeps going off and you keep telling yourself you'll get up at the next one, then the next one, then the next one, but no matter how hard you focus on sitting up and getting out of bed, you can't move. When I think logically about eating the breakfast bar and drinking the water, it seems easy, but the reality is that I have to force myself with every single bite I take and sip I drink. Each one feels like a momentous task with potentially life-threatening consequences.

I hear a huge roar coming from the crowd. But every time I even think about putting my skates on, my heart starts beating faster and my breath comes in shorter and shorter.

"How are you feeling, Casey?" asks the medic.

"I don't think I can do it."

"You don't want to skate? You've got a lot of color back in you, and it seems like the panic has subsided a bit."

"I want to. I just … Every time I think about skating, I start feeling weird again." I hold my hands out in front of me, and they're shaking. "This happened at the last game as well."

"How did you start feeling better then?"

"My girlf— My teammate helped me out. She told me everything was going to be okay." I can remember the certainty with which I knew that Imogen would fix anything that could possibly go wrong. I remember her steadying presence being like a tonic to me, something I could drink down and feel as though I could take on the world. And then I remember her losing control at practice and the look on her face like she was falling deep into something she didn't really understand. I can feel a pit open up beneath me and it takes everything I have not to fall straight into it, the place where I'm all alone and no one is there to help me if something goes wrong. Where no one can ever reach me. No one ever has, except Imogen.

"Sometimes that's all we need: someone to tell us everything is going to be okay."

"But she's not here this time," I say. I can feel my breath coming in quicker again.

"Do you think you could tell yourself everything is going to be okay?"

"I keep trying that, and it's just not working."

The medic pauses, then says to me more gently, "You know it's okay to not skate today, right?"

"But my team—" I protest immediately.

"Your team loves you and cares about you, and all they want is for you to feel okay."

"And my sister, she's in the audience."

"She was coming to see you skate?" she asks. I nod. "Well, she can come another time."

I finally finish the breakfast bar and start methodically shredding the packaging. Logically, I know she's right. But all I can think about is my team out there without me, when they were counting on all of us. I think of Billy in the audience, and how annoyed she's going to be if she got childcare for the day and won't even get to see me skate. I feel a sudden stab of panic at the thought that she might have brought Mark with her, but I soothe myself that he would rather be down at the pub with his friends on a Saturday than sitting in a cold sports hall watching his sister-in-law do a women's sport.

"But what if they lose?" I ask, not really expecting an answer.

"Everything will still be okay if they lose."

I finish on the breakfast bar packaging and decisively pull my skates towards me before I can change my mind. Slipping one onto my foot prompts my heart to beat faster, and my palms start to sweat as I do up the laces.

"I want to try," I tell her.

"Okay then."

I stand up on my skates and shift my weight back and forth, making sure I feel secure in them. I check my pads, pop in my mouth guard and do up my helmet strap under my chin. I take a deep breath in, blowing it out forcefully.

"Shall we go out?"

I nod decisively, and skate slowly out of the changing room and into the hall. The sounds of the crowd and the announcers get louder, but I try and tune them out as I make my way slowly over to my team's bench in between jams. Mel spots me first and grins widely, opening up her arms for a hug. I sit down on the bench next to her and gladly accept.

"How are you feeling, babe?"

"Not good."

"You want to skate?"

"I want to."

Yasmin walks over to me and crouches down, reaching a finger into her bright yellow hijab (team colors, of course) and scratching her head.

"How are you feeling, Casey?"

I gulp loudly. "Okay, I think."

Fi joins her and says, "Want to go on the next line-up? We could really use you out there."

"Sure."

"Okay, I'll put you on as a blocker."

The score is 35-55 to the other team, and when our players come back over after the jam I can see they're more tired than usual. We're only fifteen minutes in, and they're already struggling with not having enough skaters today.

"Good to see you here, kid," Venom says, punching me lightly on the arm.

I stand up on my skates, and my heart is gripped in a vice. No matter how much I tell myself everything is okay, I don't believe it. I watch myself skate over to the track as if in a dream, and to my dismay I hear my own voice, unusually loud, saying, "I can't do this."

"What?" Lucy asks, frowning at me.

"I can't. I'm sorry."

I skate back to the bench. I can sense the confusion happening around me and eventually Mel is sent on in my place, but I'm too full of shame to pay attention to anything that's happening around me. When I got over to the track, all I could think about were "what ifs": what if I break a bone and have to go to a local hospital and Mum can't visit me and I have to stay there for weeks? What if I get so nervous that I throw up on the track and then everyone in the crowd starts throwing up in sympathy? What if I'm just shit, so singularly terrible that the crowd starts laughing at me? I'm paralyzed by "what ifs" and I can't see beyond that to even think about tactics or the rules or the hits I need to make.

The next few jams pass in a blur. I'm just sitting staring at my skates, vaguely aware of people coming over to pat me on the back or say kind words. Eventually I admit defeat and unlace my skates, then carry them over to the wall and sit on the floor. I watch my teammates struggling to keep up, and it's obvious by the end of the half that they're just too exhausted to play effectively against a full roster of fifteen skaters. I keep on beating myself up and telling myself that if only I was able to get over this block in my head, I would at least be able to even things up a bit for them, take off some of the pressure. There's a gaping hole in me where Imogen should be, and I think about the safety and security just having her around gave to me during the last game. I think about the strength she lent me that's no longer there, and I just feel sick. Clearly she was the thing keeping me going. Without her I'm not worth anything to this team. My roller derby journey started with her arriving into my life, and maybe it'll end with her exiting from it.

~

I've been avoiding looking for Billy in the crowd. When the rolling halftime whistle sounds I know I can't hide forever, so I pull myself up from the floor and walk towards the seating area. She spots me straight away but stays in her seat, waiting for me to come to her with a confused look on her face.

"Hey, Billy," I say, sitting down next to her in a seat that's just been vacated.

"Why haven't you been skating?" She dispenses with the formalities and goes straight in with a challenge.

"Are you enjoying it so far?" I ask her. She fixes me with a stare.

"When I got here I saw you get on the track but then get straight off, and you took your skates off. What happened? Why weren't you skating?"

I really don't want to tell her the actual reason why. I have a feeling she won't understand the intense anxiety shooting through me that stopped me skating.

"I, uh, I twisted my ankle." I realize too late that I've walked over without a limp. "It's not too bad but the medic said I shouldn't skate on it."

She narrows her eyes at me. "I didn't see you twist your ankle." Rumbled.

"I just couldn't skate," I offer as a substitute explanation. "I had a … I was feeling bad before the game and I tried to skate but I couldn't—the medic said I shouldn't."

"You were feeling bad?" She's always been like a dog with a bone. She sees right to the core of me, always has. It's usually more of a hindrance than a help, like when we would play poker as a family. She wouldn't even have to sneak a look at my cards (although she usually would anyway, just to be sure), she'd know by glancing at me whether I was bluffing or had a brilliant hand. Imagine growing up with a sister who instantly knew the quickest way to make you give her your brand-new sparkly top, cutting straight to the words she knew would cut me the deepest: "Oh that's a … nice top, Casey. Are you sure you want to wear it out of the house?" she'd say with a tiny crinkle at the corner of her mouth.

"I just couldn't skate." I settle for no explanation being better than the truth. "I couldn't do it."

She looks at me hard for a second, then stares out into the sports hall.

"I got a babysitter so I could come here today, you know."

"I know, Billy. I'm sorry."

"Mark's always got his football on Saturdays and I was going to go to the library with some other mums and babies. They do Baby Boogie once a month."

"I'm sorry."

She continues like she hasn't even heard my apologies. "But do you know what I said? I said, 'My sister's playing this new sport and she says she's really good. Mum says I should go and see her because it's just a fiver and only half an hour away on the bus. She says it's only the second time she's done a game and she'd love to see a friendly face in the crowd.'"

"Billy, please—"

"What are you even doing, Casey?" She turns to look at me and gestures vaguely at my skates. "All of this costs you so much money. Money you should be saving for uni. You know Mum wanted you to be able to focus just on studying and not have to find a job, you know how worried she is that you'll burn yourself out like she did."

"I know, Billy."

"It's like Mark was saying to you at Christmas. Why are you making this your life when it won't go anywhere? You can't make money from it. It's not a career. Mum tells me you're out skating three nights a week now. I just think you need to be a bit more sensible about this. You've got chances I never had and I worry that you're throwing them away."

As she gathers her things around her, I can't even look her in the eye. My throat is tight. It's taking everything I have to not start crying in front of her.

"You're leaving?"

She stands up and looks down at me. "I know where my priorities are, Casey. Think about yours."

~

As soon as I get into Sam's car after the game I plug my earphones in, then close my eyes and try to forget about the whole day. Mel tries to get my attention a few times, but I know that as soon as she says anything remotely soothing I'm going to be crying in her arms for the rest of the journey. I don't want to put that on her. So I smile and squeeze her hand, and I stare out of the window, willing myself not to completely break down.

When I get home, I don't want to tell Mum what happened. It's too embarrassing. I tell her that we lost and try to change the subject, but she is dogged in her determination to get me talking about it.

"It's the first game you've lost, isn't it? Is that why you're so upset about it?"

I sigh and put down the forkful of shepherd's pie. "We lost because of me."

"I'm sure that's not true—"

"We were four people short anyway, and then I couldn't play."

"Why couldn't you play, sweetheart?"

"I don't know, I just couldn't."

Mum looks at me in silence. I rest my elbows on the table and my head in my hands. I can hear her open her mouth a couple of times and close it again, carefully testing the words out before saying them.

"Was it because Imogen wasn't there?" she asks gently.

And that's it. That's what sets off the tidal wave of feelings. My face crumples into my hands and I nod. She comes round the table and hugs me from behind, murmuring soothing sounds. The fact that it was my brain that stopped me from skating is just too depressing to think about. I thought the panic at the last game was just a one-off that Imogen helped with, but if this is a thing, if I'm having panic attacks now, then I don't know if I'll ever be able to skate at a game again. And that's even before all the things Billy said to me as well.

Mum sits next to me.

"They said …" I take a deep breath. "They said I had a panic attack," I tell her, turning my head to look at her. Her expression goes from empathy to concern immediately, which is exactly the thing I always try and avoid. But I can't bring myself to regret saying it, like I usually do when I tell her about things I'm struggling with.

"A panic attack?"

I nod.

"What was it like?" she asks.

It takes me a little time to find the words.

"You know when you walk down the stairs without

looking, and you think there's one extra step but there isn't and you get that jolt? It was like that, except constantly. Like I was floating a few centimeters outside of myself. I couldn't even feel my skates on the floor."

"Oh honey, that sounds really scary."

"It was horrible. I started panicking and Mel tried to calm me down but I felt like I couldn't get any air into my lungs, and nothing she was saying was helping. I fainted and missed the warm-up, then when I tried to skate I just couldn't. I had this dread in the pit of my stomach and all I could picture was me falling and breaking a bone or tripping over my own skates in front of the whole crowd. Or that I'd just suddenly forget how to skate. I couldn't even think about tactics, staying upright was difficult enough."

"Have you ever felt anything like it before?" Mum asks.

I think for a moment. "Not like this. But I get that pit in my stomach sometimes."

"Like when?"

I hesitate. "When I think about going to uni."

"And what stops it turning into a panic attack?"

This takes me a moment to figure out. "I just stop thinking about it," I eventually say.

"Well, that's not going to solve every problem. Are you sure it's anxiety? Excitement and nervousness can feel very similar sometimes."

I roll my eyes. "No, it's not excitement."

She nudges my shoulder with hers. "It's worth considering, you know. I feel very anxious about some things, but if I sit with that feeling for a little bit it usually turns out to be at least part excitement."

"Maybe Billy is right and I should just give it up."

"I was going to ask if Billy helped you out today. I know she's not the most …" Mum pauses for a moment, "enthusiastic about roller derby. But I thought she would be supportive of you when she saw you play. She does love you very much."

"Well, she didn't see me play. I tried to skate once and then I gave up, just sat at the side and watched my team lose."

"Oh, sweetheart. That's so difficult. But I certainly don't think you should give up. Is there anything I can do to help you feel better?"

I shake my head.

"Why don't we take the rest of our dinner into the living room on trays and watch some old *Bake Off* episodes?" she offers. I wipe my eyes and nod.

As we go through to the other room and get set up, Mum tells me it's not my fault. That I can try again next time, that I can definitely get through this, that if I'm not afraid of anything then there's never any need to be brave. But I just don't believe any of it. The dream is over.

Chapter 21

"I shouldn't be here, I shouldn't be here," I mutter to myself as I warm up, skating around the track and loving the responsiveness of my body. I glide around the apex, scissoring my feet and twisting my upper body to the left, feeling the momentum push me around the corner and back down the straight. I lift each knee up to my chest a few times, then kick my bum a few times and do some slow windmills with my arms. My muscles warm and loosen, and I shake my shoulders out before going down into a deep squat, skating for one, two, three laps, until my thighs start to burn. Then I pull out of it and shake out my legs before circling my ankles in front of me.

This first practice after the game is the only exercise I've done since—four days without skating or running or anything—and my body is loving it. I can feel all the knots and tension leave my body, and I remember why I fell in love with this, and that makes it so much more difficult to give it up. Just one more session, I tell myself.

A brief stretch in the middle of the track, and then I'm ready for practice. It's the first time the new fresh meat are running strategy drills after learning the theory. We start out with the Four Corners drill, giving everyone a chance to work offense, defense and jamming. I relax into it, keeping my hits light and slow to give the newest fresh meat a chance to shine.

We start out with a jammer at the jammer line and a blocker near the first turn, ready to come in as soon as the jammer starts skating. The blocker practices their positional blocking, physically putting their body in the way of the jammer. It's a blocking drill, so the jammer's job is to gently test the blocker, moving around quickly and challenging their reflexes and agility. As they round the second turn, a second blocker joins and they practice their teamwork, using both of their bodies to keep the jammer from passing them. Then at the third turn, an opposing blocker enters the track to try and break up their team and get their jammer through. They have one more lap to make this happen. This is when the jammer really starts to work hard, working with their blocker on offensive strategies to pass the other team.

I switch around the roles but find it difficult to hold myself back against the newbies. My body is screaming for me to push myself—hard hits, fast stops, hopping about on my toe stops. But I keep calm and focus on creating a good learning experience for the newbies. Watching them make their unsteady hits reminds me how far I've come from that first time on skates at the roller disco with Imogen. I'm good at this, I remind myself, but only if there isn't an audience watching. And roller derby is a spectator sport, which makes me useless.

After that drill we move into some endurance, and I can't wait to push myself until it hurts. We form a massive pack, all twenty of us, and we practice falling and recovering and dodging fallen skaters, keeping close together in low squats until my thighs are screaming at me.

Timed laps are up next—a challenge to see how many we

can do in five minutes. I manage 30, which is better than my previous best of 29.5. And to finish up we work on some hitting drills. When I describe roller derby to someone who doesn't know how it works, I focus on the rules, the strategy, and the safety measures we take because it's a full-contact sport. I tell them about how women and nonbinary people don't get many opportunities to play sport outside of school, and about how it's a grassroots sport—by the skaters, for the skaters. But honestly, the best part of roller derby is hitting people. Zoning in on exactly where you're aiming for then slamming right into that spot. Our bruises are trophies, and if you deliver a painful hit you're much more likely to get a high five than a nasty look from the one who received it.

Those of us who are more experienced are told not to hold back, that the newbies need to learn how to take repeated, heavy hits. They've been practicing them at low speeds, and it's time to test what they've been learning.

"Okay, folks, we're going to work on our can openers. It's a good hit, and most of us can do it already," Venom booms from the center of the track, "but it's easy to see it coming. We need to work on it being a fluid movement, so it's less predictable. Obviously we all know it's coming because this is the drill we're doing, so I just want everyone to skate round the track in their own time and hit as many people as you can. Shoulders only. This is a free-for-all: give it all you've got but keep it safe."

I'm in my element. I don't even think about the fact that I'm on skates—my wheels become a part of me and part of the movements. I hit people again and again and again, taking pleasure in the "oofs" I hear as I skate around the track. I come up behind Charlie, one of the newbies, who's just taken a big hit and isn't paying attention to what's happening around them. I dart left behind them, then scissor my feet and cut right in from of them, dipping down and bringing my shoulder back, hard, into their sternum.

Crack.

"Agh!" Charlie cries. It happens in slow motion this time. I pull my shoulder away and immediately stop skating, turning around to face them. Their face is part shock, part agony. They fall almost gracefully to the floor and stay there, swearing profusely. I'm not sure whether the moistness on their face is from sweat or tears. Maybe both.

"Shit, Charlie, I'm so sorry. What happened? Are you okay?" I drop to my knees in front of them. "Stop everyone! Stop! Charlie's hurt!"

"Something hurts … Something, agh. I can't move."

"Do you need an ambulance?" I ask them, desperate to be able to help.

"I … ahhhh shit … Yeah, I think so."

"Call an ambulance!" I shout. More people are gathering around. "Give them some air. And someone bring over something warm."

My heart sinks as Charlie's face starts paling.

"What can I do? What hurts?"

Yasmin strides over with the medical kit and a hoodie, which she places carefully over them. She starts taking off Charlie's left skate, slowly and carefully. I start on the right one, trying to emulate Yasmin's calmness.

"I think my rib is broken," Charlie says, letting out a short bark of laughter before a cry of agony takes over.

"I'm sorry. I'm so sorry."

Yasmin nudges me. "Number one rule of roller derby?"

"Don't say sorry?"

"Don't say sorry for delivering a hit. You're a safe skater, it was a legal hit. Don't be sorry," Yasmin says sternly.

"Yeah, don't apologize," Charlie agrees between groans. "I wasn't looking at what was happening around me."

"I've called an ambulance," Rae says, skating over with another hoodie and a bottle of water. "Here"—she hands me a hoodie—"get this one under their head."

I fold up the hoodie and un-clip Charlie's helmet, lifting up their head carefully to place it underneath.

"Keep breathing," I remind them. They have an iron grip on my hand. "Just keep breathing."

"How's my face? Am I pale?" I recognize the panic in their voice.

"You're fine."

"Tell me the truth."

I pause. "You do look a little pale. Just take slow, steady breaths. You're going to be okay."

Charlie's face has moved from paling into greying. They're shaking violently and a tear runs down the side of their face into their hair. I loosen the straps on their elbow pads and wrist guards and slip them off carefully.

"Cavalry's here," Yasmin says to us both, nodding to the doors where a paramedic team are walking quickly towards us. Charlie draws in a slow, rattling breath and smiles, tears still streaming down their face.

"Can you … I mean, could someone come with me?"

"I'm coming with you," I say firmly.

"I'll follow in my car," Sam calls from behind me.

"I'll come with as well," Mel adds.

Charlie squeezes my hand. "Thank you."

The paramedics take over. I step back and Mel puts her arm around me.

"They'll be fine. It's not your fault."

"I know. I just … I wish it didn't happen. I wish I hadn't hit them."

"You can't think like that, Casey. We all know the risks. We all sign the agreements. We all know that it's not a case of 'if' you get injured, it's 'when.' I saw the hit, and it was safe and legal. It could have happened to anyone."

I nod, and she puts her arm around me as we follow the stretcher out of the sports hall.

The ambulance trip goes by in a blur, and soon enough we're waiting in Accident & Emergency at the local hospital up the hill. Charlie was triaged quickly and taken for an x-ray. Sam had to get home, so Mel and I sit in the waiting room.

"Will I get us a coffee?" she asks.

"Hm?"

"I saw a machine."

"Oh. No, I'm fine thanks. Thank you."

"Okay."

"Do you want one? Do you need any money? Look, I think I've got some change." I start rustling in my bag and stand up to feel in all my coat pockets.

"Sit down, chick. I'm grand. Sit down."

I don't. There's a silence, punctuated only by the hospital noises around us. I can't stop shifting from foot to foot.

"Jesus, how much longer is it going to take?"

"Sit down, Casey. Breathe."

"We're not family. The hospital isn't going to give us any information about them."

"They'll find us."

"What if it's really bad?"

"Charlie is going to be fine. Okay? They're going to be absolutely fine."

I wring my hands. I can't keep still.

"I can't do this anymore. I just can't."

"What, hospitals?"

"Roller derby."

"Casey …"

"I'm serious. I can't play in games because I panic. I hurt people at practice. I don't think I can do it anymore. What's left for me to do?"

"You can just skate, you don't have to be on the roster. You can just come to practice."

"But I hurt Charlie, Mel. They're a newbie, and now they're going to have to be off skates for months while they heal. They might not even come back at all."

"Casey, please—"

We're interrupted by a nurse coming over to us.

"You're friends of Charlie Nowak?" he asks.

"Yes, that's us," Mel confirms.

"You can come and see them now."

He walks off at such a brisk pace that I don't have time to ask what's happened. We walk out of the A&E waiting room and down some corridors that all look the same. A left turn takes us into the Acute Medical Unit and Charlie is grinning at us from a bed.

"Charlie!" Mel exclaims. "Oh, love. How are you?"

We sit in plastic chairs by their bedside, only marginally more comfortable than the squeaking metal ones in the waiting room.

"You broke two of my ribs," Charlie tells me, offering a fist bump in my direction. I tap my knuckles against theirs, certain that I'm going to throw up from the guilt that's just washed over me. Mel throws her head back and laughs.

"Shit, Case. Two ribs!" She nudges me in the arm and I know they both want me to laugh along with them, but I can't think of anything less funny than breaking my friend's bones.

"And pneumothorax. Guess I'm putting the punk back into punctured lung," Charlie adds with a smile, mostly talking to Mel at this point. "It involved a big needle and wasn't even a little bit fun. I got some fun painkillers though, and they're keeping me overnight to make sure my lungs are okay tomorrow."

I can feel myself going deathly pale and there's a buzzing in my ears that has nothing to do with the hospital noises around us. I feel like I can't breathe.

"But it's only six weeks off skates." Charlie adds quickly, maybe noticing that I'm not coping too well with the news. "And another four weeks without contact. Then you can hit me again!"

"I have to go to the toilet," I announce, too loud, and leave them chatting as I push my way through blue curtains and out into the hallway. Instead of looking for a toilet, I just press my back against the hallway wall and screw my eyes closed, balling my hands into fists. My breathing comes in too quickly and I have no idea how much time passes or how many weird looks I get before I stop feeling dizzy. The only thing I can think of is that I need to get home. For a brief moment I consider just walking out without saying anything, but I think about the scared look Charlie gave me when they heard they had to go to hospital and I know I can't abandon them like that.

When I walk back into the ward, Mel and Charlie are attracting some scandalized looks from the mostly elderly patients in beds surrounding them, and a quick glance at the clock confirms that it's definitely too late for the volume of their conversation and laughter.

"Hey, you," Mel says to me, a hand on my arm. "Is it home time now? We should let Charlie sleep."

A glance at Charlie's face tells me they're totally fine with this. We say our goodbyes and get up to leave.

As we walk back through the ward, my phone rings in my bag. I fish it out, making apologetic faces at the disapproving nurses on duty.

"Gimme a second, Mel, it's my mum calling," I say, rushing through the double doors into the corridor.

"Hey, Mum!"

"Casey, love, there's nothing to worry about."

My hackles go up.

"What do you mean?"

"I'm fine, you don't have to worry, but I'm in hospital and I need some help getting home."

I feel like I've swallowed a rock.

"You're in the hospital? *I'm* in the hospital! What happened? Where are you?"

Mel is mouthing something at me and has a hand on my shoulder but I don't know what she's trying to communicate to me. I can't quite get over the fact that Mum is in hospital. This is what I've been afraid of.

"Stay calm, love, I'm just at the entrance of A&E. Why are you in the hospital?"

I hold the phone away from my face. "My mum's in A&E," I tell Mel. She takes hold of my arm and steers me down the corridor quickly until we're back in the waiting room. I scan the seats frantically and hang up the phone when I see Mum sitting in a wheelchair next to a row of plastic chairs.

"Mum! What happened? Why are you here?"

"Casey, slow down, why are *you* here? I'm fine."

I wave my hand dismissively. "There was an injury at practice, we were just leaving. What's happened to you?"

"I fell down the stairs outside our front door," she says.

"Are you okay?" Mel asks, taking the seat next to Mum.

"I'm absolutely fine," she replies, smiling. The rock in my stomach is still there but it feels a little smaller.

"What happened?" I ask, scanning her body for injuries and finding a support brace on her ankle. "Did you hurt your ankle?"

"I slipped when I was taking the bins out this evening," she tells me.

"Mum, I was going to do that when I got home from practice."

"I know, it was just a good energy day and I thought I'd

take advantage of it. But there was already a bit of ice and I twisted my ankle then fell down the stairs. Belinda next door was just coming in from her car and she gave me a lift here but she had to get back so the babysitter could go home, so I was just calling you to see if you could pop up here with the wheelchair and we could go home together."

"Is your ankle okay? Is there anything else wrong?"

"Casey, I'm fine. It's a small sprain and I have to keep weight off it for a couple of weeks. A couple of bumps and bruises other than that, but nothing that a few hot baths and some arnica can't solve."

Mel reaches out and takes my hands. "She's fine, Case. Everything's okay. Here, sit down, love." She stands up and gently pushes me towards the seat. I sit down numbly and realize my breath is coming in too fast. My first thought is to find Imogen because she knows how to calm me down, but then I remember she's not here, not even contactable, and I start to panic more. I've got Mel's hand in my left hand and Mum's in my right, and I look from one to the other. They're both looking at me with kind, open, concerned faces. I take a deep breath in and force myself to breathe it out slowly.

"Everything's okay?" I ask.

"Everything's okay," they reply in sync. I can feel my hands shaking and try to focus on the fact that no one is gravely injured and nothing terrible is happening. But it just feels like I'm going to die.

I turn to Mum and ask her, "What if Belinda wasn't there?"

"Then I would have shouted for someone to come and help. We live on a friendly street, sweetheart; someone would have come to help me out."

"I should have been there."

"It's okay that I'm by myself sometimes," she tells me.

I focus on taking slow, deep breaths and the feel of Mum and Mel's hands in mine. The rock in my stomach slowly starts to feel more manageable, more ignorable.

"Everything's fine, love," Mel repeats to me. "We're all okay."

"I'm sure we can borrow a hospital wheelchair to take me home tonight, and you can return it tomorrow," Mum says.

"I'll go and check." Mel gets up and walks towards reception.

Mum smiles at her then turns back to me. "Is this a panic attack?"

I nod.

"Is there anything I can do?"

I shake my head. "Let's just go home," I say. "Some fresh air is all I need."

We head out of the A&E entrance together. As we reach the exit to the street, Mel turns to me.

"Will I walk you two home? You look a bit peaky," she says.

I shake my head but can't make any words come out.

"Casey … You'll be at practice on Monday?" Mel asks.

"I don't know."

"I'll see you on Monday," she says firmly, searching my face for some kind of confirmation. I force a smile.

"Maybe."

"And I'll see you soon, Laura. Heal well," she says to Mum before turning and walking up the hill.

"Let's go home."

Chapter 22

I've just brought the biscuit tin through to the lounge to provide sustenance for our movie marathon when Mum looks at me quizzically.

"It is Monday, isn't it?" she asks.

"Yeah, I think so," I reply.

"Why aren't you at roller derby practice?"

I sigh and put my half-eaten chocolate digestive down on the arm of the sofa.

"I'm not going anymore."

"What? Why?" She shuffles to sit up straighter without hurting her injured foot and stares at me, shock written all over her face. I've hinted at parts of this to her, but I've never put the pieces together in so straightforward a way. I sigh, closing my eyes, then look at her and spell it out.

"I told you already. I hurt someone, Mum, and I couldn't skate at that game. If I can't skate at games because of panic attacks, and I hurt people at practice, what's left there for me?" I can feel this emptiness open up inside me when I say it out loud.

"But you love roller derby." She's still shocked, and I can understand why. Roller derby has been my entire life. When I'm not skating, I'm exercising so I'm better at skating, or I'm watching gameplay to learn strategy, or I'm reading theory to know the rules better. All the friends I have, I made through roller derby, and all we do when we hang out is talk about it.

It's been such a vital part of my life.

"I know. But I just don't think I can do it. You saw what I was like after the game when I had that panic attack. Am I just going to be like that every time? Just keep trying and not being able to do it. That's going to be so embarrassing. Why would they ever roster me if I just can't play? Why would I spend so much effort on something I can't do all of?"

"You got through the panic once before." Mum's tone is kind and gentle. I know this tone. When she doesn't think I've thought through a decision enough, she will gently present alternatives. Alternatives that I've already thought of.

"That's because Imogen was there. She calmed me down."

"Can you not calm yourself down?"

I'm getting impatient now. "No, Mum. I've tried. Yes, I love it, but there's nothing there for me anymore."

There's a short silence. "I just can't believe you're giving it up," she says. "I've never seen you so passionate about anything."

"Mum, please. Can we drop it?"

She holds her hands up in defeat. "Fine, dropping it. But I think you're making a bad decision."

"Okay, thanks for voicing your opinion," I grumble. She shoots me a look, but doesn't say anything more, and we get settled in for our movie marathon. It's partway through *The Matrix* that Mum nudges me.

"Have you sent off the forms for your uni accommodation? Isn't the deadline for that really soon?"

I twist in my seat. "Not yet."

"Well, you need to get on that sooner rather than later."

"Mm," I say noncommittally.

Mum reaches across for the remote and pauses the film.

"Casey, is there something you're not telling me?"

"Can we just watch the film?" I don't have the energy for another questioning.

"I dropped it about roller derby. I don't think I can drop it about university." Her expression is now very serious.

"I know, I just … I don't know if I want to go." The emptiness is turning into a bottomless pit, where anything outside of what I'm doing now feels terrifying. Even the thought of leaving home makes me feel like I'm going to fall into something and not be able to get back out again.

"Why?"

"It's a long way from home."

"It's only an hour and a half away by train." Mum's tone is starting to irritate me now. She says it like getting on a train for an hour and a half isn't a big deal, like it hasn't always terrified me.

"What if you need me?" I know I'm deflecting. But I don't care.

"I'm going to have carers coming round."

"But what if they're not available, or just don't pick up their phones?"

"Casey." Mum sits up straighter and tries to take my hand. I pull it away. "I'm going to be okay here. You don't need to worry about that."

"I can't leave you."

My breath starts coming in shorter, and I recognize the pounding heart. I take a slow breath in and blow it out through my mouth.

"Sweetheart, I thought we talked about this when you

decided to defer? You're going to love living in London."

"But what if this keeps happening?" I gesture broadly.

"Where has this all come from?" she asks. "Do you think it's still about Imogen?"

I make an impatient sound. "This was never about Imogen." I can feel myself raising my voice, but instead of being powerful like I want it to be, it's high-pitched and desperate. "The thought of playing roller derby made me feel like I was going to die. What if I get another panic attack while I'm at university and freak out my flatmates? What if your new carers take advantage of you and start stealing money from you? What if they just don't show up at all and you have to just manage by yourself?"

"Casey—" Mum reaches a hand out to me again.

"No!" I stand up, taking a step back from her. "I'm scared. I'm scared of it happening to me again. What if there's not a medic around next time? What if I pass out in the supermarket? What if it happens during a lecture?"

"Sweetheart, there are people you can talk to about things like this."

"How is talking going to help me?"

"They're trained professionals. You could get some counselling. It sounds like you really need to talk this out with someone."

"And now you want to send me to therapy. Great." I throw up my hands. "Just great. Now I'm too crazy and I need to be shipped away, is that what you're saying?"

She breathes out heavily through her nose. "Of course I'm not saying that. But there are options here."

"There aren't any options."

I don't wait for a response and run out of the room, taking the stairs two at a time. Once I get into my room, I close the door firmly and sit on my bed. I hold my hands out in front of me and they're shaking; I'm shaking all over. I hadn't even realized that I'd started crying, but the tears are running down my face in streams. I fling myself down onto my bed and let the tears come, gripping onto a pillow and holding it to my face.

~

I must have fallen asleep at some point, because I wake up confused by my phone. It's an unknown number, and it's 10 p.m. I dither on answering, but I worry it might be some kind of emergency. I don't think I know anyone who would call me at 10 p.m. without texting first unless it was an emergency.

"Hello?"

"Hey, kid. How's it going?"

It takes me a while to place the voice. "Venom?"

"Yeah. You didn't come to practice tonight and I wanted to check in on you after what happened with Charlie."

I sit up and rub my eye with one hand, blinking at the harsh light.

"I'm sorry I didn't let you know," I say.

"Want to tell me why?"

I twist the duvet in my hands. "I just didn't want to come."

"Bullshit."

"What?"

"Bullshit. You love skating."

"Well … Yeah."

"So why weren't you at practice?"

Wow, she's like a dog with a bone. "I don't think I can come any more." I'm trying to deflect, trying not to give her a straight answer.

"Why?"

It's one thing saying it to Mel, or even saying it to Mum. But it's so different saying it to Venom.

"Well, I can't skate in games and—"

"Also bullshit."

"And I hurt people at practice."

"Case. About the game: you had a panic attack. So what?"

Anger flares up in me at this. There's no way she would say that if she knew what it was like to have a panic attack. If she knew that feeling of deep and unending terror, the certain knowledge that this is it, this is the end.

"I felt like I was going to die," I protest.

"But you didn't. It was one time."

I feel like she's not understanding me. I sigh impatiently. "The same thing happened at my first game as well," I tell her.

"And you skated then."

"Imogen talked me down."

"So talk yourself down."

There's barely any time between what I'm saying and her replies. It's like this is a script she's following—except I don't know my parts. "And about Charlie," she continues, "that was a legal hit. I specifically said not to go easy on the newbies, so you didn't. I respect that. Maybe Charlie wasn't ready to be hit that hard, but they still agreed to skate with us. They'll be back on skates in no time at all. You haven't put them off, they're just even more determined—they came to practice tonight to sit on the side and cheer us all on. It's not your fault."

"Venom …"

"Look, kid, I'm going to go against my 'don't inflate the ego' rule here. You are an incredible athlete. I've never seen such determination since … well, since I started skating. You can make something out of this."

"Like what? There's no such thing as a roller derby professional league; it's not like I can make a career out of skating."

"Well, you're going to uni in London next year, right? One of the best teams in Europe are there. You could train with them. You could be on Team England within a couple of years or whenever the next World Cup happens. I have no doubt. You turn up to every practice and you put in the time. You're single-minded in getting better constantly and consistently."

I don't know what to say. I open and close my mouth a couple of times, determined to come back at her with some reason why I can't do that.

"Skip practice on Thursday if you need to," she tells me. "Hell, skip it for a few weeks. But just promise me you'll be back when you've sorted your shit out."

"I can't promise that."

"Promise me."

I can't make the right words come out of my mouth, so I change the subject instead. "How do I sort my shit out?"

"Kid, I'm not your therapist. Make sure you do the right thing. I just wanted to check in on you and make sure you weren't making a terrible decision."

"Okay. Thanks for checking in, Venom. I'm sorry."

"Don't be sorry. Be smart. See you soon."

The phone call leaves me stunned. I wipe away what was left of the tears on my face and pull my legs up onto the bed. Mum suggesting I see some kind of therapist felt insulting. I feel like I should be able to deal with my problems myself, and if there's anything I can't deal with then I'm just not trying hard enough. But Venom telling me in a roundabout way that the key to sorting my shit out is to talk to a therapist hits differently. Maybe that's just the solution. Maybe there is no way to try hard enough to fix my own problems. Maybe I do need some outside input here.

Mum is still up when I go back downstairs, watching some kind of reality TV show, but as soon as I walk in the door she switches it off.

"I'm sorry, Mum," I say.

"I know, love. Want to come talk about it?" She pats the cushion next to her on the sofa, smiling at me sadly. I sit down and shift backwards onto the sofa, pulling my knees in towards me and tugging my sleeves over my hands.

"I shouldn't have got angry at you; you were just trying to look out for me. And I should have told you about stopping roller derby and being worried about going to university."

"I know, sweetheart. Apology accepted."

I take a deep breath. I want to talk to her, but I don't know how to start. "I'm just really scared. All the time. I'm scared of leaving the house, and meeting new people, and anything I can't control. I'm scared of never being able to skate at a game without Imogen there. I'm scared something bad has happened to her. I'm scared that if I leave for university, she'll come back for me and I won't be here. And I'm scared that you'll really struggle without me here."

Mum reaches out and takes my hand, stroking soft circles onto the back of it.

"You're scared of a lot of things, aren't you?"

"I'm scared that if I sit up too quickly when I wake up, that I'll pass out and hit my head on the bedside table and knock myself out and fall with my mouth and nose in my elbow crease and I'll die from suffocation."

Mum stifles a laugh, then sees my stricken expression and arranges her face into something more serious. "That seems very unlikely."

"I read about it happening to someone."

"It's very unlikely it would happen to you."

"But it could happen," I insist. "And I'm spending all of this time worrying about the things that could happen and not focusing on the things that are actually happening. When I was at the game and I couldn't skate, I was just so scared of hurting myself or embarrassing myself."

"But what would happen if you hurt yourself or embarrassed yourself?"

I consider this question for a moment. "Everyone would laugh at me."

"I highly doubt people would laugh if you broke a bone."

"Maybe it would hurt so much that I throw up on the track. Then people would laugh."

"And so what if they do?"

The terror this question evokes in me is unreal. I take in a deep, shaking breath.

"I can't think about that."

"Maybe you need to. But with someone who knows what they're doing and can help you process it all."

"Therapy."

"The young people's center in town does free counselling if you're under twenty-five. We can get you signed up tomorrow."

A wave of self-doubt hits me. "What if they think I'm just being silly?"

"Sweetheart, you're not being silly. You're really struggling. Having counselling could really help you. I think it would be good to have a space to talk about things, things that you've never really talked about before. Like your dad leaving, and university, and everything that happened with Imogen."

"Yeah, okay. I'll try it."

Chapter 23

I do end up staying away from practice while I wait to get to the top of the outrageously long waiting list for counselling, like Venom suggested. I miss being on skates, but it's good to have some space from the reminder that I broke Charlie's ribs. Luckily only a week into waiting, the youth center calls me with a last-minute cancellation that no one else can make because it's at lunchtime on a Wednesday.

My counsellor, Paula, is a woman in her thirties with tanned skin and blonde curly hair. It's easier to talk to her than I thought it would be, and it only takes me about half an hour into the first session to get over the fact I'm talking to a mental health professional and start opening up to her.

We spend the first two sessions talking about my past. Paula tells me she prefers a psychodynamic approach, which looks at your past to try and explain how you feel in the present. She says that the main thing she can offer in therapy is to take all the things that are floating around in my head and get them out to have a proper look at. Partway through my second time seeing her, we start talking about Imogen. I realize that when things started happening between us, I thought everything else would settle down. Like that was the big thing in my life that I was worrying about, and once there was a conclusion to that, all the other problems would stop. But actually, it turned out there were more problems than a potentially unrequited crush, which I only started seeing after she left.

A little while into my third session, we start talking about university.

"I've got an unconditional place to study English," I tell her. "But it makes me feel really anxious to think about. I need to apply for housing soon, and then over the summer we'll have to hire carers for Mum." Roller derby and Imogen kind of distracted me, but now they're both gone the worries are back with a vengeance.

"Which of those is worrying you the most?"

I think for a moment. "Both of them. I'm scared to live with strangers and to not know anyone there. And I'm worried that we won't be able to find anyone good to care for Mum."

"Are you feeling anxious that no one will look after her as well as you can?"

"Yeah, I think so. They'll only be able to come in for a few hours each day and she's going to be alone at home a lot."

"She's got friends, hasn't she?"

"Yeah."

"And you said your sister comes down to visit sometimes, with her son and sometimes her partner."

"Yeah, she does."

"So it sounds like she's not going to be lonely. And you're going to move away from home one day; all parents are prepared for that eventuality."

It takes a moment for this to sink in. "I guess so."

There's a short silence.

"What are you thinking about?" Paula asks me.

"I never really considered that this isn't how the rest of my life is going to be. I always figured I would go to uni and then just move back in with Mum, because she needs someone to care for her. She talked me into applying to a uni in London, and I thought that was just because then I could experience what it's like to live away from home for three years."

"How does it feel to think about leaving home permanently?"

"... Scary."

We sit with that for a moment.

"Really scary."

"Can you imagine what your life will look like when you're at uni?"

"No. It just feels impossible."

"Well, maybe that's an exercise you can do before our next session. Look up some videos and blogs of what life looks like at university and imagine yourself there."

I nod. It feels doable.

"We're coming to the end of our session today. How are you feeling?"

I take a moment to consider the question. "I'm okay. I feel a bit anxious but it's not overwhelming. Thank you. I'll see you next week."

Chapter 24

I try to focus on my homework over the next few days. I spend some time watching videos people have made about moving into uni accommodation in their first year. For the first time, thinking about moving to London doesn't just fill me with dread. I start to think about who I might be living with and how excited I am to delve deeper into some amazing literature. Mum and I even talk about making some phone calls to sort out her care for when I'm gone. It starts to become real and not just that I feel like I might really die if it happens.

I start running again every day and doing some weight training, and I pass the five-minute mark on the plank. My core muscles feel strong, full of potential, but I'm still worried about skating. It's difficult to think about going back into that world without Imogen, considering what happened in the first game I tried to play without her around. I wander into the kitchen one evening to find a plate of whole-wheat toast and peanut butter with a smoothie next to it sitting on the breakfast bar.

"It's got blueberries, a banana, some strawberries, a bit of melon and I chucked in a bit of peanut butter as well. I'm sorry if it's gross," Mum says, smiling up at me from her seat at the table.

"What's the occasion?" I ask, pulling myself up onto a bar stool and taking a bite of toast. "This is good workout fuel, you know."

"You're going back to training."

"I'm what?" The days are slipping by so fast that I have to do some quick maths in my head to figure out that it's Monday. Practice night. These evenings used to be practically tattooed onto my brain but after more than a month without them they just pass me by.

"I spoke to Venom," Mum continues, "I've never seen you skate, and she said I could come and watch tonight."

"How did you speak to her?"

"I messaged the team's page and she called me."

I take another bite of my toast and chew it slowly, mulling it over. My heart seems to be stuck between leaping at the thought of being on skates again and dropping to my stomach when I think about hurting someone or having a panic attack.

"I don't know. What if I can't ever play because I panic? That was so embarrassing."

"No one else thinks it was embarrassing." Mum stands up and walks over to me, resting a hand on my forearm.

"And I broke someone's ribs! I mean, that's really bad. It's like I don't know my own strength."

"Casey, love, it's a full-contact sport. Injuries happen. If someone accidentally injured you as a result of playing roller derby, would you want them to never play again as a result?"

I take a moment to think about it. Imogen hurt me accidentally and I don't want her to stop playing.

"… No."

"Well, then."

I take a deep breath. "But what if I get injured? Like, really badly? I know someone who got a spiral fracture in her ankle and dislocated it at the same time, and she was in plaster for months. You'd have to look after me. Or my flatmates at uni would have to."

Mum squeezes my arm and looks at me seriously.

"Casey, I want you to hear me very clearly on this one. I am not your priority. I am the parent here and I get to say what I can and cannot handle. You've been looking after me for a long time, and it makes sense you're worried about that, but we'll both be fine if you hurt yourself. I promise."

I can feel a sting at the back of my throat and my eyes start welling up with tears as Mum continues.

"Sweetheart, you are *my* number one priority. And you're miserable without roller derby. As long as you're happy, we'll figure everything else out. Okay?"

The tears spill over as I nod at her. I push my plate away and curl up in her arms.

The night is warmer than usual as I push Mum to the sports hall in her wheelchair. I walk quietly into the practice hall, and Venom looks over and shoots us both a thumbs-up.

"Where shall I sit?" Mum asks.

"Here is probably fine," I say, maneuvering her over to the wall where everyone is kitting up. There are a lot of smiles and waves in greeting from the rest of the team, and I smile back. I set my bag down and start putting on my pads, wincing at the smell that comes out of my kit bag after it's sat in my bedroom without being aired out. I'm kicking myself for not checking the group chat to see if anyone said anything specific about this practice. It kills me that I haven't prepared for this as well as I could have, but maybe the endless preparation would have stopped me from coming at all. Maybe it's good that Mum surprised me with this.

Mel walks over and wordlessly sweeps me up into a long, rocking hug.

"Welcome home. We missed you."

I smile and duck my eyes, knowing that I'll start crying again if I make eye contact with her. "I missed you too. It's been so weird."

"So weird," she agrees.

"What did I miss?"

"Um … nothing too big. We're playing in London soon, so that should be fun, and I think we're doing a home game a couple of months afterwards."

"Has the roster been posted yet?"

"Nope, you could still be in the running."

I laugh and squeeze Mel's arm before securing the Velcro on my elbow pad. "Even after last time?"

"Of course, you silly billy. Oh, and we can't hit Charlie yet. They won't be doing any kind of hitting drills anyway but, you know, don't hit them any other time."

"I'll try and remember not to punch them in the face."

"Ah, you knobhead." She laughs at me.

Mel dashes back off to finish kitting up. I finish putting on my knee pads and get to work on lacing up my skates. The motions feel instinctive, even after so long. I wonder how it will feel to be back on wheels again.

I'm done with my kit and turn round to talk to Mum, who's sipping a bottle of water.

"Are you okay?" I ask her.

"Fine! Go and skate."

"If you get too cold here, we can just go home." I know I'm fussing but I can't help myself.

"Don't be silly."

"I've got a little hand heater in my bag; do you want it?"

"Go and skate!" Mum says for the second time, and this time I listen to her. I stand up hesitantly, testing the floor with my wheels. I look at Mum, and she smiles at me. I turn around and head to the track.

It feels like flying. The air is slicing past my face as I do a few laps to warm up my muscles. People are skating slowly round and chatting as they stretch, but I'm in my own head for this. I do a quick set of moving stretches and plunge down into a deep squat, pumping my arms and legs into the cross-overs all the way round the track. Even though my body is working so hard I'm sweating already, I feel calm. It feels … right.

The first hour of practice is focused on endurance, so no hitting of any kind is necessary. We're doing turning sprints up and down the hall, and I fall into the routine of skating straight at the wall, then at the last second falling to one knee, turning 180 degrees and pushing my entire body down onto the floor as I spin around, then pulling up again, hopping onto my toe stops and sprinting back where I came from. As my body gets warm and loose, I can feel something stretch inside me that doesn't feel like muscles. I'm using my fast brain, the one that makes quick decisions and doesn't over-think things. My roller derby brain. Man, I missed this.

The endurance just keeps on coming and I keep up with the team. Clearly the treadmill and weight training has paid off, but there's only so much running I can do before boredom hits. Endurance drills on skates are exactly what I've been craving.

No one comments on the fact that I'm back. I get a few claps on the back and more understanding smiles than normal, but other than that everyone is business as usual, which I appreciate. My team knows me well, and any kind of scene about me being back would just make me feel anxious, so they're just being really chilled about it.

An hour in, Venom whistles for everyone to gather in the center of the track. I reach up into the side of my helmet with a finger to scratch my head, then take the opportunity to stretch my shoulders out a bit. They're screaming at me, but I know I'll feel that good muscle ache tomorrow, the kind that benefits from a long bath.

"You've worked hard today and now it's scrimmage time." There are a lot of smiles and a couple of groans, and I immediately feel like I need to tap out. Hitting people is a step I'm not sure I'm ready to take. I turn around and catch Mum's eye, who slowly shakes her head and points firmly at the track. The last thing I want to do is to have an argument with her in front of everyone. I would never live it down. I turn back around and Mel grabs my hand, as well as one can do while wearing wrist-guards, and gives it a squeeze.

"You'll be grand, chick. Just skate."

I'm handed a yellow bib that doesn't smell too fresh. I pull it on and head to the track. My teammates line up beside me and then the whistle blows and it's all happening so quickly. I'm reminded of my very first scrimmage, when I didn't really know the rules very well and couldn't remember what I was supposed to be doing. We all jostle for space, and I'm hit, hard, and land directly on my bum. For a split second, I consider staying there, just dragging myself into the center of the track and refusing to play anymore. But my body knows better. It's been trained well, and I'm back up on my skates before I even realize it. Instantly I'm checking over my left shoulder, looking for the other team's jammer. I can see Sam and Gem struggling to hold her back and skate over to them, facing backwards on the track and providing a stable body for them to hold onto and push back against the jammer. My plank skills are paying off, because now when I engage my core it's like there's a steel cable running from my stomach down to the ground.

"Inside, inside!" I shout as the jammer takes a step back and comes at us again, angling her body to try and skip down the inside line. But we're not letting her. My teammates and I are a solid team as our jammer gets through the pack with help from Lucy. After the jam, I skate back to my team's bench and squat down over my skates to watch my teammates play.

Just like that, the bug is back. I get that itchy feeling inside my skin, and I stand up on my toe stops, reminding myself how agile I can be on them. I catch Mel looking behind me and smiling, and I turn around and Mum is sending a knowing smile back at her. They both know I can never just stand still; I've always got to be doing something. Lifting hand weights when I'm watching TV, ankle circles in the cinema, balancing on one foot in the queue at the supermarket. Or, I guess, running on the spot on my toe stops while I wait for it to be my turn to skate again.

I haven't quite got the agility that I had before though, and I put my weight too far back on my skates, leaning on my front wheels instead of my toe stops. My leg flies out in front of me and my body instantly reacts, twisting in mid-air to land heavily on my right thigh and bum cheek. That'll be a big bruise tomorrow.

"Welcome back, clumsy," Mel says loudly, giving me a slow clap and grinning widely.

I respond by hopping straight back on my skates and sticking up my middle finger at her, before practicing my toe stop work again. Besides, that's what pads are for, right? To catch you when you fall.

It's been ages since I've been to Mel and Rob's flat. He's plugged into his PC setup with headphones on, playing some complicated game about maintaining spaceships. Mel reassures me that he can't even hear Sparkle yelling for dinner above the sound of his game, and she's got a loud meow.

"So, you're back?" she asks me as we settle on the sofa.

I can't stop the smile spreading across my face. "Yeah. I think I'm back."

"How did it feel to be on skates again?"

"Amazing. I missed it so much."

"We missed *you*," she tells me, poking my shoulder with her finger. "We dealt with losing Imogen, and then …" Her face falls as she realizes what she said. "I'm sorry, I didn't mean to—"

"I'm okay to talk about Imogen," I tell her, interrupting.

"Really. It still sucks, but I've been working a lot with my counsellor on thinking and talking about difficult things without spiraling."

"How's that going?"

I take a deep breath. "It's okay. It's like I've found a bit of a happy medium between how I was with her and then without her. I think she became, like, my safe person. It used to just be my mum and so it was difficult to go anywhere without her, and it felt like I was getting a lot of freedom but really I just transferred it onto Imogen. You saw what happened at the game where she wasn't there. I just couldn't cope."

Rob yells at something on the computer and we laugh at him. I warm my hands around my cup of tea.

"How do you feel about skating now?"

"I think I can do it. It still feels scary, but I feel more like I can calm myself down rather than relying on Imogen."

"And you know I'm always there to help as well," Mel says, shifting on the sofa to allow Sparkle to curl up next to her.

"I know," I tell her, "but I feel like that's not really the point. I don't want to shift that onto you now." If Mel is hurt by this, she doesn't show it. In fact, she smiles warmly at me.

"That's good. You can do it by yourself, but I'm here for backup."

"That's what we're working on, anyway."

"Have you heard from Imogen at all?" Mel asks me.

"No. I've texted her a couple of times but nothing. She hasn't blocked me though, which is something. Have you?"

"Not since she sent me that text to tell everyone she had moved away."

"I wonder where she is."

We settle into silence and watch a few jams of the roller derby game she's put on the projector.

"I just want to talk to her," I say after a while. "I want closure. We were dating and then she was just … gone. She didn't even break up with me. She just left. I want to know what actually happened. Not for her to come back, or for us to be girlfriends again, I just need to know."

"I know, chick," Mel says, reaching over and squeezing my arm. "It's not fair."

We watch a few more jams.

"You're a bit like her," Mel tells me, pointing at the jammer on the screen.

"Who, Gladiator?"

"Yeah. You're strong like her. We've really missed you on the team. You always keep everyone focused."

"Do I?"

Mel turns to look at me. "Do you not see yourself, Case? You kick arse. At least once a week when you were gone someone said how much they miss you. You're a triple threat—jammer, blocker and pivot. I always know what I'm meant to be doing when I'm on track with you."

Now I reach over and squeeze Mel's arm. "I like that."

"We like you!"

As we watch some more derby, I think more about what she said. I always felt a bit like the odd one out on the team. Like I was Imogen's kid sister who she dragged along and everyone felt like they had to humor me. I feel like I can give myself a bit more credit than that, considering what Mel has just told me. Maybe I do have a place on the team that isn't just the one who panics and the one who broke Charlie's ribs. Gladiator is the kind of skater I aspire to be, and it feels good to know I'm at least part of the way there.

~

At the next practice, I have to prove I'm still fit enough to play roller derby by skating at least twenty-seven laps of the track in five minutes. We do a group warm-up then a few of us stagger ourselves around the track, getting ready for the pain that comes with this endurance drill. Rae is counting my laps, and I'm seriously happy with myself when she shouts, "Seven!" before the first minute has passed. I push harder and harder, but as always lose a bit of steam towards the end. I finish with thirty-one laps in five minutes. It's my best yet and Venom squats down to clap me on the shoulder as I lie star-fished on the floor. "That's roster material, kid. You're in."

When I'm recovered sufficiently to stand up, I skate a couple of laps in the opposite direction to make my screaming muscles feel a bit more evenly in pain, then head back into the middle of the track, stretching my arms behind me and tilting my head from side to side as we wait to hear what's happening this training session.

"Okay, this session is scrimmage central. We're going to be trying out different line-ups and seeing what works. We've got some refs and NSOs and we're going to be playing two full halves with all the rules, just switching up line-ups and bibs, so get ready to change what you're doing at a moment's notice."

I nod and smile. This is going to be fun.

Chapter 25

I spend the whole time in my next session of counselling talking about Imogen. About how she just came along out of nowhere, in the weirdest of situations, and completely changed my life. About how she made me realize that I wasn't broken, just didn't fancy Ryan, or even know what fancying someone really entailed. And most of all, about how it ended. How she still hasn't spoken to me or anyone else on the team that I know of, other than to tell us she's safe and she's not coming back.

I end the session feeling angry for the first time, rather than hopeless and heartbroken. Angry that she didn't give me the courtesy of actually breaking up with me, just left. On my walk home, I text her.

Imogen, this is ridiculous. I need to talk to you. When is good for me to phone?

Not apologetic, not pleading, just stating the facts. I'm not expecting a text back but it comes immediately.

Are you playing the London game?

Yes. Why?

Meet you in the park by the museum at 11?

It's a couple of weeks away, but it's better than nothing. I think I can hold onto this feeling until then.

While I've got my phone out, I open up my messages with Anna. Because I didn't tell her about Imogen, I couldn't find the words to tell her about what's happened since she left. Our next game is during the time she's next visiting home, and I send her a quick text with the details and say I'd love it if she came along to see what I've been doing while she's away. If I'm doing one reunion, I might as well do them all.

~

To my surprise, Anna says yes straight away. I'm still upstairs getting ready on the morning of the game when I hear Billy answer the door and their polite conversation. I grab my things and head down the stairs.

Her hair is longer, but otherwise she's still the same. She smiles at me. We walk towards each other wordlessly and hug, squeezing each other for a long time.

"I missed you," I say into her hair.

"Missed you too," she replies.

We have about an hour to spare before we've got to leave, and we spend the time catching each other up on everything we missed. If she's surprised about my relationship with Imogen, she doesn't show it.

"I'm sorry I wasn't there," she tells me. "It sounds really tough."

I shrug my shoulders. "You had other stuff going on. I get it."

It sounds like her first almost-year at university hasn't been quite as rosy as she painted it to be in her texts. We're still talking nonstop when Mum pops her head around the living-room door and tells us it's time to leave.

Billy's hired a car to take us all to the game in London. She says she tried to convince Mark to skip the football for a week, and I think I believe her.

"You're not going to skip out on this one as well are you?" she jokes as I get Mum settled into the front seat with a couple of cushions. I scoff outwardly and try to squash the note of panic that's entered my throat, not just about the game but about seeing Imogen again. I awkwardly stow Mum's wheelchair in the tiny boot of the car and get into the back seat with Anna.

"It's just we've got Mum here this time, and it's over two hours in the car. You sure you're up for it?"

"Billy," Mum scolds quietly.

"What? I'm just asking."

"It's fine, Mum. Yes I'm going to skate this time. I've got it under control." This is more to comfort myself than anyone else in the car. I touch my anti-travel sickness wristbands and check my tote bag for the millionth time. Phone, wallet, brown paper bag in case I puke, medical kit in case of emergency, a steady supply of snacks to make sure my blood sugar doesn't dip low enough to make me feel panicky. My kit bag is in the seat next to me, and I've already checked and double-checked the contents a million times. I settle back into my seat and take a couple of deep breaths. Billy pumps 80s bangers through the car to get me pumped up and Anna and Mum sing along loudly. I still feel jittery, but I manage to lose myself in staring out of the window at the retreating houses, then the fields as we cut through the country on a motorway towards the venue.

It's not lost on me that the team we're playing today are the team I'll be trying out for when I move to London in September, and they use the same venue that I saw my first game in. Even though they're the C team of the main league, it's one of the best leagues in Europe and I'll have to fight tooth and nail to earn a place in it. I slipped back into my place at the team so easily after those first couple of practices and my cross-training in the meantime really paid off. I'm faster and more nimble than when I quit, and it takes a solid unexpected hit to get me to move an inch on the track these days. I'm amazed at the ways my life has changed since that first roller disco. Mum and I have never been closer or more open with each other, and my good times with Billy are finally outnumbering our squabbling sessions. It feels like the first time we've connected as friends, not just bickering sisters. She's not completely happy with all of my life choices, but now that I've actually booked my place at university she's chilled out a bit. No more giving me hassle about playing a ridiculous, violent, made-up sport. I can't quite believe she's helping me bring Mum to this game after my embarrassing display at the last one she attended, but I think it might have had something to do with a long phone call she and Mum had a few weeks ago.

I've been added to a group chat with all seven of my future housemates in university accommodation, and they're not the antisocial tyrants I had imagined they might be. In fact they almost seem … nice? And some of them seem just as anxious as I am about this big life change. I'm still worried about leaving Mum in an empty nest, but I'm pretty excited about starting my course.

When we arrive, Billy puts the blue badge on the windscreen and I push Mum to a nearby café for them to wait until the doors open for the audience.

"I'll see you later," I say and turn to go.

"Wait." Billy touches my arm and I turn back around.

"What?"

"I just … I'm looking forward to seeing you play today. I shouldn't give you so much shit about it."

I look behind her at Mum and Anna. Mum shrugs at me while smiling.

"What do you want?" I ask suspiciously.

"Nothing! Can't I wish my sister good luck in her game?" She's outraged but smiling, and I move in to give her a hug. She squeezes me for a moment and lets go, and we grin at each other.

"Good luck, sweetheart," Mum says to me.

"Can't wait to see you skate," Anna says.

I give them both hugs as well, then heft my kit bag up onto my shoulder and set out for the museum gardens.

~

I feel Imogen's presence before I see her. A twisting in my stomach as I sit on a bench and enjoy the cool spring day, and a few seconds later I see her turn the corner into the park. She's wearing cut-off jeans and a band t-shirt. It doesn't take long before she's sitting next to me on the bench. Neither of us says anything for a moment.

"Hi." I don't know what to say to her. I pull both of my thumbs into fists, squeezing, and I feel my knuckles crack.

"Hey."

There's a short silence as we look at each other. I can't quite believe she's here. It's been so long.

"So, how are things?" I ask. The question feels too light for what I want to ask.

"Oh, you know," she says.

I'm about to smile and agree when I realize I really don't know how things have been for her.

"No, I don't," I say.

Imogen smiles sheepishly. "No, I guess you don't. Sorry. Well, I'm living in Leeds with Nathan now." She gestures towards the corner she arrived from, and there he is. Sitting on a bench and reading a book. He's just as gorgeous as ever, and I get a strange pang of jealousy even though I know they're not dating.

"Oh, okay."

"Mum kicked me out. Well, I don't know if she really meant to. But she told me she wouldn't tolerate me being … you know … and living in her house. That I would need to change myself, to stop liking girls. So I said that I couldn't do that, and that I would move out. I don't think she thought I would actually do it."

"Wow. I'm so sorry," I say. I go to reach a hand out and nearly stop myself, but I push through the awkwardness and pat her lightly on the arm. She looks down at my hand then back at me, smiling, before taking my hand and squeezing it briefly then dropping it.

"Yeah. There was a lot of crying. I came to practice that night to take my mind off it. I didn't realize I'd had that much to drink."

"It was kind of scary," I admit.

"I'm so sorry. I never meant to hurt you. How's your nose?"

I touch it gently. "It's fine. Don't worry. I understand."

"I wish I could take it back." Her face twists with embarrassment or maybe shame, but when I told her it was fine I meant it.

"Really. It's okay." I smile at her.

Another short silence.

"I joined a support group as well."

"What for?"

"Help with my alcohol problem." She tries to play it down, but there's a proud smile on her face that she can't stop from coming out.

"Oh, wow. That's huge, Im!"

"Yeah. I didn't really know I had a problem until the shakes started, you know? And then I discovered that the shakes would go away if I had a glug of something in the mornings, and before you know it I'm waking up in my own vomit at six in the evening."

"That's tough." I don't mention that even though there were times I suspected she relied on alcohol a little too much, this shocks me.

"Yeah. It's been difficult without you guys. You know, all the derby crew. I'm sorry I disappeared."

"I get it," I say, automatically going to reassure her and tell her everything is okay. But then I remember talking about Imogen with my therapist, and her expressing concern about how I would always agree with her or go along with what she wanted even if I thought something different. I take a breath. "It really sucked. I didn't know where you were. I didn't know what was happening."

"I know."

"You just left. You didn't reply to any of my texts."

I'm expecting her to twist uncomfortably or look embarrassed, like I would if I was in her position. But she sits upright, looking directly at me.

"I'm sorry," she says to me, "I couldn't … I didn't know how to talk to you. I was meant to be the one looking after you, you know?"

"You're allowed to be vulnerable though, Imogen."

At this, she dips her eyes. "I'm learning that."

"I get why you had to disappear though. Just needed a clean start, right?"

"Yeah."

We look at each other. I cried over her for so long and I kept picturing what I would do if I saw her again. My imagination ran the gamut from punching her in the face to pulling her in for a long kiss, but I don't want to do either of those now. We're starting on new journeys now, ones that might not include each other. We feel … done.

"Are you skating up in Leeds?" I ask.

"Not yet. I think I need to sort myself out a bit before I restart. How's it going down here?"

I pause for a second before saying, "I stopped skating for a while."

"What?" She grabs me by the arm. "What happened?"

"I broke Charlie's ribs."

"Charlie?"

"Fresh meat."

"How many ribs did you break?"

"Two. And a punctured lung."

"Fucking hell. Nice going!" She grins widely and punches me on the arm. I make a face; it doesn't feel like a good response. Sure, roller derby is badass and we hit each other a lot, but the goal is never to hurt someone. I don't know if Imogen really gets that yet.

"Why did you stop?" she asks.

"I just …" I blink hard. I wasn't expecting tears to come to my eyes. "At practice, I hurt Charlie. And at games, I didn't feel like I could play. I had a panic attack before the last game and I couldn't skate."

"I remember you freaked out a bit before your first game, but I thought that was just first game nerves. Shit, Case. I'm sorry."

"So I figured there wasn't really any point. But then I went back and it just felt amazing. Today's the real test to see if I'll panic again. But I'm definitely going to uni. Sorted accommodation and everything—I move in October. So if it goes well today, I'll be trying out for the London team."

"That's amazing."

"Yeah, I think so. I'm just nervous about today."

"I get it." She leans over and taps me on the temple, lightly, with two fingers. "There's too much going on in here. You need to do, not think."

I smile. "Easier said than done."

"Hey, if I can stop drinking, you can stop thinking."

"I doubt that."

"The drinking or the thinking?" Her eyes sparkle as she asks me.

"The thinking."

"I'll make you a deal: we can swap. Okay? I'll do all your thinking. And you can start drinking in the moment. Not stopping to think about the consequences and what might happen and all the possibilities. Just drinking it all in. And I'll try and exercise my brain before acting. Deal?"

"Deal," I say, laughing. Imogen reaches out and pulls me in for a sweaty (on my part) and unexpected hug. She pulls back slightly, nose-to-nose, and rests her forehead against mine. On autopilot we move in and press our lips together, briefly. It doesn't feel like we're restarting something, though. It feels like an ending. We've had different journeys on our way to this place, and it feels good to know that she's seeking support for her more impulsive behavior, at the same time that I'm trying to be a bit more daring.

"I've got to get to warm-up," I tell her.

"Kick their asses. I'll be watching. See you around, Timberlake. Don't be a stranger."

"Bye," I say, running my hands down her arms and squeezing her hands before letting go. She chucks me under the chin and I get up, turn around and walk away.

The rest of my teammates have already arrived and are in the process of getting ready in the changing rooms when I walk in and set my bag down on a bench.

"How are you doing, chick?" Mel asks me, nudging my shoulder with hers. "Feeling level?"

I look at her and smile tightly. "Yeah I think so. Just about."

As I say it, I realize it's true. I'm feeling level. The anxiety is there, but it's like it's behind a glass panel. I can hear it, but it's muffled. Instead, I've got the mantras I developed in my counselling sessions floating around in the foreground of my mind: "I'm safe," "I can look after myself," "there's nothing so bad I can't come back from it." I've had enough practices without Imogen now that it seems normal to not have her in the changing room. We've grown and shifted as a team to accommodate the space she left, and we're complete. We're whole. I look around the room and feel such a fierce love for my teammates, and for myself. We know each other so intimately and trust each other so completely. A surge of pride and energy comes to me as I realize these people are my friends. They're my support system. And no matter how far any of us moves away, there will always be a place for each of us on the team.

I strap my pads on, checking and double-checking that the Velcro is stuck down properly, and I'm still not panicking. We skate out into the hall together just as the doors open, and I spot Billy, Mum, Anna and Imogen in the front row. Imogen and Anna are chatting animatedly and I try not to think about what they might be saying to each other; Anna has a track record for holding grudges on behalf of her friends. I give them a small wave before heading over to our team bench. We briefly go over our strategy for the game and head out onto the track for our warm-up. I can hear the announcers calling out our names as we go through our pre-game drills and the roar of the crowd as they cheer for us. I remind my body what it feels like to have a single purpose, to be connected to my teammates and to work as a whole, and the anxiety is still behind that glass pane. Even as the hall fills up with spectators (I'm told the game is completely sold out), I only get tiny glimpses of my last experience playing an open-door game. I'm safe, I can look after myself, there's nothing so bad I can't come back from it.

We go back to the bench to allow the London team to warm up on the track. Everyone has their own pre-game ritual, and it turns out my new one is to stay quiet and focused. I watch the other team run exercises and take note of who their jammers and heavy hitters are. I can feel the same wild energy buzzing within me that I felt when I was in this same hall as a spectator with Imogen, Rae and Lucy. I remember that famous line about roller derby in *Whip It*, about falling in love with the sport, and I get it so deeply within myself. Since I first strapped on a pair of skates, I've discovered what it means to fall in love. With myself, with Imogen, and with this ridiculous, violent, made-up sport and all the people who make it happen.

It's time to start the game, and Fi lets me know that I'm on the first line-up as a jammer. I take the star helmet cover from her and pull it on, then line up on the track. The audience is cheering so loudly I can barely hear myself think, but I repeat my mantras in my head one more time before looking beside me to see who I'm up against for the first jam. She's short and has dark brown skin and two long black pigtails coming out of the back of her helmet. Her shorts are bright pink and impossibly tiny. She grins at me.

"Ready?" she asks.

I return her smile then squat down, balancing on my toe stops, and look in front of me at the task ahead.

"Ready."

A Note from the Author

When I first watched *Whip It* in 2009, I thought roller derby was a fictional sport. I had endless daydreams about being as badass as those skaters and knocking people over, but I resigned myself to the fact that it was just made up for the film and didn't exist in real life. Clearly my Google skills were sorely lacking.

My friend Cerys took me to my first bout on May 1, 2011. It was at York Hall (the venue where Casey sees her first game) and we saw the London Rockin' Rollers play Central City Roller Derby. There was a punk band at halftime. Much like Casey, I went out and bought skates a couple of weeks later and have never looked back.

I skated and officiated with a couple of women's leagues* until my partner Finn came out as trans in 2014 and we started an all-gender league in Brighton, where we lived together. B-Town Brawlers was officially formed in 2014, and I started coaching and doing a lot of organizational stuff behind the scenes.

In 2017, Finn died by suicide after a long period of illness. He was so loved by so many people, and we kept the league

* In roller derby, a league is a collection of people under one name, like London Roller Derby. Each league will have one or more teams, e.g. London Brawling, Brawl Saints, Batter C Power. These are rostered skaters who compete in games. The league is the overarching collective, rather than a 'competition league' like in other sports.

going for a year or so after his death, but it just couldn't live without him. The trauma of his illness and death caused me to develop M.E. (the same illness Casey's mum has) and, as it worsened quickly, I stopped being able to skate. I spent three years needing a full-time carer, and roller derby left my life completely.

In September 2022, I visited Los Angeles and went to see an LA Derby Dolls game; the fire got re-ignited. When I got back to my home near Bristol, I started volunteering to NSO (non-skating official) at local games and met a few people from Bath Roller Derby who mentioned they had a newbies course coming up in a really convenient location for me, and so I rejoined. Instantly I got the bug again. I came along with my wheelchair and skated some very wobbly laps around the track, and then kept coming back. It's been a difficult journey—I'm not physically able to skate very much at all and will sometimes spot Finn out of the corner of my eye at practice and get very emotional—but it's brought so much joy back into my life. I was even voted in as Head NSO of the league in 2024.

The thing that has really kept me engaged is officiating. I'm a huge clipboard nerd and loved learning all the different roles that NSOs perform to make games happen. I now lead teams as Head NSO and travel up and down the country, meeting some great new friends as I do so. We're always swapping hints and tips for making our work more efficient as well as having a lot of fun officiating. I use a wheelchair a lot of the time and struggle with the more physical parts of officiating, like shifting furniture around and setting up projectors, but there is always someone there to help.

Bath Roller Derby has such a brilliant mindset on officials.

Refs, NSOs, and bench crew are as much a part of the league as any of the players. The community aspect of roller derby is so important; it's a grassroots sport and we build everything ourselves. The sport has grown to be incredibly inclusive and there really is a role for everyone, no matter their ability. I'm currently a Divisional Head Official and part of the stats processing team for the Five Nations tournament, and most of that work is done from home. If I'm too ill to come to practice, my team sends me lovely messages to say they're thinking of me, and we always keep each other in the loop on Discord.

We've reached a point where most people have multiple leagues local to them. If you want to get involved, I can't recommend it highly enough. Each league has different priorities and ways of working, and if you don't find what you want from one then you can always try another. Mine and Casey's stories aren't unusual—most of the roller derby people I know have found the sport life-changing in some way, and I hope you can see that you don't have to be on skates to be involved. Be your own hero!

This book was born during the time of one-minute penalties and knee-starts (iykyk) and has kept me company through my entire journey with roller derby. It feels very exciting to put it out into the world, and my greatest hope is that it might make you feel like it's time to try something new and scary. It might change your life.

Thank you for reading,

Acknowledgements

This whole "writing a book" thing is actually quite difficult, it turns out. It's been a real adventure, and there are so many people who helped me along the way.

First of all, thank you to my agent Lucy Irvine for seeing the potential in my roller derby book, and to Silvia Molteni for championing *Learning to Fall* across the pond. It's a story I loved telling, and it's a real privilege to have you believe in it. Thank you to the rest of the team at PFD who worked behind the scenes to make it all happen.

To my editor Allison Moore—endless gratitude for helping shape and refine this book to be the best it can be. You and everyone at 8th Note have made this whole process smooth and easy. Let's do another one! Thanks also to Renata Sweeney, Bengisu Onal, and Jacob Bronstein, and to Jill Sawyer for copyediting.

Huge thank you to Claire Wilson, Alice Sutherland-Hawes, Sarah Juckes and Gemma Cooper for your invaluable advice as I worked to query this book, and to LD Lapinski for running the Twitter competition that linked me with some of this advice. Thanks also to Jess Green for the mentoring session that encouraged me to focus on finishing this book.

My very first readers, Cat and Snoogs. Thank you for motivating me to write "The End" and for loving this story since it was a tiny baby in your email inboxes.

I had so much wonderful feedback from my beta readers, thank you to Esmeralda, River, Katie, Liza, Lois (the original Toxic Block Syndrome), Mum, Maria, Dad, Sass, Amy, Gin and Vic. You helped me work through a lot of sticking points and gave me the confidence to keep going. Slab and Acer, thank you for sitting down with me to hash out the plot. To Marchie for listening as I read it out loud for the first time. Thanks also to T.S. Ferguson.

Thank you to all the members of They//Us, the best non-binary writers' group around. Your thoughtful feedback shaped the first chapters of this book. Long live For Books' Sake's legacy, and Bridge you are a superstar. Thanks for bringing us all together and keeping us on track for as long as you did. Gays are a tricky bunch to wrangle!

Hellions—it's truly the best thing to share hell with you. You forever challenge me to be my favourite self and I give you all a big sloppy smooch. Honey gives you a big poo.

To the Dank Weasel Party Crew, we dragged each other through lockdown and beyond, and you tolerated my 3 a.m. questions about roller derby minutiae. Thank you for being wonderful.

In chronological order, thank you to the Brighton Rockers, Eastbourne Roller Derby, B-Town Brawlers and Bath Roller Derby for being my home away from home and playing this ridiculous violent made-up game with me.

To my parents and my brothers, thank you for believing I can do anything I want to do. And to my closest people, family and friends, you know who you are. If you're wondering if this includes you, yes it does. You love every version of me, and I am made up of parts of all of you.

Finn. I can't believe I'm doing this without you. It feels silly to write something down when you are with me every second of every day, but I'm doing it anyway. This whole book is for you. You know which parts are ours. My roller derby romance, I love you.

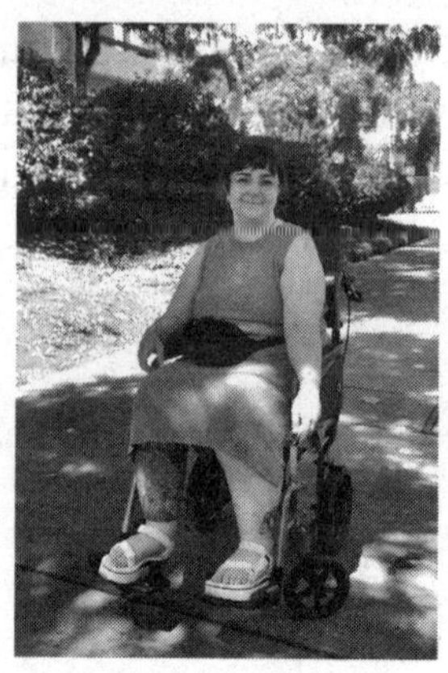

About the Author

Peach Morris (they/them) is a queer, disabled writer living in Bristol, UK. Peach has been skating and officiating since 2011 for various roller derby teams and co-founded and coached the B-Town Brawlers from 2014–2018. They were the writer in residence at Trans Pride Brighton 2018, and had a short story, "Pivot," published in For Books' Sake's Derby Shorts. *Learning to Fall* is their first novel.